Border Crossings of My Youth

(A memoir.)

Eugene McElhinney

Published in 2015 by FeedARead.com Publishing

Copyright © Eugene McElhinney

A CIP catalogue record for this title is available from the British Library.

Dedication

To Monica, Angela, Brendan and Peter
who shared a large part of my early journey.

A special word of thanks to Angela for checking
the manuscript and suggesting improvements.

This is a true story but, in the interests of confidentiality, the names of some people and places have been changed.

Contents

Prologue 7

Chapter 1: My Village................................29

Chapter 2: Donegal...................................54

    Part 1: Finner...54
    Part 2:Templenew..................................88

Chapter 3:Rathdangan...............................200

Chapter 4 Philosophy, Cork 226

Chapter 5: Theology, Rathdangan 251

Prologue

The Border in the 1940's

Sergeant Cecil Stevenson tightened the belt of his large overcoat and fastened the last brass button under his chin to keep out the cold of a late November night. Visibility was poor on Clady Bridge but even though in his mid-sixties he had keen eyesight and still didn't need spectacles. This combined with his military style moustache and large stature equipped him well for his work as a policeman. He didn't particularly care for night surveillance but it meant extra cash at the end of the month. This could be a long night, he thought, but he was prepared to wait it out. Nearby were two junior constables. He knew they were reluctant to be with him, crouching in the darkness as they waited for Sweeney. But then they didn't share his zeal about stamping out smuggling along this stretch of the border between Donegal and Tyrone. In fact Cecil knew that a lot of petty smuggling went on, which neither he nor his colleagues could control, but Sweeney was different. He was the local Mr. Big of smuggling. He knew Sweeney only too well, chiefly through the smuggler's capacity to operate his lucrative business with impunity.

Through the darkness he could see the red glow of a cigarette. Despite having warned his junior colleagues about smoking openly one of them had ignored his order. He quickly moved across to the other side of the bridge and hissed,

"Hide that cigarette Thompson!" and returned to his own position. These young constables did not understand that a veteran smuggler like Sweeney could spot the glow of a cigarette from a hundred paces and take evasive action. Stevenson didn't mind his men having an odd smoke to while away the night but not in a manner that would blow their cover. He had smoked himself when he was younger but had given them up so he understood the craving. But it was his discipline and attention to detail that had served him well in his career. That and his Presbyterian work ethic ensured that he was promoted quickly and put in charge of a section of the border area. For him smuggling was not just illegal but immoral. He knew that view was not shared by the smugglers.

Ever since Ireland had been divided in 1921 according to political rather than physical or ethnic factors, the three hundred mile border that ran from South Armagh to South Tyrone provided countless opportunities for smuggling. Now it was different given that the war had created an economic imbalance that made smuggling really profitable. With no rationing in the Republic of Ireland there was a surplus of products there such as sugar, flour, tea, butter and meat, all of which were in big demand in Northern Ireland. Northern nationalists referred to the Republic as the Free State following partition, a term with indicated where their sympathies lay. As a northern unionist Cecil Stevenson was happy to patrol the border for king and country and of course it provided him with a secure job. Born in nearby Sion Mills in 1880 he had lived through the war of independence following the 1916 Easter Rising in

Dublin and had progressed from being a shop assistant to a senior position in the Royal Ulster Constabulary.

In the old days before partition there was less political distance between Protestants and Catholics. Since the division of the country some tensions had emerged, particularly in border areas. Splinter groups of The Irish Republican Army made the odd foray into Northern Ireland to attack police stations and post offices. Sergeant Stevenson knew from his own experience about such incursions. Just three hundred yards from where he was standing such an incident had taken place in the recent past. He had been summoned from the R.U.C. Police station in nearby Strabane to investigate an attack on the Post Office in Clady. He found the postmistress, Mrs. Rebecca O'Flaherty and her two daughters in a state of shock. They had told him that they had to lie on the floor as a volley of shots was fired through the front window of the post office in the early hours of the morning after the postmistress had denied them entry. The sergeant had seen the bullet holes for himself in the walls. He had been informed that this was the second time the post office had been attacked. And then there was the incident when a local IRA man had been killed when a bomb he was assembling exploded. In these circumstances it was understandable that border patrols were carried out by an armed R.U.C.

Twelve feet beneath him the cold water of the river flowed by with just the faintest of gurgles as its smooth flow was interrupted by the seven arches across its span. A few miles north of Clady Bridge it made its uninhibited and permanent incursion into Northern Ireland. Long before the arrival of the Celts and the Planters it had drained the Finn Valley after the last Ice Age and in relatively recent history had marked out the division between the land of Eoghan and the land of Conall. From its source in The Donegal Hills it flowed eastward as far as Clady before turning northeast to join the river Foyle. Before the construction of the bridge in the early eighteenth century there was a ford at this point. After prolonged rainfall the level of the river is raised enough to ignore political boundaries and flood the village. Tonight the water level was high but not in danger of causing a flood.

Just then Cecil thought he saw lights approaching from the Donegal side of the border. The lights of a slow moving car continued past the junction that led to the bridge. As it was now two in the morning it was probably smugglers scouting for the presence of police patrols. It would just be like Sweeney to have organized some reconnaissance before making his move. The sight of the passing car raised Cecil's spirits for that reason. As the car disappeared into the night in the direction of Lifford he could faintly hear the strong and steady flow of the river Finn below but could see nothing.

Smugglers rarely ventured out on moonlit nights, unless they needed some visibility when swimming pigs across. This was risky and seldom tried, even though it was the most profitable of all. He knew that cattle were sometimes forced to swim across at certain points in broad daylight. He had been informed that a recent arrival to the village, a certain Hugh McElhinney, who was a

10

cattle dealer, was a suspect in cattle smuggling. He had taken some land on each side of the river, a real indication of unlawful intent. The same gentleman had other talents, from writing short plays to composing songs and ballads. He had even the audacity to compose a short play called 'Border Blunder' making fun of the constabulary. One of Cecil's junior officers had overheard a song from the play being sung in Sweeney's pub much to the delight of the revellers within. He couldn't remember it very well but there were a couple of lines that went something like,

"There was bread and flour and rice went o'er the border,
Never talk about the candles or the tay ,.............
and Stevenson could be seen a mile away".

Apparently this was sung to the tune of Galway Bay. Well, Cecil was intent on having the last laugh. He hoped it would be tonight, the last week before retirement, with the arrest of the publican smuggler. Cecil also knew that McElhinney's wife Teresa, formerly O'Flaherty of the local Post Office no less, had a shop of convenience on the Donegal side of the border from which she smuggled certain items on her person while travelling back to the village. With few female customs officials available for body searches he was powerless to intervene. And of course the odd time he had a female officer her searches proved fruitless. His informants had provided him with lots of information but it was not always easy to get these smugglers in the act. What puzzled him was that despite flouting the

11

law they were devout in their religious practice. Ironically, they had to cross the border every time they went to religious services in the parish Church of St. Columba. It wouldn't have surprised him if they combined church attendance with a bit of smuggling at the same time. The village was predominantly Catholic though there were a few prominent Protestant families there too. To the best of his knowledge the active smugglers were the Catholics. He was well aware of the political dimension of course. He knew that the Catholics resented the border for it cut them off politically from family and friends. In some instances the border ran through their land. So, night or day this illegal activity was going on. The daytime smuggling tended to be minor. All the more reason to be on patrol on the dark nights. The smuggler he was chiefly interested in was a master of darkness.

Jim Sweeney was a large ruddy faced man with a hearty laugh and a twinkle in his eye. He owned a pub in the village just about three hundred yards from the border. He also had a small shop on the Donegal side. Apparently he had spent a number of years in New York during the prohibition era of the twenties where he had learned his trade in speakeasies and illegal clubs in the Bronx. Needles to say, the shop on the Donegal side was a front for the movement of smuggled goods but since such commodities such as flour, tea and sugar were sold out of open bags it was impossible to identify what was smuggled without catching the smuggler with contraband on his person.

Sometimes animals such as pigs mysteriously made their way into Sweeney's back yard behind his pub and just as mysteriously disappeared without trace, as Cecil Stevenson knew only too well, for instance the night when he and several R.U.C. officers sat up late in a surveillance operation of his premises. Adjacent to the pub was the yard with outhouses in which he kept a few cows and feedstuffs of one sort of another. At about two in the morning they had heard the squeak of his gate opening signalling that contraband was more than likely passing through it. When Cecil knocked loudly on the front door of the premises Sweeney opened it dressed in his pyjamas and yawning asked what the problem was. Needless to say the ensuing search was fruitless.

Tonight was different. A few days earlier Cecil had learnt from his intelligence sources that Sweeney would be moving contraband on the following Friday night. He knew that this was his big chance. So he waited and waited............

.

****

13

Rebecca O'Flaherty, with the aid of her walking stick, slowly climbed the stairs to her bedroom for her afternoon nap. Since turning eighty-six she found that she tired more easily, so the afternoon nap became an important pick-me-up. As she entered the bedroom she could see herself in the mirror of her dressing table. Recently she had taken to checking her appearance more often for any signs of deterioration. She didn't mind the wrinkles around her eyes, which were evident, but her skin was still clear and her cheeks smooth though her hazel eyes no longer had the old sparkle. A cataract in one eye had left her needing a stronger left lens but by moving close to the mirror she could read the signs of aging in her face with her good eye. Being slim and of average height she had managed to maintain good health helped by hard work and a healthy lifestyle. But now she needed to rest more often.

The nap also gave her a bit of respite from her five grandchildren who ranged in age from two months to eight years. So, turning around from the mirror she went to the door and turned the key to ensure privacy for an hour. She loved her grandchildren dearly for they were the only O'Flaherty grandchildren she had. She was pleased that her remaining daughter Teresa had married, even though she had left it until she was thirty-five. Hadn't she herself married her first husband Patrick Bonner in 1881 when she was twenty-one? And hadn't she given birth to seven children within ten years? Seven births, but just five that lived. The death of twins at birth broke her heart at the time but she had had to live with that bereavement and more in the course of her long live. She realised that these thoughts had been triggered by the date- November 15th, Lena's anniversary.

As she sat on the bed she heard the doorknob turning gently but she ignored it. It was probably her third grandchild Eugene. Although just turning five he had taken upon himself to be her minder and used to check on her whereabouts from time to time. Indeed if she needed him, all she had to do was tap the floor with her stick and he would come racing up the stairs exclaiming to his mother or father, 'That's my granny calling'. The eldest grandchild Peter used to be her minder but lately he had abandoned her, preferring to spend more time out on the street socialising with the other village children, not always to his mother's liking.

Before closing her eyes for her nap Rebecca took one of her heart tablets as her doctor had prescribed. She knew herself that her heart was weakening but the tablet was supposed to be essential at her age and condition. For some reason taking that heart tablet always reminded her of Lena, not that she needed much reminding for Lena's death had been devastating for her and her second husband Michael O'Flaherty. How could she forget the joy on Michael's face on that February 16th 1898 when his first born arrived? The pain and incredulity she saw on that same face twenty years later was a poignant reminder of life's apparent cruelty. Both Lena and her younger sister Teresa had been struck down by the Spanish Flu. When Dr. Brown examined them he informed Rebecca and Michael in a matter of fact sort of way, "The dark one will survive but the fair one won't". Thankfully her strong religious faith had sustained her through this and three other bereavements.

On her bedside table were some of her treasured photographs. Pride of place went to one of her mother, Catherine Donaghy who had married Peter McCrudden. Rebecca was very proud of this photograph because when it was taken the art of photography had only recently been invented. To go to a photographer's studio and pose for a photograph was quite an event in the 1860's. It took several days for the photograph to be processed. Calling at the studio to inspect it and purchase it was exciting.

Looking at the picture now she could see a woman of quiet stoicism. Although dressed in an ornate shawl with an equally ornate bonnet tied under her chin, her mother's gaze was fixed on a point beyond the photographer. Even though her lips were closed there was just a hint of a smile. Looking at the inscrutable face Rebecca knew that the serious pose revealed the struggle of raising eight children to adulthood and burying Bernard when still an infant. Rebecca's own picture stood next to her mother's. She recognized the likeness and could see the same stoic countenance. She was beautifully attired right down to the toe of an expensive shoe appearing at the hem of her long flowing skirt. Unlike her mother she was gazing directly at the camera. In her hand was a book. She liked this portrait a lot because it projected her as a person of good taste, intelligent and cultured. Herbert Cooper, the photographer, who had his studio in Strabane, always seemed to capture the personality of his sitter. All her family portraits had been taken by him.

Today, of course, the third picture on her bedside table, that of Helena evoked the old sadness of 1918 when the Spanish Flu arrived in Clady, brought probably by soldiers returning from the Great War. Unlike the photograph of her mother and herself, Lena's face and upper torso filled the entire space revealing a close and intimate portrait. The photographer had composed the picture to accentuate Lena's beautiful youthful face. He had captured her in the middle of playing cards with one hand about to place a card on a table but with her gaze directed at the camera through pinz-nez glasses. With an ornate blouse, a broad bow tying back her long-flowing fair hair and a pearl necklace high on her neck Mr. Cooper had captured the beautiful, talented, eighteen year old Lena. She would not have known it at the time but the card she was playing was about to be cruelly trumped. Helena had been born in 1898 and even though she had been diagnosed from an early age with an enlarged heart the condition was not life threatening. Her birth had marked a new and important stage in Rebecca's life.

Rebecca remembered the first time she had crossed Clady Bridge. She had cycled from Glencairn, a country district of hill farms between Convoy and Letterkenny where she had been born to Peter and Catherine McCrudden in 1841. She still remembered the hardship of growing up on a small farm with her eight siblings. She didn't remember Bernard who had died in infancy. The four youngest had emigrated to The United States of America in their early twenties. Rebecca corresponded with them regularly, knowing that her letters eased some of their homesickness. Her two older siblings still lived in the old homestead in Glencairn and she visited them from time to time.

Tragedy had struck herself and her first husband John Bonner with the death of twins at birth. Her other five children had survived but Rebecca became a widow in 1890 just nine years after marrying John. She still remembered the hard years following John's death trying to eke out a living on a small farm. Fortunately she had always been resourceful. Families had to be self-sufficient in those days. Animals and fowl raised on the farm provided food and revenue when taken to market. Home-grown potatoes and vegetables were part of a staple diet and turf cut from the local bog provided fuel. Like most women of her generation Rebecca could bake a wide range of breads and cakes and when it came to knitting and sewing she was accomplished. Like most of the rural community she had left school at fourteen. By that time she had accomplished all the grades that the teachers had set for her and so she left school confident in her ability. She had liked school and her success had given her confidence to improve her lot.

Meeting and marrying Michael O'Flaherty had given her ambitions a boost. Michael gave up a butchery business in Dromore and he and Rebecca bought Urney Post Office which was situated at the lower end of Clady Main Street. This was a great opportunity for Rebecca to put her talents to good use. Having the Post Office gave them financial security but Rebecca opened a drapery business and with her sewing skills was able to provide undertaking facilities through making shrouds. Her undertaking service extended to preparing corpses for burial. It was with a sense of pride that she made her entry in the 1911 census; Rebecca O'Flaherty, Post Mistress, Shopkeeper. She did not know it at the time but five short years later events in Dublin, one hundred and forty miles away would adversely affect her business. The Easter Rising of 1916 set in train a period of conflict and instability that would lead to a war of independence from Britain. The outcome of this was the Government of Ireland Act of 1920 and the partition of Ireland. With a border three hundred yards from her Post Office her customer base was greatly reduced. She was helped in both businesses by her daughters Mary Bonner, Catherine Bonner and Teresa O'Flaherty. However, Catherine decided to follow her brothers to the United States in 1913. Further income came from providing lodgings for Miss Feely, the local primary schoolteacher.

While the deaths of her Bonner twins, her O'Flaherty daughter Lena and her second husband Michael had been sore on her she also grieved sorely at the departure of James, John and Catherine to Philadelphia in the intervening years, for she knew she would never see them again. On this November afternoon she allowed all these painful memories to intrude. Reaching over to the bedside table she picked up her rosary beads and began slowly to recite the Joyful Mysteries not expecting to say them all for she could gently feel the drowsiness overtaking her.

****

Teresa McElhinney sat down at the piano in the parlour to practise 'Waves in a Storm' a very difficult piece that she had learned while attending the Convent School in Strabane. Mr. Franklin, her piano teacher had always encouraged her to interpret the music. "Tell your story, tell your story" he would exclaim as he listened to her rendition. So she needed to brush up on it because that evening a group of friends was arriving to play whist. It was normal to have some tea after the cards and more often than not the evening's entertainment would end with a sing- song around the piano. Teresa's mother Rebecca had bought the piano for Lena and herself in Phillips of Derry in 1912 and both of them had become proficient on it. Lena was a gifted musician but Teresa had worked with great determination to achieve her grades. With Lena's death it was left to her to carry on the musical tradition.

Teresa liked these gatherings because they provided a means of keeping in touch with the sort of people with whom she liked to socialise. This circle of friends from both sides of the border included other business people in the village- the Simpsons who had a grocery business opposite the Post Office, the Wilsons from just up the street on the opposite side who had a hardware shop, the Boyles from The Green, prosperous farmers and of course the Gallaghers from Castlefin. Willie Gallagher was godfather to Teresa's third child Eugene. Molly Gallagher, his sister had been Teresa's best friend at school but had entered a Dominican contemplative convent in Drogheda. Another sister Catherine had graduated from

University College Dublin with a Master of Arts Degree in music.

Teresa's mother Rebecca and her half –sister, Mary Bonner liked these gatherings also because they helped to brighten up the long cold winter evenings. Teresa's husband Hugh was a keen card player and greatly enjoyed playing whist. Fortunately Rebecca's granddaughter Margaret Bonner, or Peggy as he was called, used to cycle over from Convoy, some fifteen miles over the border in County Donegal, to look after Teresa's children on such occasions.

Just before the guests arrived Teresa's husband Hugh said he was going around the corner to collect some 'stuff' from Jim Sweeney but said he would be back in good time for the whist. "Okay, but don't let him delay you. You know what he's like once he gets started", warned Teresa. "Don't worry; I'd rather be playing cards than listening to Jim's views on the forces of law and order!" "Okay, just remember how punctual our guests are. They like to start playing on the dot of 7:30."

The guests duly arrived, six in all. With Teresa and Hugh they would have eight players. After the usual pleasantries the players sat down at two tables that Teresa had set out for them in the parlour. There was a lively fire in the hearth and all they needed was for Hugh to arrive. After five minutes Teresa called on her sister Mary to sit in for Hugh until he arrived. "I warned him not to be late and not to let Jim Sweeney detain him with his grand yarns about you know what," apologised Teresa. With a knowing chuckle from the guests the whist began without Hugh.

Although Mary Bonner was happy enough to oblige her sister she didn't like card playing that much. She always felt the tension building up in the competitive atmosphere of whist. Her doctor had told her not to get over excited because of her high bold pressure. Lately she had not felt well but did not tell her younger half-sister whom she knew depended on her as a confidante and mentor in the Post Office. Lately she had begun to worry about Teresa's future. With her own poor health and an ageing mother Rebecca, she worried about the future. She hoped Hugh would not be delayed long.

They had just finished the first game when Hugh arrived back and addressed them all with, "Sorry for being late but I just had to hear Jim Sweeney's latest escapade. You won't believe it but just last night he outmanoeuvred the constabulary again. Apparently Sergeant Stevenson was on the bridge with a couple of constables waiting for Jim. He says he doesn't know how they knew he was going to be on the job last night. The scout car hadn't seen a thing and Jim had four men lined up to follow him over the bridge. Well, half way over out stepped the Sergeant. You'd need to hear Jim himself telling it, but before they could arrest him he dumped the bag over the bridge into the Finn pretending that he was drowning a dog that had been eating his wife's chickens!" At this disclosure the entire card school burst into laughter. All agreed that Sweeney had done it again. "It's a pity that incident didn't happen last year for you could have included it in your 'Border Blunder', said Catty. Did I tell you about our newest smuggler said

Teresa, feigning a serious tone?" "No. Who is that" enquired Willy Gallagher. Someone we know?" "Yes, exclaimed Teresa, my second son, six-year old Brendan. I was coming across from my 'shop' over the border with a blanket wrapped around me under my coat as I have done many times. When I got into the house here what had the bold Brendan stuck up his jumper but a pot of jam?! It's a good job there were no customs women on duty"! "Well, would you believe it" said Trevor Simpson "and sure Brendan is a quiet shy child, you'd think butter wouldn't melt in his mouth"! "Wasn't there some other story about Jim Sweeney, Hugh that you told me? I don't think the others have heard it", remarked Willie Gallagher. "What was that one"? enquired Hugh. "About the cow" said Willie? "Oh right. Jim had a cow that was half blind. Johnny Doherty of Foyfinn was interested in it. So Jim says to him, "Johnny you'll have to come and take the cow away at night for if the villagers hear that I am selling her there will be a riot. Sure she's a walking creamery"! More bursts of laughter. "Right, enough of Jim Sweeney and you other smugglers, old and young" said Mary Bonner mischievously," I'm handing my place over to Hugh. I'll check if everything is okay with Peggy and the children.

The next day Teresa was interrupted in her work in the Post Office with a commotion down the hall that led to the living quarters. Mary Anne Doherty was in the kitchen with four- year–old Eugene all covered in mud. "What happened you Eugene? Look at the sight of you!" exclaimed Teresa. "Paddy Boyle pushed me into the mucky stream at the bottom of the street", blurted out Eugene. "Teresa, I saw it from my own front door," interrupted Mary Anne. "Eugene was going past with a toy windmill and Paddy Boyle and his brother Jack came over, snatched the toy and pushed Eugene into the burn. I ran over and rescued him. Those rough Boyles hit him hard. He was lying mouth down in the mucky water. It's a good job I was there or he might have suffocated", added Mary Anne. "Well, thanks be to God you were Mary Anne", said Teresa. Go out to the scullery Eugene and take off those filthy clothes and I will get you cleaned up. "It's not the first time those Boyles have picked on your children", said Mary Anne, "but as you know Teresa I keep an eye out for them. I have a good view of the whole street from my front door". "Thanks again Mary Anne, I am much obliged to you", said Teresa as she left her neighbour to the front door.

When Mary Anne had left, Teresa washed Eugene's face and hair and put dry clothes on him. Returning to the Post Office she related the incident to her older sister. Mary listened and after a pause she said, "Teresa, you know that I have already mentioned to you that you should be planning for your future somewhere other than Clady. I have noticed mother lately and I am a bit concerned about her health. You know that my own health is not good. I don't want to alarm you but Dr. Brown has told me that I need to reduce the stress brought on by Post Office work. My deafness is getting worse and that makes me more stressed when trying to take down telegraph messages. I don't want to interfere but Hugh has fallen out with a few neighbours over that plan of his to build a picture house across the street. You know how he talks about buying a small farm. Well, my advice to you is that when mother and I are gone, sell the place and take Hugh and the children to where they won't be harassed the way Eugene was just now. I have been meaning to say this for some time and today's incident convinces me that that is what you should do. You know you are a bit highly strung yourself. As a matter of fact, ever since those two attacks on the Post Office I think both of us have been worrying that it might happen again". Teresa listened intently to Mary. Since Lena's death her older half sister and she had become very close. She valued her advice and deep down she knew Mary was right. "I know Mary but mother and you are not that frail", insisted Teresa and sure Peggy is a great help to me. And don't forget Eugene's godmother Marjorie. She is so good to come all the way from Rathmullan for the odd day to help. I wonder what she would think if she saw her precious godchild covered in muck". Both of them gave a little laugh at the thought of Marjorie McElhinney finding her precious Eugene just out of the gutter.

Neither Teresa nor Mary would have agreed with the old expression that it takes a village to raise a child. Their view might have had something to do with the size, location, and population of their village. Clady was one of those small Irish villages that had been adversely affected by the partition of Ireland in 1921 and Teresa, as Postmistress, knew a lot about her customers. She was aware of their financial situations and was privy to aspects of their family affairs through her work as telephonist for the community. She knew only too well the political and social divisions and petty jealousies that beset the village. She was determined that her children would be raised according to her standards and aspirations and not the collective standards of the village. Her parents had raised both their daughters to have high standards and high expectations. They made sure that Lena and Teresa got a good convent education. Buying a piano for them was a financial sacrifice at the time but it contributed to their development as cultured young ladies. Later, with Michael's help and approval, buying Teresa a motor car so that she was the first woman in the village to own and drive a car reinforced the O'Flahertys' importance in village life. Apart from the other business people, the inhabitants of Clady worked for employers in the area. A mile or so to the east of the village on the road to the town of Strabane was a small chocolate factory while half a mile to the west was a flax mill. These provided employment for some of the villagers while others worked on the surrounding farms or in shops in Strabane.

With the death of her father Michael in 1930 Teresa was left with her mother Rebecca and her half-sister Mary. That situation changed in 1938 with Teresa's marriage to Hugh McElhinney, a cattle dealer from Ballydun, Co. Derry. In those days a popular resort for excursions and summer holidays was Bundoran, some sixty miles westwards on Donegal's rugged Atlantic coast. In the summer of 1937 Teresa went there with a couple of girl friends and met the tall dark handsome Hugh. Teresa was thirty-four, two years older than Hugh. Friendship blossomed and the opportunity to take the relationship to the next level must have seemed attractive to both. If Teresa was to marry and have a family Hugh must have appeared as a suitable partner; for Hugh the prospect of marrying into a small business would have been an attractive proposition. And so it came to pass and on the 23rd February 1938 they were married in Melmount Chapel Strabane and had the wedding reception at home in Clady.

On the 7th September the following year their first child, Peter Joseph Anthony was born. Their second son, Michael James Brendan arrived on October 25th 1940. Three years later a third son, Eugene Patrick was born on March 8th 1943. The following April 1st Teresa was delivered prematurely of her first daughter Kathleen, Mary Angela and two years later Monica Josephine Helena was born on September 19th 1946. Teresa was forty three years old at the birth of her last child. It was not unusual in those days for women to have children into their early forties partly due to the fact that large families were the norm. All five children were born at home which was also normal in those days with the local GP overseeing the births. Teresa's first experience of giving birth was very difficult and dangerous, largely due to an incompetent doctor. The damage done on that occasion affected Teresa for forty years until she had corrective surgery in her seventies for a genitourinary prolapse.

In keeping with Teresa's determination to raise her family according to her preferred social values she ensured that each child was christened with a name which could not easily be abbreviated. So, Peter Joseph Anthony was

27

referred to as Peter, Michael James Brendan was called Brendan, Eugene Patrick was Eugene, Kathleen Mary Angela was Angela and Monica Josephine Helena was Monica. This proved to be a successful strategy until Peter joined the Irish Naval Service in 1959 and was referred to by the Irish version of Peter which is Peadar. He has been Peadar ever since.

That was the political, cultural and social context into which I was born on March 8th 1943.

****

Chapter 1: My Village

One of my first memories of Clady was the day I accompanied my father to the bus stop to collect a box of day-old chicks. When the bus arrived in the village the bus conductor handed my father a flat cardboard box with an array of little round holes on the top. It was like a musical box because all I could hear was the cheep, cheep, cheep, of day-old chicks. I asked if I could carry the box, so my father handed it to me as we approached the house. It was heavier than I expected. It seemed to be almost alive because it was warm, and throbbed with the energy of twenty-four chicks, and it sang. When we got to the house my father took the box to an outhouse in the backyard and released the yellow feathery contents into a little chicken run which was sitting on a table covered with wire mesh. There was a big bulb hanging down over the chicken run which gave off a lot of heat. In the middle was a container of water and a drinking trough. The smell of meal filled the air.

I used to go in to see the little fluffy chicks regularly but after a couple of weeks I was disappointed to see that they had grown into young chickens and seemed to spend a lot of time pecking each other. Especially vulnerable were the weaker ones. Sometimes a dead chick, stripped of many of its feathers lay among the bird droppings. The sweet smell of meal was now mixed with the smell of bird shit and gone was the chirpy music, so I left them to grow and fight among themselves, if that was what they wanted. Anyway I had too many other things to do. I had the whole village and beyond to explore.

Even though my grandmother, Aunt Mary (or Aunt Mia as we called her), and my mother warned us all about being mannerly when out on the street and not to be imitating the ways of the rougher children it was difficult to avoid the reality of village life. I seemed to have the run of the place for I used to walk with my brothers and other children the half mile or so over the border to St. Columba's Church in Doneyloop for Sunday Mass and various devotions in May and October. My father took me up to a field in Inchenny that he had taken for growing flax and sometimes out the Strabane road to another field where he had some cattle grazing. On another occasion he took my brothers and me over the border where he had some cattle that he herded into a low part of the river and swam them across. But there were other times when I roamed the surrounding countryside with a small group of village children, usually in the summer months.

At four years of age I knew nothing about Sigmund Freud's theories about psychosexual development but looking back on one afternoon's stroll through the fields outside the village I realise that my childhood friends and I experienced manifestations of elements two and three of a five stage model i.e. the anal and phallic elements. According to Freud, children of that age are curious about bodily functions and gender difference. Well, he was right in our case. Paddy

Rogan who was four and a half decided that he needed to go to the toilet immediately, out in the middle of the field. We were right beside him and as he dropped his short trousers to relieve himself we had a worm's –eye view of the whole business. We lay on our stomachs and watched and understood how that part of the anatomy worked. Whether out of respect or just intense interest little was said. Except for four year old Jimmy Kelly who had the best view of the process, who exclaimed, "I see it coming". And with that it was over. Paddy had performed in a very quick and efficient manner so that he did not even need toilet paper. He simply pulled up his pants and we all moved off without any sense of guilt or shame. This episode must have emboldened us, for on another day sometime later we proved Freud right again when we moved effortlessly to the next stage. One of the boys, I forget which, sat down and a girl in our company sat astride across his lap. Another girl did the same with me and then repeated this with a third boy. These childhood embraces lasted only seconds and looking back were nothing special. Their closeness felt warm and tingly but that was about it. Again, nobody said anything. We simply resumed our walk through the fields not knowing that we had learned something fundamental about human psycho-sexual development. Even though it did not seem at the time to register as anything unusual to children of four and a half, it clearly did have a subconscious effect otherwise I would not have remembered it. In fact all my memories have some element of disclosure about them.

Like the time my sister Angela and I were in Strabane with our mother. It was September 1948 and I think my mother was buying us shoes. We came to Gibson's chemists. Just as we got inside the shop Mr. Gibson called my mother over. "Your husband Hugh was on the phone a few minutes ago. He said to tell you to get home right away; your sister Mary isn't well. I ordered a taxi for you so you'd better get going". In that instant our carefree shopping day was transformed. We rushed outside where a taxi was waiting for us. All the way to Clady my mother sat leaning forward trying almost to make the car go faster. She didn't speak but we could sense that she was in shock. As the car raced homewards I still remember the tall row of leafless beech trees half a mile from the village whizzing past that meant that we were fast nearing our destination. As soon as we reached home my mother jumped out of the car and raced to the front door to be met by my father. "Mary's dead", he said as my mother rushed past him and up the stairs where she found her sister Mary lying dead with one foot out from under the clothes as if she had been attempting to get out of bed.

That death was very sore on our mother because she and Mary had been very close. My brothers and sisters and I were whisked away to stay with the Boyles of The Green until after the funeral. We did get a chance to return to the house before the burial to view the remains. I was brought up to Mary's bedroom. She was laid out on the bed and my mother lifted me up to kiss her goodbye. What I noticed most about her was how purple her face was. It was the first time I had felt the coldness of a corpse and the first time I had smelt the odour of death.

My recollections of Aunt Mia's death are more vivid than those of my grandmother. Rebecca O'Flaherty had died six months prior, on January 20th 1948. I remember large plumed horses arriving, pulling a glass hearse, but not much else. As with Aunt Mia my siblings and I were looked after by the Boyles of The Green during the time of the wake. Considering that I had been granny's 'minder' I don't know why I did not get a chance to say goodbye to her like I did with Aunt Mia. Maybe it was because Mary had died so suddenly.

Before the term was invented I was a 'joy rider'. In fact I can probably claim to be the first and youngest joy rider in Ireland. It all began one day in that eventful summer of 1948. Bob Simpson was one of the few in the village to own a motorcar, a black shiny one that had a running board and externally mounted chrome headlamps. Both of these items were to play a part in an incident that was to turn me from a law abiding five year old into a fugitive from justice.

Bob's car, which was parked up the street from our house, attracted the attention of the village children. In fairness to Bob he didn't seem to mind us playing around it or leaving our sticky fingerprints all over the shiny paintwork. Anyway, there I was this day with Paddy and Joe, both seven year olds, Jimmy and John both five, like myself. The older boys discovered that by standing on the running board and reaching in and moving the gear stick they could knock the engine out of gear and get it to move a few inches. Now this was really exciting and so a game of dare began. The two seven-year olds managed this effortlessly. So now it was my turn. Well, to my surprise it was not that difficult to move the gear lever but in doing so I couldn't reach it again to reengage it and stop the car. In no time at all it had moved on to the street and was gaining speed at an alarming rate. Instinctively I jumped clear before it ran into the side of our house and broke a headlamp.

So there I was, the first and youngest joy rider in Ireland having just crashed my first vehicle. To make matters worse I immediately left the scene of the crime. In an effort to avoid detection I raced up Simpson's brae, ducked through the hedge at the top, hopped on the stepping stones over Kelly's burn, raced through Mrs. Kelly's garden, ran down along the river and, making sure to 'juke' behind the gorse bushes, and casually sauntered up our back garden only to find the towering figure of my father waiting for me. He lectured me on the enormity of my crime, saying that I would have to go to prison, produced a small suitcase and started to pack it with what I would need in jail. On seeing this, my young sister Angela began to cry. Fortunately my mother entered a plea of mercy and after what seemed to me like a very long trial I was reprieved. The strange thing is that even to this day I sometimes dream of being in a car that doesn't slow down when I apply the brakes.

Our house on the main street seemed to be a busy place with the daily comings and goings of the villagers to the Post Office and visits by friends and relations to the living quarters. Our cousins Peggy and Lena Bonner used to cycle over from Convoy in Co. Donegal, about fifteen miles away and Marjorie McElhinney, who was my Godmother used to travel from Rathmullan, also in Co. Donegal. They came after births or to help my mother with housework from time to time. Marjorie was very neat and tidy and if she tidied the house she expected us children to keep it that way. Any dissent was greeted with, "Don't you talk back to me, and that's all's about it". On one occasion after tidying the upstairs she challenged Brendan, who was climbing the stairs with, "Where do you think you're going"? To which Brendan replied, "Don't you talk back to me and that's what it's all about!" much to Marjorie's amusement.

My Godfather, Willie Gallagher, used to call to play cards or to 'ceili'. I remember him as a tall thin man with ginger hair and freckles. He used to bounce me on his knee and tell stories or recite rhymes like 'The Crooked Man'.

'There was a crooked man, and he walked a crooked mile.
He found a crooked sixpence upon crooked stile.
He bought a crooked cat, which caught a crooked mouse,
And they all lived together in a little crooked House'.

He also liked to tell us the story of the three pigs. And of course he had to repeat the stories every time he called. My father used to do the same though he seemed more awkward at that sort of thing. He would relate the story of 'Tom

35

Thumb' and did his best to dramatise the story vocally. My mother used to wig our toes with the 'this little piggy went to the market, this little piggy stayed at home, this little piggy ate bread and butter and this little piggy ate none. And this little piggy said, "wee, wee, wee, all the way home".

My uncle Peter called one day and he and my father spent some time in our back garden. I was with them and as we walked down the steps from our back door Uncle Peter took out a penknife and cut a six- inch length of branch from a boor tree bush. The branches of these bushes are hollow so by cutting an opening on the top side of the six-inch length he had made a basic flute for me. My friends and I were more used to using these hollow branches as pea-shooters. Now I had a basic musical instrument. However, what pleased me more was that I had been acknowledged in a special way by my uncle in fashioning the flute for me.

My grandmother O'Flaherty liked to take a nap in the afternoon. Since I was her 'minder' at that stage I observed her routine closely. When she climbed the stairs and went into her room I could hear her turning the key in the door. That meant she didn't want to be disturbed. If she knocked the bedroom floor with her stick that was her signal that she wanted me for something or other. What she didn't know was that she wasn't the only one to take a nap in her bed.

One afternoon my mother got alarmed because I was missing. The house was searched to no avail. My siblings knew nothing of my whereabouts so the adults in the household began to get anxious. My mother had a fear of water and had warned us about the danger of getting too close to the river. She told us to stay away from the mill race that turned the waterwheel for the scutching mill. She searched the house again and tried my grandmother's door but it was locked and so assumed that her mother was taking her usual nap. On coming down the stairs she saw her mother in the hall and realised that someone else was in her mother's room. Going back up she used the spare key to get inside only to discover me fast asleep on my grandmother's bed with her key clutched in my little fist. This penchant for napping has stayed with me to the present day.

MaryAnn Doherty had a little cottage at the corner of Urney Road. It was she who had saved me from the mucky burn outside her house after I was pushed into it by a few rough boys. Like my father she used to get some day-old chicks and rear them. Sometimes the chicks developed respiratory problems. I remember one day on my way home from school seeing her using a piece of thread to fish out some obstruction in some of the chick's gullets. Sometimes I went into her house. She had always a great fire burning because she burned the 'shows' from the scutching mill along with wood or coal and this combination made a great blaze. The 'shows' were the dry outer shell of the flax plant that came off the flax when it was scutched in the mill just down the road from Mary Ann's house. There was a bed in the kitchen up close to the fire so I lay down on the bed and with the great heat from the fire I was fast asleep in no time.

The main street of the village divided into two just fifty yards below our house. The branch to the left led past Mary Anne Doherty's and on past the primary school on the left. Further along on the left was the scutching mill where locally grown flax was scutched and half a mile further was St. Columba's Catholic Church. The branch to the right led past the village forge and five hundred yards past that was Clady Bridge over the river Finn. Looking back on it the road to the left had a part in shaping my future because of the influence of the school and the church.

Mrs. Maguire, who was the teacher in charge of the junior classes, told my mother to send me on to school at just over four years of age as she felt that I could cope with the demands of junior infants and would give her a break from child-minding. Peter and Brendan were already in the school. Peter, who was eight, was in the senior side of the school with Master Brown. The said Master Brown was fond of using his strap to put manners on all of us. Any time Mrs. Maguire was absent Master Brown folded back the partition between senior classes and junior classes and imposed a strict regime of study. Slackers and disrupters were lined up and given a few short sharp slaps which established order until the next lapse of concentration.

The two schoolrooms were heated with coal-fired stoves. The older boys were in charge of bringing in coal from a bunker in the school yard. The yard itself was not that big. It had a high retaining wall at the back opposite the school building. Our coats hung from pegs at the back of the room and in wet weather there was always the smell of wet coats drying out on account of the heat generated by the coal stoves.

Brendan was in the junior side of the school with me and one day he was being chastised by Mrs. Maguire who wigged his ear. A few days before this our dog Doughery had nipped Brendan on the ear and the wound hadn't fully healed when Mrs Maguire tugged on it. In keeping with his quiet nature Brendan didn't say anything so I took it upon myself to inform Mrs. Maguire that she had pulled on Brendan's sore ear. She didn't apologise but a few days later I arrived at school with wet clothes and she made a fuss over me and even insisted that I sit up in front of the stove to get dried. She had never done this for anyone else.

After prolonged rainfall the river Finn used to overflow its banks and inundate the lower part of the village. The water used to come right up our back garden almost to the back door. The resulting flood at the lower end of the village cut off access to the school. A local fisherman had a small boat which he was able to use to evacuate anyone cut off by the water. The flood lasted a few days which gave us a welcome break from school. My last memory of the school was of being present at a retirement function for Mrs. Maguire.

The road to St. Columba's, Urney Road as it was called, featured quite a bit in my childhood. It was my road most travelled because of the school and the church. St. Columba's played a big part in village life generally. All the Catholics attended Mass on Sundays and Holy days. My mother played the harmonium and trained the choir. Peter and Brendan were altar boys. Large crowds used to attend October and May devotions. When Peter and Brendan were not on duty as altar boys they accompanied me to the church, which was just over half a mile from the village. Most people walked, some cycled and a few travelled by pony and trap. Going over in that company I felt very much part of the village community whatever about my mother's reservations about getting in with the wrong crowd.

At five years of age the church was a place of wonder with its tinkling bells, flickering candles and the rich aroma of incense. The mixture of long monotonous-sounding prayers by the adults and the priest with the melodious rise and fall of organ music and choir made the long services bearable. On one occasion during the Stations of the Cross I ventured down behind the priest and his clerks to get a better look. Nobody paid any attention to me and when my curiosity was satisfied I returned to my customary seat half way up on the right aisle.

The Church was built in a cruciform style, but not in a pronounced way so that the transept was not too wide. The organ loft was at the back of the main aisle where my mother played the harmonium. In the porch of the right transept there was a long thick rope that reached up to the bell in its tower. The end of the rope was just about reachable to a five year old boy.

Whether it was the droning sound of the priest and congregation as they recited the rosary, fatigue on my part or a combination of both I dozed off one evening during the October devotions of 1948. Peter and Brendan obviously did not notice me or else they had been acting as altar servers because they made their way home without me. As I slept, anxiety grew at home about my whereabouts. I had not returned from the chapel and there was no sign of me on the street. A search of the village proved fruitless.

Meanwhile I was roused from my slumber by Mrs. Gallagher the sacristan. She had finished her chores for the evening and was just about to lock up the church when she had spied a curly headed boy of five and a half fast asleep at the end of a seat on the right transept. After ascertaining who I was she locked the church and put me on the back carrier of her bicycle and set off for the village. A few hundred yards from the church as we crossed the border a customs man stepped out and asked Mrs. Gallagher about her cargo. Seeing that it was human cargo he waved us on and a few minutes later the sacristan delivered her parcel to the Post Office much to the relief of my parents.

In the debriefing that followed I was quizzed about how I would have managed had Mrs. Gallagher not spotted me. The general consensus was that had I awakened with the dark church shut and everyone gone I would have pulled on the bell rope in the porch to alert the village of my plight. It would be flattering to think that a five and a half year old would have had that presence of mind to effect such an escape. We shall never know.

The road from the church to the village featured in my young life the following autumn. I was making my way home from Mass with a few other boys. About half way home I noticed a few wasps circling around their nest half way up a grassy bank at the side of the road. Someone had pushed a crab apple into the opening of the nest, partially blocking it. This made it difficult for the wasps to enter. I stopped to investigate but my companions walked on. I don't know if I felt sorry for the wasps or just curious to see what would happen if I pushed the crab apple further into the opening. Anyway I grabbed a stick that was lying nearby and proceeded to push the crab apple inwards. This worked because suddenly a swarm of wasps flew out of their nest and proceeded to attack me. As they launched their attack I pulled off my tweed jacket to fend them off. This strategy didn't work very well and after receiving several stings I flung the coat at the attacking wasps and ran home.

Bounding into the house, yelping with pain, I told my mother what had happened. I had several stings, one even on my tongue. My mother got out a bottle of gentian violet and treated my stings with it while my father was dispatched to retrieve my jacket. Despite the severity of my pain and discomfort my parents seemed amused at my plight. From my point of view there was nothing funny about it.

My mother's misgivings about letting her children roam the village at will had some justification. There were always older boys who could be a bad influence on the younger ones. The incident of me as a 'joy rider' was a case in point but there were other incidents that would have alarmed her had she known about them. For instance the dangerous practice of getting halfpennies flattened on the railway line. The Donegal Railway Company had a rail service between Lifford and Stranorlar which passed close to Clady on the Donegal side of the border. By crossing the bridge it was possible to get access to the railway line. Never one to resist a dare I was quite happy to assist some of the older boys in placing our pennies and halfpennies on the line and wait for the next train to travel over them. We hid in the bushes of course when we saw the train approaching and then dashed up the embankment to check if our halfpennies had been turned into pennies. Peter and Brendan were probably in the same gang.

Another dangerous practice unknown to my mother was the construction of mini bombs with the aid of carbine and empty tins. We learned from the older boys that by placing some carbine on the base of a tin and then depositing a generous spit of saliva on it and closing the tin tightly we had only to wait a few minutes for the tin to blow its lid with a loud bang. The combination of saliva and carbine started a chemical reaction which filled the tin with gas which led to the explosion. Carbine was used in bicycle lamps in those days so it was not difficult getting a few ounces for our bomb making. At six years of age we didn't know the science behind the bang but it was exciting to be part of a dangerous game.

I followed my parents' wishes in being mannerly on the street and if I happened to bring any 'bad words' or coarse language from my frequent tours of the village into the house I was quickly corrected and told not to use that sort of language. One word that didn't pass the test of acceptability was 'shite'. The memory of being chastised for using it escapes me but to the present day it is a word that is not part of my vocabulary.

Children are very perceptive and are quick to notice differences in the speech or manners of their friends. Equally I was aware of different standards and recognised when older boys were deliberately emphasising the difference. One way was through singing bawdy songs, not that the ones I heard were that bad, lines like, 'Swimmin' with naked women in Honolulu Bay' or the more daring, "My auntie Mary had a canary up the leg of her drawers. When she was sleeppin' I was peepin' up the leg of her drawers". I knew that these songs represented the coarse language of the street and ignored them. There was no need to mention this in the house. Even at five years of age the differences between some street language and the language of the home gradually became apparent.

This tuning in to language extended to the words of the popular songs of the day. Two songs that I remember from that time were 'Five Minutes More' and 'Buttons and Bows'. Lines like 'Give me five minutes more, only five minutes more, let me stay, let me stay in your arms' sounded very grown up. A number of homes in the village including ourselves had a radio so the popular American songs were known to us. The radio was particularly important for listening to the All-Ireland series of Gaelic matches. In 1947 Kerry was playing Cavan in the final which was played at the Polo Grounds in New York. I was too young to know much about the football scene but my oldest brother Peter and my father were tuned in to the match. Apparently John Joe O'Reilly was the star player for Cavan. Like the other boys of similar age football was beginning to be important to Peter. He even asked Santa Claus for a football that Christmas but to no avail. Obviously Santa, like my mother, had decided that putting a football in Peter's stocking would only encourage him to spend too much time on the street with the rougher boys of the village.

Radio wasn't the only medium to open up a wider world to the villagers. This was the era of the travelling Picture Show. My father, who had an interest in drama, brought my brothers and me to a screening of 'Mutiny on the Bounty'. The film was shown for a week in a tent in a field just beside Clady Bridge. Other films on offer were of Laurel and Hardy and Charlie Chaplin. These 'movies' were a big hit with the villagers who turned out in big numbers. Going to these picture shows gave my father the idea of building a 'Picture House' on a site that we owned across from the Post Office. However, some of the neighbours objected so the scheme never got off the ground.

Great was my curiosity in those closing years of the forties. Whether with my young friends roaming the fields around the village or with my father checking up on his cattle on land he had taken out the Strabane road or going with him to watch the lint being pulled in fields out the Urney road I covered the village in every direction. After the lint had been pulled it was tied into bundles and steeped in the flax dam to break down the outer skin. Peter and Brendan and my father and I used to go to the flax dam to tramp down the flax. We were not allowed to go there on our own because there was some danger in this operation. After several days of soaking in the summer heat the flax gave off a putrid smell which was a sign that it was nearly ready to be hauled out, dried and taken to the scutching mill.

For any young boy there were some areas that were off limits, even for the adventurous. For some reason my parents told us not to get too close to a particular property on a broad corner of the Strabane road just a little way from the village. According to them there was a wild man living there in a dark old house behind a high wall who had a large knife who was to be avoided at all costs. I never did find out what the real reason for their warning was but I always passed this man's house as quickly as I could on the opposite side of the road. I learned much later that he was mentally unstable.

Another no-go area was the forge at the bottom of Main Street just around the corner from Mary Ann Doherty's cottage. Jimmy Toal was the blacksmith, a large muscular man with a blackened face and large moustache. He had a large dirty looking handkerchief tucked into the belt of his leather apron which he used from time to time to mop the beads of sweat from his brow. The inside of the forge was dark except for the red glow of the fire which surged with every squeeze of the bellows. I always kept my distance passing by but was curious enough to get close enough to see the bright red of the fire and the spray of sparks as Jimmy hammered the glowing red and white metal on his anvil. As he dipped a newly fashioned horse shoe into the trough of water outside the forge there was a hiss off the cooling metal and a mist of vapour rising. Sometimes a horse was brought to the forge for shoeing which the blacksmith carried out in a very methodical way. Holding the horse's hoof between his knees he removed any old nails and then pared the hoof. Sometimes he reheated the new shoe and placed it over the bare hoof to track its position. When he did this there was a strong smell of burning hoof but to my surprise the horse didn't flinch. After cooling the shoe he placed it over the track he had made and nailed it to the hoof. I couldn't figure out how the horse could be so co-operative especially when Jimmy hammered in nails or used a rough rasp to smooth the rough edges of the metal shoe.

The blacksmith was not the only man to impress me with strength and daring. My father was an expert at killing fowl, whether hens, turkeys or geese. If a hen was to be killed my brothers and I gathered to watch. My father lifted the hen by the legs, placed his first and second fingers around its neck and with a sudden and powerful downward motion he broke the hen's neck. This sickening tug was followed for about twenty seconds by the sound and the sight of the hens' wings beating violently, then gradually slowing down to a stop. At this point the dead hen was handed over to my mother or Peggy to be plucked and hung up in the scullery. My father assured us that the hen had not suffered and that the violent beating of the wings was just the twitching of muscles. Going out to the scullery later I would find the stiff and lifeless body of the hen hanging from a peg on the wall, small clear drops of water dripping from its beak. The largest and healthiest of my chirping fluffy day-old-chicks now hung in silent featherless shame.

As 1949 drew to a close arrangements were being made to sell the Post Office and move across the border to Finner, a district between Bundoran and Ballyshannon in County Donegal. With the deaths of my Grandmother Rebecca and Aunt Mary my mother didn't want to carry the burden of running the Post Office even though she had employed an assistant postmaster a few years earlier. My father had heard from one of his cattle dealer friends that there was a farm for sale at Finner which would serve as an alternative source of income to the Post Office. Although there was a certain amount of risk involved my mother decided to follow her sister Mary's advice and move. She knew that my father needed a farm to supplement his cattle dealing. He had already created some friction in the village over the plan to build a picture house on a site which belonged to the Post Office on the opposite side of the street. In addition he had taken the pledge a couple of years earlier when he realised that he was drinking too much, so a fresh start looked like a good idea to both of them.

And so in early September the following notice appeared in the Derry Journal.

Important Auction of Old- established
Border Business Premises
Dwelling-House, Garage and Building Site
(Vacant Possession)
I am instructed by Mrs. McElhinney to SELL BY AUCTION at my Salerooms, The Diamond Derry, on Wednesday, 14th September, 1949 at 1 o'clock in the afternoon-   IF NOT PREVIOUSLY DISPOSED OF:-

All that old-established Business Premises and Dwelling House known as "McElhinney's, Main Street, Clady, Urney, Co. Tyrone together with Garage and Plot of Ground suitable as Building Site for Hall or Picture House situate at the foot of the opposite side of the street, all held in Fee Simple, Free of Rent, P.L.V. £11.

The House is substantially built of stone and slated, has a wide frontage and contains a well laid out Shop with Back Store, Kitchen, Scullery, Dining Room, Drawing Room and four Bedrooms; also large rear with Coalhouse, Byre, Flush Lavatory and enclosed Garden Plot used as a hen-run. The House is fitted with Electric Light and was recently papered, painted and decorated and is in an excellent state of repair.

Vendor's parents started business in Clady over 70 years ago and carried on a most successful Drapery, Grocery and Funeral Undertaking Concern which was continued by the family. The Trade Position today is really wonderful due to the close proximity of the BORDER TOWNS of Urney, Castlederg and Castlefin and to the prosperity of the farming community.

Anyone in quest of a 'good stand' with opportunities for developing would do well to consider this Sale.

For Cards to View, Title and Conditions of Sale, apply:-
Wilson & Simms, Solicitors, Florence O'Sullivan, Auctioneer
Bowling Green Strabane; The Diamond, Derry
Phone 2096

Before we left, my mother went into the house to take a last look at the place of her birth. My father and Peter had gone ahead to the new house to await the rest of the family. Some of the furniture had been sold and the rest transferred by a removals company earlier in the day so the house was bare and lacked the ambience of her familiar home. Nonetheless she did a tour of the property, planning to go into every room to recall the significance each one had in her memory. She was not sentimental by nature but she wanted to take her leave formally as one shakes hands with friends and acquaintances on leaving them. Crossing the hall she looked into the living room which had been the main room in the house for day to day events. It was here that the children had hung up their stockings by the fireplace at Christmastime over the previous ten years. It was here she had overheard Peter and Brendan learning their Latin responses for serving Mass. Still visible on the wall to her right was the track left behind where a picture of St. Patrick had hung. Seeing the demarcated blank space reminded her of the occasion when Eugene had been asked by his grandmother who it was and he had said "That's me and my big beard!"

Making her way down the hall she checked out the kitchen on her left. In many ways this room had been the hub of the home, where meals had been cooked and served, where the family had gathered round to listen to the wireless or say the rosary and where the heat of the range had drawn all together on cold winter nights.

Going through the pantry she opened the back door to have one last look at the garden where she and Lena had played as children and where her own children had played and squabbled and laughed and cried. It was at the bottom of the garden below the leafless trees that her group wedding photograph had been taken twelve years earlier. To her right was the little gate that had been the subject of a court case that her mother had won against a neighbour who had objected to it. At least this was something to smile about chiefly because of the wording of the judge's verdict. "Go home Mrs O'Flaherty and paint your little gate red".

Returning to the house she went upstairs to view the parlour. It was unusual to have a parlour upstairs but this was the case because one of the front rooms on the bottom floor had been incorporated into the Post Office. It was in this upstairs parlour where over the years visitors had been entertained and special events had been celebrated. Gone was the piano that her mother had bought for Lena and herself. Many were the hours they had spent practising and playing for visitors. That same piano had been locked for a full year following the deaths of her sister Mary and mother Rebecca. She recalled in particular that it was here she had gathered with her new husband and family and friends following her wedding on February 23rd 1938. Although empty and echoing her footsteps she stood for a few moments to recall the scene. She realised that by leaving none of her children would have similar celebrations there. She decided not to look into the four empty bedrooms. She was still coming to terms with the recent deaths of her sister and mother in two of the rooms. It was in one of the other rooms that Lena had been taken and she had been spared. So, instead she went down the stairs and walked along the passage way that led to the Post Office for a last look at the business end of the property which was intact and ready for business the following day when the new owner was due to move in. With a final glance at the wall where several bullets had lodged at the time of the armed raid she retraced her steps, locked the back door and left by the front door pulling it shut as she stepped down on to the footpath.

As she walked towards the side of the house, where the taxi was waiting, she looked up the main street for a final look. Many of the villagers had called at the Post Office in the preceding days to say goodbye and wish her well. With that she got into the car which headed for the Bridge over the Finn.

As the car moved slowly over the bridge I got my last look at the place of my birth, until I would return many years later to see it. We crossed the border and turned left towards Castlefin. For about a mile or so we could see the spire of St. Columba's Church receding behind us but still reminding us of the central place it had been in our lives.

I was in the back seat with Brendan, Angela and Monica. At three years of age it was Monica's first time in a motorcar. She had baulked at getting into it but with some persuasion she eventually agreed, got in and sat in the middle of us in the back seat. Not having travelled in a car before she was surprised at seeing houses seemingly approaching. "There's a little house coming up"! she exclaimed, and with each subsequent house "There's another little house coming up". She kept up this refrain as we sped southwards through village and town and on through Barnesmore Gap en route to Finner. As a six year old I was just looking forward to seeing my new home.

The village that I had just left had played a bigger part in my upbringing than I realised.

Chapter 2   Donegal

Part 1 Finner

We reached Ballyshannon early in the afternoon of January 11th and a new phase of my life began. It was exciting to see a new large town but I did not have time to take much of it in as we travelled down the steep main street past the large clock that stood out like a beacon on the lower end of the street. As we crossed the bridge over the River Erne we were crossing the border between the dioceses of Raphoe and Clogher. "Just another couple of miles and we will be there", said my mother as we watched the buildings of West Port flash past. A mile out of the town we began to climb Corn Hill and from the top my mother pointed out our destination in the distance.

Our new home was a pebble-dashed bungalow with bay windows at the front set back about ten yards from the main road. The front garden had a patchy lawn bounded by a small wall with a wrought iron front gate. A concrete path led to the front door. A larger gate attached to pillars gave entry to an area at the left side of the house from which there was access to the back door. Another large iron gate marked an entrance to the field at the right of the house. We later discovered that this gate allowed access to a neighbouring farmer who had a right of way through our farm to his property two large fields away.

We jumped out of the car and rushed in to see what the house was like. We discovered that there were four bedrooms and a kitchen, all on the same floor, which was a novelty to us. As children the house was just another house. We were more interested in the outside because of the wide open spaces and the proximity to a main road. There were outhouses behind the main house comprising of a haggard and a byre and at the very end was an outside toilet. Two brand new wooden henhouses were located in the field behind the house. A solitary donkey grazed in the field nearby.

Behind and to the side of the house were sixty-nine acres of arable land marked off into fields by stone ditches. There was scarcely a tree to be seen. In the background there was the soft rhythmic sound of the Atlantic Ocean breaking on Tullan strand on the outskirts of Bundoran, the popular seaside resort just two and a half miles down the road. We noticed a cluster of buildings just up the opposite side of the road from us which we later discovered was Finner Army Camp which operated only during the summer months. Directly opposite and within the grounds of the camp was a football pitch for the use of the soldiers.

About fifty yards behind our farm buildings was a pond. Our mother immediately declared it out of bounds, warning us not to get within ten yards of it, a warning that we heeded during the three and a half years that we lived there.

As it was January when we arrived we didn't have much time to explore before dark and by the time we helped with unpacking, had something to eat and worked out our sleeping arrangements it was time for bed. That first night in Finner we quickly drifted off to sleep to the lulling sound of the Atlantic breakers making landfall on a beach that seemed nearer than it actually was. In the following days, weeks and months we got to know a great deal about Finner and the towns on either side.

The priority for our parents was to make arrangements for our schooling. Ballyshannon had a joint primary/secondary school for boys run by the De La Salle Order, so Peter, Brendan and I were sent there. On the first day of attendance the Head Brother assigned a local boy, Hugh Doherty to be our minder until we found our feet. Peter was placed in fifth class with Brother Timony, the Head Brother while Brendan and I were assigned to second class with Brother Michael.

Monica was too young to start school but Angela, who was almost six, needed to find a place either in Ballyshannon or Bundoran. There was a primary/secondary school in Ballyshannon run by the Sisters of Mercy and in Bundoran there was a similar school run by the St.Louis Sisters. Because there was a school bus service from Bundoran to Ballyshannon the logical thing was to send Angela to the Sisters of Mercy School. However the St. Louis Sisters had a better reputation as educators so Bundoran was chosen even though this meant that Angela had to get a lift to school in a bread van that plied that route. Unfortunately the bread van didn't do the return journey which meant that Angela had to spend many weary afternoons after school waiting for her bus home.

For my brothers and me getting to school was not a problem, just as long as we were ready when the bus arrived. Like many young boys we were difficult to rouse in the morning and often had to scurry across the road to the sound of my mother shouting, "Quick boys, there's the bus coming,' as munching on our toast we raced out in time for the bus driver to see us. There were times of course when we didn't quite make it. Luckily, Master Moran who lived in Bundoran drove to school and always passed our door a little later than the bus. Thankfully, he used to stop and give us a lift. I appreciated his kindness at the time but later when I moved to the secondary side of the school I changed my view of him because of the manner in which he administered corporal punishment.

We had to pay for our transport, a few pence each way, but with the improvement of the weather in late spring we used to save the fare by cycling to school. Even some boys from Bundoran cycled. Climbing Corn Hill was always a struggle on the way home but sometimes we were lucky to get a tow from "Paddy Go Aiasy". Paddy Slevin had an old Model T truck that had a top speed of about fifteen miles per hour. He used to deliver furniture for Stephenson's' Hardware and Furnishings shop on Castle Street. If he happened to be going out the Bundoran Road we tucked in behind his slipstream and caught on to the back of his truck with one hand for a tow up Corn Hill at five miles per hour. Only two cyclists at a time could do this so there was a bit of competition to hook on for a tow. We never discovered if Paddy approved of our reckless behaviour but we thought it was great fun.

The original school bus was a single-decker, but it was replaced by a double-decker which became very popular. There was always a scramble to get on the upper deck. Although as schoolboys we were not particularly interested in the scenery that unfolded before us from the vantage point of the front of the top deck of the bus, nonetheless the images of the broad sweep of the Erne estuary unfolding before us in the ever-changing light of the seasons as we sped down Corn Hill seeped into our subconscious leaving an indelible mark. Images of the ruins of the 12th Century Abbey Assaroe and the small clock tower of St. Anne's Church of Ireland on the hill above Ballyshannon, unknown to us were being etched in our memories. Every school day we passed Inis Saimer on the approach to the town, reputedly one of the earliest settlements in Ireland. At least we knew about the history of the little island because we were told about in our history classes and so we took great pride in its historic place in Ireland's distant past. To us it made our town important. The bus stopped at Milltown, an area at the edge of town and we all walked a quarter of a mile up the West Rock to the school which was situated opposite St. Joseph's Church.

In order to get the return bus we had to walk down from the school on The Rock to the bus station across the bridge beside the big clock. In 1950 the Hydro Electric Station, which harnessed the waters of the Erne at Kathleen's Falls a quarter of a mile upstream from the bridge was just being completed and we could see as we crossed the bridge some of the rail tracks on which small buggies rode bringing materials to the builders of the dam. Always up for a dare I used to join local Ballyshannon lads sneaking in to get a spin on one of the buggies unknown to the workmen who were otherwise engaged. I later discovered that the father of one of my classmates had been killed in the construction of the dam or 'cementation' as it was referred to locally.

In those days there were conductors on the buses. Some of the older boys used to be allowed to ring the bell to start or stop the bus. We quickly learned on our return journeys from school how to disembark from the back of the bus before it stopped by leaning backwards as we jumped and the boy 'conductor' timed his bell ringing to synchronise with our departure. Needless to say our parents were oblivious to such antics.

As we settled into school we quickly made friends and embraced the ways of our neighbours. Joining a new class in a new school was challenging at first. Not having learned Irish in Clady we were at some disadvantage learning to read Irish or when prayers were being said in Irish. In Brother Michael's class the local boys, not untypically, had a habit of raising their hands and shouting out, "Brathair, Brathair", when wanting to answer his questions. As they moved up the school this practice died out. Brother Michael had two different grades in his classroom and at the end of the 1950 school year Brendan, who was two and a half years older than me, moved on to Brother Thomas's class and I stayed for another year with Brother Michael. The following year 1951-'52 Brendan moved on to Brother Francis'

59

class and I joined him having skipped the year with Brother Thomas. We stayed with Brother Francis until we sat the Primary School Certificate examination in the summer of 1954.

Learning came easy to me in the Primary School and I was quite content with my lot. We liked Brother Francis even though he could be cross especially with the slow learners. There was an area in town known as Falcarragh Park which was socially disadvantaged and some of the boys from there struggled academically. At lunchtime the school provided a free cup of cocoa with bread and jam for boys of poor parents. The person in charge of providing this sustenance was Maggie O'Neill who dispensed the food in a no nonsense manner. She did not tolerate misbehaviour of any kind and one look or loud rebuke kept cheeky boys in line.

One day I had a particular argument with a boy over something which ended with me challenging him to sort it out after school. This was code for having a fight. Sure enough a venue down The Mall was agreed upon for sorting out the problem. I had made the mistake of challenging a boy who was a lot taller than me but once the challenge had been made it would have been cowardly to back down. So, after school a number of us trouped down to the patch of ground off The Mall for the showdown. These 'duels' always attracted a crowd, so as soon as we threw off our coats, we squared up and started throwing punches at each other. It wasn't long before the other boy's longer reach began to break down my defence and suddenly he caught me on the nose which started to bleed profusely. This marked the end of the affair. Some older boys intervened at the sight of blood and stopped the contest, much to my relief. Nothing more was said. Everyone knew who the winner was. I had learnt my lesson.

Living between two towns had several advantages. Bundoran, as a seaside resort had the glamour of hotels, restaurants and souvenir shops, a beach with mighty Atlantic waves, entertainment malls and amusements that included swings, hobby horses, dodgems and the Dive Bomber, a mechanical arm with pods at either end with seats and a glass canopy which rotated high into the air and down again at great speed. On the beach were donkey rides and an amphibious craft that took passengers along the beach and then out into the wave strewn ocean and back again. There was an outdoor swimming pool that had its water replenished with every flow tide. Further on from the beach was a walkway up past the Great Northern Hotel, called Rougey which gave stunning views of Donegal Bay to the West and the Ox mountains to the South and was a favourite meeting place for courting couples.

In the summer of the early 50's we spent a lot of time in Bundoran. A bus from Ballyshannon passed our front door so, with our parents we were able to travel on Sunday afternoons to the resort and joined throngs of day-trippers who came on excursions from far and near to avail of the town's amenities. At that time the Great Northern Railway Company still operated a train service from Belfast which brought hundreds of visitors from mostly West Belfast. The hotels and boarding houses were usually full in the high season and with this influx of visitors the town

61

was very busy at weekends. Sometimes our cousin Peggy would arrive and she accompanied us on our Sunday trips. She and my mother liked going into the amusement arcade to try their luck on the slot machines. We didn't have any interest in them and really wanted to get to the beach for a paddle but we had to spend some time in the arcade en route. "Pull the handles gently please" was the constant refrain of the proprietor as throngs of people tried to force the spinning cylinders to go a bit faster in the hope of hitting the jackpot. My mother did get the odd jackpot when coins came tumbling out of the mouth of the machine and fellow gamblers helped to pick up coins that had spilled on to the floor. She took a childish delight in her success and like a child she proceeded to feed the coins back in again. A siren sounded when a jackpot was won and this added to the excitement. In a quieter section of the arcade patrons played Bingo with the numbers being decided by throwing a ball into a grid made up of a hundred small numbered compartments. The amusement arcades blared out lively tunes and popular music to entice passersby inside. One tune that was popular in the early 50's was 'Walking my baby back home'. As an eight year old boy I didn't quite figure out how anyone would expect a baby to walk home with its parents.

There were a few street traders on the main route to the beach but one in particular was a great attraction because of his wit. He called himself the Bargain Man and sold an array of products such as cutlery, dinner sets, delft, cameras, binoculars and a range of fancy goods. He used the Dutch auction style of selling to lure his clients and did so very successfully. He interspersed his patter with the odd witticism that entertained the crowd and kept them long enough to get interested in another bargain. He was not liked by the owners of the traditional shops so he would make jokes at their expense by asking the crowd if they had ever heard about the legendary Ali Baba and the forty Bundoran shopkeepers!

We were too young at that stage to learn how to swim but we enjoyed paddling in the sea. Afterwards we liked going into the amusement park to join people of all ages on the merry go rounds and the dodgems. A popular attraction was the hall of distorting mirrors which had a 'laughing policeman' with his infectious laugh.

While the house at Finner was adequate to our needs it was a little bit cramped so my parents decided to build on an extension at the back which would function as a kitchen/dining room. This meant that the original kitchen could be turned into a sitting room. The McGranaghan Brothers were employed to do the building which was a straightforward operation. They spent about six weeks building the extension and during this time our father was away at fairs or at markets in England. My mother decided to kill one of her chickens for a Sunday lunch, so of course since my father was away she asked Paddy McGranaghan to kill a fat hen for her. She assumed that any man could kill a chicken as skilfully and humanely as her husband. Not so. First, Paddy was reluctant to even try but when my mother explained to him the technique that my father used he agreed. This was a big mistake on my mother's part. Paddy botched the first attempt and in a panic he proceeded to bash the half alive hen against the wall of the new extension. The poor hen had no chance and eventually expired. Paddy rather sheepishly handed the mangled carcass to my mother and set about cleaning the blood off the new pebble dashed wall. Paddy's failure to kill the hen in the manner of my father surprised me. He somehow seemed to be a lesser man.

When Mick Magee sold the farm at Finner to my parents he told them that they would make a good living from it. Apart from the good grazing for raising sheep and cattle the soil was fertile for growing crops. With the proximity of the army camp there was a ready market for dairy products. Another attraction was horse racing. Every year on the August Bank Holiday Monday the farm became a racecourse for the day. The race meeting was referred to as the Bundoran Races over the Finner Course. There was great excitement in the weeks running up to the event. Posters had to be ordered and displayed in shops and public places in Bundoran and Ballyshannon. My father hired a car with a loud speaker and toured the two towns a few days before the meeting inviting the public to attend. I used to accompany him in the car.

Some preparations had to be made to turn one of the fields into a racetrack. The large field furthest away from the house was ideal because it was raised in the middle which meant that the race goers had a good view of the track which ran around the perimeter. Mick Magee, who had run the races before my parents bought the farm, was able to assist my father in the preparations. A couple of local labourers, Bartley and Charlie, came and helped us to put up the fencing for the finishing straight. This entailed hammering posts into the ground and stringing a couple of strands of bull-wire between. Other posts were placed strategically around the perimeter of the field to mark off the track. A couple of field toilets were constructed with high posts and hessian cloth. My brothers and I enjoyed being out with these local men helping them as best we could. We had a horse and cart which came with the farm for transporting the posts and wire. The horse was white all over. We called him 'Snowball'.

On the day of the races we were up from early morning as final preparations were made for the day's racing. Peter and Brendan were posted strategically to sell programmes while I, being that bit younger had the freedom to roam as I pleased. Gradually horse owners began to arrive in their vans with horse boxes attached and several hucksters paid my father a fee to get in and set up their stalls for selling minerals, ice cream, sandwiches, confectionary and such like. Extra buses brought race-goers from Ballyshannon and Bundoran and by mid morning there was a great buzz on the race course. On the top of the hill at the centre was a public address system which consisted of a loudspeaker mounted on the top of a motorcar. This was the control centre of the meeting which gave out information on forthcoming races and announced the results as each race was completed. Nearby was a line of on-field bookmakers each with their unique stands with mark-up boards for displaying their odds for each horse. Standing under their brightly coloured umbrellas they shouted out the names of the runners and the odds they were giving. An assistant kept the odds up to date on the board while keeping an eye on what odds the other bookies were offering. Each bookie had a bag slung around his front for storing the punters' bets and a bunch of personalised tickets in his fist for assigning to each bet. As the race-goers milled about each bookie called out his odds inviting business. "Get your bets on here for the 1:30. Six-to-one Black Shadow, seven-to-two The Millerman, evens Twinkle Toes, forty-to-one bar these. Get your bets on for the 1:30 here".

Not having an official job for the day I was able to roam round the racecourse taking in as much of the event as I could. I met some of my schoolmates, out with their parents for the day and observed the brightly coloured jockeys as they mounted their horses down by the starting line. In one of the races a jockey was unseated. He wasn't injured because he got to his feet immediately. I went down to where he was walking in off the course. The owner of the horse was doing the same. As soon as the two of them met the jockey came out with a string of curses the like of which I had never heard in my young life. I was shocked to hear such an outburst. This glimpse into how some people behaved was a revelation to me and dented my innocent view of adults. At eight years of age I was becoming aware of an ugly side to life. Although I didn't know it this incident was the beginning of the end of my carefree childhood. From now on the real world would gradually assert itself.

On the day after the races Peter, Brendan and I had to help with the clearing up. The field was covered in litter of all sorts so we had to go around with bags and lift it all. Bartley and Charlie arrived and removed the posts and wire and dismantled the field toilets. Mick Magee called and he and my father balanced the books and shared the profits and discussed plans for the following year.

In the carefree days of the summer of 1950 we gradually got used to farm life. My father stocked the farm with sheep and cattle and planted potatoes and vegetables while my mother was busy running the home and catering for all seven. My brothers and I were gradually getting more involved in farm work because our father was combining farming with cattle dealing. His routine was to go to fairs in the West of Ireland, buy some cattle which were taken by lorry to Larne and shipped across to Stranraer, from where they were transported to markets in Northumberland. My father and his fellow cattle dealers sailed with the livestock and sold them to English farmers for 'finishing'. This meant that he was away from Monday to Thursday or Friday during spring, summer and autumn.

Because of the proximity of the army camp we had bought six cows to produce milk that we could sell to the camp. We gave each cow a name derived from the fair in which it was bought. So, for example, we had 'Kinlough' and 'Dunkineely. Another cow was a 'dexter' so we just called her 'Dexter'. One outstanding cow suckled three calves plus her own so we called her the 'Four Lifer.' She was my favourite cow and moved with us from Finner to our second farm in 1953. We quickly learned to milk the cows and did so before school during term time. However, Kinlough was difficult to milk as she didn't have a strong flow of milk from her teats. This was a problem for us when trying to get the milking done before setting off to school. The solution was to enlist another milker. Our mother volunteered and so she was given the task of milking Kinlough.

As with any flock of sheep some lambs are abandoned by their mothers. Experienced shepherds have ways of getting ewes to adopt a stray but we were not familiar with such techniques so when we had our first abandoned lamb our mother started feeding it with a bottle and teat just like a baby. In no time at all we had a pet lamb and a spoiled one at that. We called her Daisy and grew attached to her, taking turns at bottle-feeding her. Then one day we found her lying on her side with a swollen stomach. An experienced shepherd would have known that our over feeding had caused gas to build up in the lamb's intestines. A quick solution was to puncture the lamb's stomach with a sharp knife. By the time we got Mr. Begley, the local vet to treat our sick lamb it had died. A period of mourning followed led by our tearful mother.

It was around this time that I learned to ride a bicycle. Peter and Brendan had already mastered the art but Angela and I were still trying to remain upright for a few yards. A problem was that the only bicycle we had was a man's bicycle which had a bar from the handlebars to the saddle which meant that children had to reach in under the bar with one leg to pedal. Before we got to the pedalling stage we had to practice balancing on one pedal as we sailed down a slope. There was such a slope from the back of the yard to the back door which became our practice area. After many attempts I gradually managed to stay upright on one pedal for longer and longer distances. With confidence growing I managed to put my other leg under the bar and pedal a few times. After several failed attempts my skill level increased and before I knew it I was a cyclist. Shortly afterwards I ventured out on the main road and was doing fine until my foot slipped and I crashed into a shrubbery at the side of the road and was pinned down under the bicycle. A couple of soldiers were out practising hurling across the fence where I had landed so they came across and got me back on my feet. A least I had escaped relatively unscathed unlike Brendan who had a similar crash some months earlier and broke a front tooth.

The donkey that came with the farm grazed in the field on the Ballyshannon side of the house. We called him Joey. He seemed to be quite content grazing at his leisure. As children we took to calling out 'Joey' until eventually he looked up from his grazing at the sound of his name. Not content to let the poor donkey be, we went further and began taunting him with his name and racing up to him and then running away. One day Brendan, Angela, Monica and I started teasing him. Joey put up with this for a while but suddenly he decided that he had had enough and proceeded to charge at us. Monica who was about five at the time wasn't quick enough to get out of the way. As we scattered, Joey caught up with Monica and trampled over her. We quickly ran to her aid and pulled her through the bull-wire fence to safety. Joey had made his point so we left him alone after that.

In the late spring of 1950 Finner Army Camp came to life with the arrival of a battalion of soldiers from the Western and Southern Commands. Lorry loads of troops and personnel carriers trundled past our front door one afternoon and the Irish Tricolour was raised on the high flagpole that was the centrepiece of the camp. Every morning after that, until late September, we could hear an army bugler sounding reveille to rouse the soldiers from sleep. Luckily we could turn over and snooze quite a bit longer. The army camp was fenced off from the public and access was controlled by a checkpoint at the main gate. Our house was situated a few hundred yards below the front gate on the Bundoran side, just opposite the football pitch which the soldiers used in the evenings. My brothers and I used to climb the fence and watch the soldiers playing football or hurling. They didn't seem to mind that we were 'unauthorised personnel'. Some of them became quite friendly towards us and if we brought over hurling sticks we could take up position behind the goals and race after stray sliothars. This saved them having to retrieve wide balls and gave us an opportunity to 'join in' on the outside. The language of the soldiers was not always what would have been approved of at home but we just put it down to soldier language. Behind it they seemed okay. Sometimes one of them would say to me, "Have you any sisters?" I knew what they were driving at so I would play along and say, "Oh, yeah, I have two sisters". Then would come the expected, "How old are they?" With my reply of "six and four" that particular conversation ended.

Every Sunday while the army camp was open Mass was celebrated in one of the huts. Local people were allowed to attend so this became a regular feature of our week. The priest used to question why so few soldiers came forward for communion. On particular Sunday hardly any one went forward to receive but I did and the priest singled me out as a good example to all present. I don't think this commendation made any difference apart from embarrassing me.

My father quickly got to know the Commandant and arranged to supply milk, potatoes and vegetables during the army's stay. 'Snowball' was duly hitched to a cart and in the early mornings we used to make deliveries to the camp kitchen with our farm produce. The army kitchen had lots of left-over food, scraps, potato peel and the like, or swill as it was called, which my father agreed to take as feed for three pigs that he had bought. We got to know a number of officers and NCO's during this time. Sometimes they would invite my father and us to Picture Shows put on for the soldiers. They set up a film projector in one of the huts turning it into an improvised cinema for the night. A number of soldiers had copies of American comics which they shared with Peter and Brendan and me.

Through these contacts with the soldiers my parents set up an improvised shop for selling cigarettes and confectionery to them at times when the army shop was not open. This lasted for a time but the demand was not sufficient enough to continue so our improvised shop closed. Some of the soldiers who were from farming backgrounds helped my father in the month of August when it came to saving the hay. This made them some extra money to spend in Bundoran. There was a hayfield opposite the entrance to the camp and when half a dozen off-duty soldiers joined us for a few hours in the evening it did not take long to turn the hay or build it into haycocks. Horse power was still very much used in those days. Snowball was hitched up to a 'tumbling paddy', a large wooden rake that gathered up a row of dried hay which then could be left in a heap when the 'tumbling paddy' was flicked over by the skilful operator. Some of the soldiers were expert at this.

Our dog 'Doughery' had travelled with us from Clady. He had been given that name by my mother because she had acquired him from a friend in Doughery in West Donegal. He quickly adapted from being a village dog to being a country dog. He was busy as a sheepdog and helped herding the cattle. In his spare time he used to roam through the surrounding countryside and spent time hunting for rabbits among the sandy soil of the army demesne. Unfortunately some men set traps for rabbits and occasionally dogs got caught. If the trap didn't snap fully shut a dog could escape. A couple of times 'Doughery' came limping home. He would then lie under a bed for a couple of days before his injured leg was healed enough for him to venture out again. We used to leave food and water for him during his convalescence and worried about his safety in the future. Sadly, he went off hunting rabbits one day and never returned. We suspected that he had been shot by a rabbit poacher. He was greatly missed by all of us. For me this was another example of one of life's little tragedies that had to be faced. We had killed the pet lamb with kindness; someone else had killed 'Doughery' through cruelty or out of mercy if he had been badly injured in a trap. Other little tragedies still lay ahead.

My mother was very resourceful when it came to preparing meals for the family. She had plenty of potatoes and vegetables from the farm and made sure we all ate our vegetables. Some of us baulked at cauliflower or onions but generally we ate what was placed before us. French fries were a big favourite, as they were for most children, so my mother used to put on lots of chips and cooking oil into a deep saucepan and cook them until they were golden brown. One day Angela, who was about eight at this time, accidentally caught the handle of the saucepan on a hole in the arm of a cardigan she was wearing and knocked it over. Monica, who was six, was standing beside her and she took the full brunt of the boiling oil. Consternation followed as we all rushed into the kitchen at the sound of her squeals of pain. My mother, realising at once what had happened lifted Monica and carrying her to the sink she applied layers of cold soap to the scalded areas and then promptly phoned Dr. Kerr in Bundoran to come and treat her. The doctor arrived shortly afterwards and applied some special anti-burn ointments on the areas that my mother had treated. He commended her on her actions and said that what she had done had protected the skin to a large degree. Monica was then put to bed in the bedroom on the Bundoran side of the living room. I was given the task of staying with her to keep her company. The doctor had probably given her something to help her to sleep but she was restless and began feeling under her left arm. I pulled up her sleeve and could see two large burn blisters that had been missed by my mother and the doctor. Racing out I brought my mother in to see what I had found. More ointment was applied but because of the delay in treating them these burn marks left a scar on Monica's arm. Eventually she drifted off to sleep and in time made a complete recovery except for the scar that remains to this day. Fortunately the boiling oil hadn't splashed on her face.

Doughery wasn't the only one who liked roaming through the army demesne. In the winter time when the camp was shut Peter, Brendan and I used to go round the various huts and look in the windows to see what each was for. Most were billets for the soldiers but others were for administrative purposes. Outside each wooden hut was a fire extinguisher. On one occasion, curious as ever, I examined one of these. Instructions on the side said that by turning the cylinder upside down it would be activated. Not quite believing this I proceeded to turn it over. To my surprise and consternation this set off the discharge of foam. Dropping it quickly I ran for home accompanied by my older brothers.

In the summertime we used to explore the area of the camp between our house and the Erne estuary which could be accessed by crossing the firing range which was used regularly by the soldiers for target practice. A red flag was flown during the times when the firing range was in operation and civilians were forbidden to enter the entire area. My brothers and I didn't consider ourselves as civilians. After all we knew some of the soldiers. We 'played hurling' with them. They helped us with the hay. So, we presumed permission to go where we definitely should not have gone. In truth we didn't realise the danger we were in. So there were times when we set off for the Finner Sand hills which bordered the Erne Estuary. The attraction of the sand hills was that it was great fun sliding down them to the beach below. Sometimes fishermen were there with their drift nets so it was exciting for us to come upon them hauling in their long nets that seemed to come alive as they were hauled ashore as large and small silver bellied salmon strained to escape from the tightening mesh of the nets.

I liked the look and the fresh tangy smell of the tall green ferns that you could roll in on a summer's day and feel the heat of the soft sandy soil beneath. Making our way through the small sand hills we came across numerous rabbit burrows and scampering rabbits. Birds were startled into flight at our approach, sometimes feigning injury to divert us away from their nests. We were carefree and full of youthful energy on those trips as we raced up and down the small sand hills and then careered down the big ones at the water's edge.

When the red flag was flying we were in mortal danger but didn't realise it. As we got close to the firing range we could hear the shooting and the whine of stray bullets whizzing over our heads. Occasionally we found spent rounds embedded in the sides of the small sand hills. On a few occasions I crept up as close as I could to the actual range. I could see targets being raised mechanically by soldiers who were shielded by a high bank while in the distance rows of soldiers lying on their stomachs were releasing volleys of shots at the moving targets. In all our time in this danger zone we were never spotted. Back home our parents were oblivious to the deadly serious dangers their sons were in.

As we moved into the early fifties my mother began to complain to my father about what she considered to be a damp house. She pointed to the condensation that at times could be seen as little beads of moisture on the paintwork. Looking back on it from today's perspective all that probably was required was better ventilation but my mother saw it as dampness. She even began removing the paint from some of the walls with safety razor blades, ones with only one sharp side. I don't think my father knew how to handle this situation. He had been the one who had recommended buying the house and farm in the first place and now he was faced with a problem that he could not solve. He probably knew that it had been difficult for our mother adjusting to farming. He had agreed to the extension to create more space for his growing family but dealing with condensation or dampness was beyond him.

I was getting on well at school and liked the De La Sale Brothers. The school had originally been a Fever Hospital that had opened in 1848 to deal with the effects of the Famine. In 1922 following extensive renovations the new school opened and attracted pupils from Donegal, Bundoran, Beleek and Ballintra. It was called St.

Joseph's after the name of the Catholic Church opposite. To us it was just a school. What we particularly liked was the spacious surroundings that allowed us to go 'scudding' at break times. 'Scudding' was a form of tag. It was basically a race round the school building with a chasing pack trying to catch the front runner.

One thing I did miss was the radio. Although we had one in Clady we didn't have one in Finner. I used to hear some of my classmates discussing episodes of Dan Dare, a popular science fiction programme and wished that I could have a radio to listen to it too. Not having a radio made another form of entertainment, the cinema all the more enjoyable. We had the choice of two cinemas, one in Bundoran and the other in Ballyshannon. In those years before television the cinema was very popular with all ages. Not only did they show films for entertainment but they also screened news stories from around the world via Pathe News. Every week patrons could see important global events that had just happened. They would already have seen still pictures of international news items in their newspapers but seeing moving pictures with commentary really brought the story alive. Younger patrons were entertained by cartoons and weekly instalments of a serial kept interest and attendance up. Sunday afternoons were ideal for young audiences. My brothers and I looked forward to these matinees. Bundoran Cinema was easier to get to as we could walk but when we learned to cycle we used to go to the Erne Cinema in Ballyshannon which was bigger. At our age we liked Westerns and Science fiction films. If a musical or mushy love story was showing we all got bored and restless. Noise levels rose and Tommy McCormick, who was a macho trouble shooter and certainly not an usher, had to march up and down the aisles hitting the sides of the outside seats with an ash plant while threatening rowdy young patrons with expulsion if they did not behave themselves.

Another form of entertainment was the Variety Show that was staged throughout the summer months in the Parochial Hall in Bundoran. Johnny Davey and his Company combined singing, sketches, comedy acts and instrumental items which were well received by the tourists. One particular year Ruby Murray topped the bill. She later went on to be the only singer to have three entries in the British Top Twenty Charts simultaneously. Her big hit was 'Softly, Softly'. My mother and father used to go to odd performance while my siblings and I only rarely.

The local newspaper was the Donegal Democrat which was read from cover to cover each week. It had all sorts of interesting local news and was essential reading. One story that aroused much interest was that a helicopter was going to be stationed for several months at Finner Army Camp from where it was going to take part in an aerial survey of the North West coast. According to the paper a hanger was going to be built for it beside the football pitch in the camp. That meant that it was going to be visible just across from our house.

Sure enough, work began on the building of a hanger and a security hut right across from my bedroom. Nobody knew when exactly the helicopter would arrive but we waited in anticipation. I had only seen a helicopter in the movies so I was looking forward to seeing a real one. I remember being out in the field on the Bundoran side of the house when I heard a strange whirring noise gradually getting louder. Looking towards the direction of the sound I was amazed to see this low flying machine approaching from the direction of Ballyshannon. I craned my neck and watched its every move as it swooped in, circled the pitch a couple of times and then slowly and noisily descended from a hovering position on to the ground. By this time a line of passing motorists had pulled in to the side of the road to watch, what for them was probably the first helicopter landing they had seen.

In the weeks that followed I watched take-offs and landings with great interest and because my brothers and I were well known to army personnel we were able to cross the fence and see the helicopter at close hand. It was guarded while on the ground by a member of the Military Police. Sergeant Duffy used to be on duty in the security hut. He didn't mind us visiting him. I remember that he had a gun in a black holster around his waist. Peter who was interested in aircraft was able to talk to him better than Brendan and me. He was a big man so I found him a bit intimidating. Living so close to the helicopter hanger and having access to it gave me a certain status with my school friends. All my Ballyshannon and Bundoran schoolmates knew about the helicopter but could only admire it from a far. Even the adult population had limited access. The aircraft was based at Finner for about two years and during that time passing vehicles used to stop and watch it when taking off or landing.

During those early years of the 50's my brothers and I combined our schooling with helping out on the farm. Milking cows, digging potatoes, saving the hay or dosing sheep were all part farm routine. With our father being away at fairs and markets in England we had to do our bit to keep the farm running. At times there was some backsliding and my mother would have to issue the warning, "Wait till your father gets home on Friday and he hears that you boys didn't weed the turnips!" This was no idle threat because occasionally, on hearing about our indolence our father would single out Peter, the oldest and give him a few 'skelps' on the legs for slacking.

Even though my brothers and I, and to a lesser extent my sisters, did our bit on the farm none of us saw it as the kind of life that we would want to live as we got older. School was opening up other worlds to us and my mother in particular was encouraging us to get a good education which she would have seen as leading to a career other than farming. Having followed a similar route herself she valued educational qualifications. With the boys and Angela at good schools and Monica about to start school she would have had high educational hopes for all of us.

In the meantime I was becoming aware of some of the harsher aspects of farming. I had heard from other boys at school about the practice of castrating bull calves and I had overheard conversations between my father and mother about a man who provided this service. My father mentioned to her that this 'bull man' would be arriving on a particular day and I wondered about what would happen. On arriving home from school the 'bull man' was out in a field with my father. He had a long rough overcoat with bits of string and small sticks sticking out of his pockets. In the same field were three bull caves. They were not their lively selves, but stood with their heads low and didn't seem interested in grazing. Sticking out between their back legs were short sticks bound with cord. I wandered into the byre and there lying in the middle of cow dung and urine like peeled onions were six shiny and bloodied bull calves' testicles. My heart sank at the sight of them for this confirmed that violence that had been done to calves that I had cared for since birth. I didn't quite know what I was feeling and I did not have the words to express it but I knew that I hated the man who had done this and I was disappointed at my father's part in it. Even though I had seen him killing hens and thought nothing of it this was somehow different. Even as a prepubescent boy I knew that something wasn't right about this. The following day the calves seemed normal again and after a few days the small sticks dropped off. By then my quiet rage had abated somewhat but my boyish innocence was gradually making way for the sometimes painful reality of animal husbandry.

A short time later I had another experience involving animal welfare that disturbed me. Mick Magee, my father's mentor on matters farming and racing arrived one day at my father's request to give his opinion on a cow that was not well. One of the cow's teats had turned solid and couldn't produce milk. I think my father suspected mastitis but needed a second opinion. Mick Magee duly arrived carrying a small jug. My brothers and I went out with him and my father to inspect the sick animal. The cow was in one of the back fields. Peter, Brendan and I herded her into a corner of the field and Mick moved in for his diagnosis. He felt round each teat and when he came to the affected one he said. "You're right Hugh, she has mastitis". "So what can we do then?" asked my father. We'll have to cut the tit clen aff", said Mick. "You reckon that's the only solution" said my father". 'fraid so replied Mick. "Okay, go ahead then if you think that's what has to be done" said my father. With that Mick took a knife out of his pocket and grabbing the affected teat he cut it off in one quick movement. The cow groaned and kicked. Mick then took the jug that he had given to my father to hold and splashed the contents over the wound left by the amputation. At this the cow kicked again. "Keep an eye on her for the next few days Hugh" said Mick. "That disinfectant should protect the wound but then you never know". With that it was over.

I didn't know what to make of Mick Magee. Other times I had seen him he was smiling and joking with my father but that day I saw another side of him. I felt sorry for the cow that had to endure a painful procedure. It did not seem fair, just like the death of our pet lamb, just like the fate of the three fattened pigs that had left the farm screeching and squealing on their way to the abattoir, just like the castration of the bull calves. I had to process these harsh aspects of farm life on my own. Neither my father nor my mother had prepared me for these experiences. In those days parents didn't have the relationship with their children or the language to talk about sensitive issues. Their solution seemed to be to let their children learn from the experiences themselves. It was, I suppose, a crude form of experiential learning.

In the summer of 1952 Peter had finished primary school and a decision had to be made about his secondary education. My mother was in favour of sending him to a boarding school. For some reason she favoured the Redemptorist College in Limerick even though this would have meant paying a large annual fee. My father, being thrifty by nature didn't think this was a great idea. When Brother Daniel, the principal of the Secondary wing of the De La Salle School heard about it he cycled out personally to convince my mother that his school would be a better choice. My mother met him out on the road in front of our house and the two of them discussed the question for an hour. During that conversation Br.Daniel also learned that Brendan was already hinting that his preference for secondary education was to go to the vocational school. That left me as the only one likely to go to De La Salle. Br. Daniel pointed out that Brendan was very well suited to a more academic route and tried to convince my mother that her three sons would flourish in his school. Despite all advice to the contrary my mother decided to send Peter to Limerick and to let Brendan go to the vocational school.

Later that summer the film The Hunchback of Notre Dame, starring Charles Laughton, was being shown in the cinema in Bundoran and my mother decided to go to it. It may have been that she had already seen Mutiny on the Bounty when it was screened in Clady as part of the Travelling Picture Show or at the Paladrome in Strabane but she informed everyone that she greatly admired Charles Laughton as an actor. Normally I would only have gone to the matinees with Peter and Brendan but for some reason it was decided that I would accompany my mother to the evening performance one Sunday. I was at the age when I could follow the story so the two of us set off and walked to the cinema in Bundoran's West End.

On our way home we talked about the film. My mother had obviously enjoyed it immensely and she explained to me aspects of the film that I had missed. I was intrigued by the exotic names of Quasimodo and Esmeralda and the pathos of the story had touched me. I never felt closer to my mother or as happy in her company before or for the rest of her life, as we walked home that summer evening talking about our shared cinema experience. It had been a very hot day and so as we walked past Finner graveyard I took off my shoes and socks to feel the hot tar of the road on the soles of my feet. We turned the corner at Mick Murphy's cottage and strolled up the hill past the home of Mrs McManus on the right. With a full moon and a sprinkling of stars to guide us we arrived home all too soon and the magic of our little journey together evaporated as we joined the rest of the family.

Shortly after this Angela and I were confirmed in Bundoran. Even though we attended different schools both of them were in the diocese of Clogher. Dr. Eugene O'Doherty was the bishop but he was ill. Normal practice was for the confirmands to be questioned on their knowledge of Catholic doctrine by the bishop before he conferred the sacrament. However, with the bishop being ill we were examined in a less stressful manner by the diocesan adviser in school. So, when we arrived at the church with all the other confirmands we were quite relaxed. The bishop remained seated throughout the ceremony. Afterwards Angela and I had our photographs taken at the house by our mother with her old 'Brownie' camera. Angela was dressed in her white confirmation dress and veil and I was attired in my confirmation suit.

At the end of the school year in 1952 Monica still had not started school. She was now almost six so it was decided that she should go to St. Catherine's Convent of Mercy primary school in Ballyshannon. Rather than have her going there on her own our parents decided to transfer Angela from the St. Louis Convent in Bundoran to St. Catherine's. And so Angela, Monica and Monica's teddy bear, 'Paddy Bear' duly started attending the convent in Ballyshannon. Because Monica brought Paddy Bear to school with her the nun in charge of her class 'included' him on the register. Each morning as she called out Monica Ni Goilla Ceannaig, Monica answered 'Anseo'. Then she called out 'Paddy Bear' and the answer was 'Anseo'.

With Angela being in a higher class, her day was longer than Monica's so Monica had to wait in the school until Angela was ready to go home. While waiting, some of the nuns would engage in conversation with Monica. They played a little game with her by asking her, "Monica, how much do you love me?" Monica would show them by opening out her arms a certain length depending on the nun in question.

By the end of that summer of '52 we had an unexpected visitor. Our mother told us that her half-sister Katherine Bonner was returning from America and would be spending some time with us. Aunt K, as we called her, had lived and worked in Philadelphia and New York for forty years and had decided to return to Ireland on retirement. She hadn't married so my mother and father agreed to let her stay with us.

So, after taking the emigrant ship in 1913 Aunt K sailed homewards in 1952 and following train and bus journeys she arrived by taxi at Finner with a large trunk. She was dressed like a Hollywood actress with a fancy hat with a feather and a pink boa. She seemed rather exotic to us with her American accent and bright clothes. Her luggage trunk was of particular interest because standing perpendicularly it opened out to reveal rows of different sizes of drawers on one side and a mini wardrobe on the other. So Aunt K was a novelty to us. She settled in to our family and seemed content to have a home. My mother found her a help around the house and a good companion. My father didn't seem to mind and he probably thought that Aunt K would be a good support to our mother. This role that she played brought her more into the centre of the family and so she began to exercise some control over my siblings and me. As we got older this relationship became strained on occasions.

Another arrival later that year was the goose. Mick Melly, a neighbouring farmer had, among other stock, a fine flock of geese. In the run-up to Christmas my father decided that instead of the traditional turkey he would buy one of Mick's geese and fatten it for the festive season. And so a lone goose arrived but didn't settle very well. She didn't mix with my mother's hens and didn't seem to be putting on weight. She started wandering further and further from the farm and one day we say her across the road running down the army football pitch which also served as the helicopter pad trying to get airborne. She was, after all just a quarter of a mile from her original flock. My father intervened and brought her back to our farm. However her bid for freedom had impressed my siblings and me. Brendan, in particular, began a campaign to save 'Goosie' as he called her. He got support from Angela and Monica. 'Goosie' had grown so much in our affections that the thought of our father wringing her neck the way he used to do with random hens was disturbing. My mother, realising that killing 'Goosie' would actually spoil our Christmas persuaded my father to spare her. We were all relieved.

Some months later we began to hear our parents talking about selling the farm at Finner and moving to a farm on the other side of Ballyshannon. My mother's continuing concerns about living in a 'damp' house must have eventually broken down my father's resistance to moving. As we heard more and more about the other farm, which had a really big house, we became more interested in the prospect of moving. There were several visits by a local estate agent and a visit by a prospective buyer before we finally heard that a deal had been done. We were too young to grasp all the financial implications of selling and buying property.

In late summer of 1953 we moved from Finner to Templenew House to begin a new phase of our Donegal experience.

Part 2   Templenew

My brothers and sisters and I were full of expectation about our new home ever since we heard that Finner had been sold and Templepnew bought. Our move from the Bundoran side of Ballyshannon to the Beleek side occurred in the late summer of 1953 just as I began my last year in primary school. Our parents had told us that we were going to live on a smaller farm than Finner but with a larger house with lots of rooms and a basement. We could hardly wait to see it.

I travelled to Templenew by car with my mother and Aunt K. Most of our belongings had already been transported but we had some items in the car including the statue of the Blessed Virgin inside its glass case. Carrying the statue, which was about four feet in height, meant that we were a bit cramped in the car. Aunt K had to squeeze in and lean on the glass case. Unfortunately, before we reached our destination the glass case had cracked under her weight, much to my mother's and Aunt K's disappointment.

Our journey to Templenew House took us out the Beleek road past Kathleen's Falls, the Hydro Electric Generating Station on the river

Erne. From there the road ran for a mile and a half parallel to the dam that had been created to store water for driving the station's turbines. Next we climbed a hill up past the entrance to Camlin Castle. We did not know it at the time but the actual castle had been submerged with the creation of the dam in the late forties. The grand entrance with its turreted tower was all that remained of its former glory. A quarter of a mile further on was Lisahully with its railway crossing off to the right which, we discovered later, was manned by Annie O'Connor. Another hill brought us within quarter of a mile of our destination. As we climbed the third and last hill we passed the house and farm of Walter Semple our nearest neighbour and just over the crest of the hill the car turned left in through ornamental gates that marked the entrance to our new farm. A gravel avenue ran from the gates around a gentle bend

As we rounded the bend Templenew House came into view. I had never seen a house like it. It's very location gave it a presence and a grandeur that even a ten-year old boy could sense. Although I did not appreciate the finer points of architecture I somehow knew that this house was special. For a start the smooth cement facade was painted in faded pink. The slate roof had two large chimney stacks with several chimney pots. The house looked huge but the appearance of size depended on one's perspective. Viewed from the turning area at the front it looked like a one story dwelling but from the side three floors were visible. Steps led up to the front door which had glass panels at either side and a lever in a niche which had to be pulled to activate a bell somewhere within. There were large windows with wooden shutters folded back at either side of the door under a fan shaped frieze. The combination of steps, large door assembly and high windows gave it an imposing appearance. Viewed from the side the house looked larger because the ground sloped down revealing three floors. We got out of the car and raced up the steps to explore our 'country mansion'. We learned later that it had belonged to a retired English Army officer called Colonel Moody.

Exploring the house for the first time was exciting as there was so much to take in. Going through the front porch we found large rooms at either side of the hall, one a dining room and the other a drawing room. Each had a high ceiling and large fireplace with a high marble mantelpiece. The dining room had a large expandable oak table that was big enough for a game of table tennis. The drawing room had a beautiful antique writing desk of French design that our mother had bought at the auction before we moved in. Each room was bright due to the large windows. The drawing room had two alcoves, one at each side of the fireplace with shelves in them.

From the wide hallway a flight of stairs ran up to a landing and then turned right via another flight of stairs to the top floor. The stairs had carpet with brass rods that made them look very smart. Racing up I found myself in the landing with a window that looked out on the rear of the house. Looking out the window I could see an orchard bounded by walls on each side and fronted by a thick copper-beech hedge. To the left and right of the orchard were outhouses. To my left, off the landing was a large bathroom. Going up the second flight of stairs I discovered four large bedrooms, the two on the left with their own sinks and running water. Each had high windows with wooden shutters. Between the rooms on a smaller landing was a box room for storage purposes.

After a cursory look at the upstairs I bounded down to the hall again to finish my exploration of the middle floor. At the end of the hall on the right was the kitchen which was long and narrow. A large Stanley range protruded from the wall just inside the door and a broad window of many panes gave a good view of the orchard and below and to the left a large concrete water storage tank. At the end of the kitchen there was a hatch for passing food into the dining room.

Retracing my steps to the hall I found three more rooms through a door at the end of the hall. One of them was a large pantry and cold store while leading off from it was a cloakroom and toilet and what looked like a spare room. High up on a wall just inside the cloakroom was a meter board and a set of fuses for electricity but there was no supply of electricity to the house in 1953 despite the fact that Templenew was located between two generating power stations, one at Cliff near Beleek and the other in Ballyshannon. The high voltage power lines passed though the farm on high pylons. Apparently this made it difficult to run a lower voltage mains supply under them to the house. This problem was solved in due course but in the meantime we were told that we would have to rely on paraffin lamps. At the entrance to the cloakroom was a door which gave access to the basement via a flight of wooden stairs.

The basement looked dark and foreboding, a bit like a dungeon. Because there was no electricity it was poorly lit by sunlight in the daytime and had to be accessed with the aid of a flash-lamp at night. At the bottom of the creaky stairs was a stone flagged passageway with various rooms leading off it. To the right of the last step was a small box room with no windows which seemed to serve as a coal bunker. Along the top of the wall facing the stairs was an arrangement of bells with wires running from them up through the ceiling. We later discovered that these bells could be rung from different parts of the house including the front steps. As these features of Templenew revealed themselves it became clear that the basement had been servants' quarters in the days when landed gentry had large houses like Templenew House.

Continuing my exploration of the basement I discovered a large square room with a fireplace that looked like it would have served as a kitchen. Among the bric-a-brac of this old kitchen were two bicycles that we would come to use a lot in the years ahead. Lying in the corner was an old tennis net and a slightly twisted racquet. On one wall there were several saws hanging up. One was a large cross-cut which had to be used by two people as was evident by the handle at each end. Opening off the kitchen was what looked like a pantry. The windows of both rooms were just above ground level and had lots of small panes of thick glass. Moving down the passage way I discovered another square shaped room that was supposed to have served as a 'ballroom' in days gone by. Alongside it was a narrow room that could have been a store or pantry. At the end of the passage just left of the back door was another medium sized room that would later prove useful to Angela and Monica as a make-believe shop.

Having made my tour of the house I was enchanted by the experience. I didn't know it at the time but the architecture, decor, furnishings and atmosphere of Templenew spoke to me in a language that as yet I did not understand but nevertheless touched me at some level. There was a sort of faded grandeur that echoed an illustrious past. That sense of grandeur grew during my years of living there and still evokes that unique experience in my memory.

If the inside of Templenew enchanted me the outside intrigued me with its layout. To the right of the main dwelling was a water pump which drew cool fresh water from a well some twenty feet below ground. Another hand pump was attached to a pipe that drew rain water from a concrete storage tank attached to the rear of the building. With the absence of electricity water had to be hand pumped up to storage tanks in the roof space. We later discovered that this required us all taking turns at pumping water, a task that no-one liked. About twenty yards down from the back door was the orchard. The front portion had a mixture of raspberry, gooseberry, blackcurrant and redcurrant bushes. Across a little stream were half a dozen apple trees and a few pear trees. Through the thick grass there were the distinctive traces of rabbit trails, something that we would exploit in time.

From the orchard I made my way over to explore some outhouses at the back left of the house. The first had a large wooden door. Inside were logs and turf left over from the previous winter. Beside this fuel shed was a general purpose stable with lots of straw on the floor for housing animals and beside it was the stable proper with three stalls with neck chains and mangers for tying up milking cows. A ladder ran up from this stable to a hay loft which extended to the fuel shed. The remains of the previous year's hay was scattered over the wooden floor.

Leaving these buildings I went across to the other side of the orchard where there were other sheds and outhouses and a very mucky yard where obviously cattle had been penned. The main shed had a large wooden door and behind this was a large square area with some of the previous year's hay still in place. A flight of steps ran up the side of this shed to a sort of loft which had a wooden floor with lots of gaps in it. We used this attic room later on as a henhouse. Through the gate at the foot of the steps was the mucky yard which was walled in and had several outhouses in a poor state of repair. This completed my first tour of the property and immediate surroundings.

Going to bed that first night in Templenew was strange. The bedroom that I shared with Peter and Brendan was huge compared to my old bedroom in Finner. Sleeping upstairs was a new experience even though I had done so in Clady but back then its significance hadn't registered with me. Even though it was clear until late we had to light some paraffin lamps to light up the house and carry a small one upstairs. As I drifted off to sleep

I did not hear the soothing sound of the sea that used to provide a quiet almost hypnotic background pulse of sound at Finner as it drifted in on the breeze from Donegal Bay. Instead there was the faint hum off the high voltage electricity wires that carried electricity from Cliff or Kathleen's Falls through our farm and across the length and breadth of the twenty-six counties. The proximity of trees outside brought the occasional squeak of branch rubbing against branch, the faint sound of bats on the wing and the gentle whistling of wind through the length and breadth of our new large mysterious mansion.

The following day I turned my attention to the larger setting of the big house. Unlike Finner where there wasn't a single tree Templenew had lots of different varieties, deciduous and carboniferous. In the same field as the house were oak, beech, spruce, chestnut and a solitary monkey puzzle spread out at random. Starting from the top of the avenue were ash, sycamore, beech and spruce. One tree in particular stood out because of the way its branches had spread out from the bottom covering a large area. This was some sort of pine or spruce. It was quickly referred to by Brendan as 'the tree that touches the ground'. It became a special tree all the time we were there. I used to love going in through the low branches and climbing up the main trunk as far as I could. With the sweet smell of the spruce and the whispering of the wind through the dense foliage the tree became a place of retreat where it was possible to feel nature's fresh and raw presence. At almost eleven years of age I was coming to that period at the end of my childhood before entering the wilderness of adolescence. The world of make-believe and fantasy was still part of my experience. Going into the tree that "touched the ground" allowed me to cross into a space that gave expression to some of my fading fantasies, where for instance, as I climbed the central trunk up to a point where I could peer out from the top I imagined myself as Jim Hawkins in Treasure Island climbing to the crow's nest of the Hispaniola to scan the horizon for any sign of Treasure Island. At other times I was Little Blackfoot of the Cherokee Indians scouting for signs of the American Cavalry on their way to their stockade in Idaho.

The experience was a bit like that of the children in C.S. Lewis's 'The Chronicles of Narnia' who crossed into a world of make-believe by entering a wardrobe which marked a border between reality and fantasy. Angela and Monica used the 'tree that touched the ground' a lot and lived out their own fantasy worlds there. Peter and Brendan were past that stage of late childhood so that particular tree did not feature much in their lives.

After we got settled into the house my brothers and I explored further. Our father had told us that there was a wood at the boundary of the farm and the dam that stored the water for the hydro electric station in Ballyshannon. We set off through the fields to find the wood and the dam. Crossing the field that led to Ednagor we found a steam and following it down its course we came to the entrance of the wood. It consisted of a variety of young trees, saplings, holly trees, silver birch and the like. In between the trees were clear spaces where over the years we discovered that snowdrops and crocuses first appeared in the spring followed by a blaze of bluebells in late summer. Birds and butterflies flew through sunlit clearances and in the darker regions lichen and moss-covered rocks were faintly visible. When we eventually got through the wood we were suddenly at the water's edge. Across the expanse of the artificial lake we could see the Knather road from Ballyshannon that led across the border to Beleek.

Part of the dam backed up into a little inlet which formed its own mini-lake. This stretch of water was an ideal place for wild fowl to nest and breed. I still remember the sight of mallard ducks gliding in at sunset on this stretch of water, a sight of pure elegance that thrilled the heart of a young boy. Unfortunately ducks gliding into their watery habitat attracted the attention of hunters as some years later, Peter when he was about seventeen, took the family shotgun and shot down one of the beautiful mallard ducks and proudly presented it to our mother as a hunting trophy. It was the first time I had seen a wild duck at close quarters. It seemed perfect in every way, with its broad yellow web feet, its thick soft outer plumage and its finer silkier inner plumage or 'down'. Its neck had beautiful dark green feathers that became finer as they reached the rounded head with its small dark eyes and fine beak.

The window sill outside the kitchen attracted lots of garden birds of different kinds. We used to put out crumbs for them especially in the winter so this kept them coming. There were sparrows blue tits, finches, wrens and robins. The narrow window sill suited these small birds so the larger blackbirds and thrushes did not interfere with them. Seeing the birds at close quarters got me interested in them to the extent that I wanted to catch some of them. An opportunity arose that winter. With snow on the ground there was little food for the birds. I set a trap for them out near the fuel shed. By spreading some crumbs on the snow and propping up a basin over them with a stick my trap was set. By attaching a long piece of string to the stick all I had to do was to wait out of sight for my first bird to arrive. It wasn't long before a sparrow walked into my trap. It didn't see me behind the shed door and quick as a flash I pulled on the string and collapsed the basin over my prey. The next part was a bit tricky as I had to slide my hand under the basin and catch the bird without letting it escape. After rummaging around I caught my sparrow. Its heart was racing and it tried to peck my fingers. It was so light and soft in my hand that I worried that I might squeeze the life out of it. Having had this success I felt guilty because the little bird was so helpless in my grip and was obviously terrified. I quickly released it, dismantled my bird trap and decided not to interfere with the freedom of the birds of Templenew. A good outcome of my bird trapping was that from then on I took an interest in birds generally and never disclosed the location of their nests. This interest has stayed with me to the present day.

As a boy of ten in 1953 climbing trees was an innocent adventure and one that I enjoyed. The big oak tree in the middle of the 'lawn' proved quite a challenge. Climbing up was difficult but getting down was not always easy but eventually I managed to master the big oak. Climbing the cherry trees had its own rewards when the cherries ripened. They were near the house and not too big but tricky as I discovered when I fell out of one of them on my way down. On that occasion I injured myself slightly when an upturned sharp part of a branch sliced into my chest. Fortunately the cut was not too deep and it healed in a few days. A small scar remains to this day as a reminder of my reckless cherry picking.

During our time at Finner we had seen how rabbits could be caught in a snare. With the evidence in the orchard that rabbits ran through there Peter bought some snares in Ballyshannon that autumn of '53 and set a number of them on the rabbit runs. To our surprise we caught a couple of rabbits at the first attempt. Being the eldest Peter killed them with rabbit punches. With this early success Brendan and I decided to try our luck and like Peter we caught several over that summer. Having caught them we then had to kill them, gut them, skin them, wash them out and cut them up into pieces for frying. They became very popular with all the family.

Our mother of course was an expert at baking all kinds of breads, pies and tarts. As the gooseberries, blackcurrants, raspberries and apples ripened through the summer she made all sorts of jams and jellies. Occasionally she bought concentrated jelly squares which she melted in a bowl and left to set in the cold store of the large pantry. Peter and Brendan knew that I used to sample the jelly before it set, unknown to our mother. One day after skinning a rabbit and washing it they planted a bowl of the reddish water that had been used to wash the rabbit in the cold store. Not being aware of this I noticed the bowl of what looked like strawberry flavoured jelly in the cold store. As was my custom I got a large tablespoon to sample the 'strawberry jelly' only to discover my mistake. My two brothers appeared from the cloakroom taunting me about my gullibility.

There were plenty of rabbits on the farm that summer and we continued snaring them in the orchard. Sometimes the rabbit was dead when we came to inspect the snares. This happened when the snare tightened on the animal's neck. At other times the rabbit's leg were snared. Picking up one of these rabbits was difficult because they seemed so soft and difficult to hold tightly. As we moved into autumn and winter sometimes our prey was dead due to exposure. In the frosty weather it was not unusual to find the rabbit dead in the snare and rigid with the heavy frost.

Two developments led to us discontinuing snaring the rabbits. On the intermediate certificate syllabus for English was a poem by James Stephens called 'The Snare' – 'I hear a sudden cry of pain, there is a rabbit in a snare, now I hear that cry again, but I cannot tell from where...... Being the eldest, Peter was the first to study this poem. For the first time he learned about snaring from the rabbits' perspective. The civilising effect of the poem discouraged him from setting snares after that, though later he used our father's shotgun to kill them humanely. A few years later when I encountered that poem I felt guilty at my treatment of wildlife despite the fact that rabbits were pests on a farm because they ate lots of grass and vegetables. The other deterrent to snaring rabbits was the arrival of myxomatosis in 1956. This disease which arrived from Australia decimated the rabbit population. It caused infected animals to have a fever and puffed up eyes and faces. Many of them went blind and ended up being killed by traffic as they strayed on to roads. I began to feel sorry for them and after school I would tour the farm and put infected ones out of their misery by hitting them over the head with a heavy stick.

It snowed quite heavily in the early spring of 1954. Brendan immediately set to work at making a sleigh. He quickly nailed some timber planks over two runners, making the front plank longer than the rest so that it protruded enough at each side for a foot rest. He then straightened two metal bucket handles along the length of the runners and the sleigh was ready. We went out to Nellie's field which sloped down towards a shallow stream and had great fun sleighing down it. We even got our father to try it and gave him an extra hard push to send him careering down into the frozen rushes that grew along the side of the stream. One spin down the hill was enough for him.

There was a really good hill for sleighing and sliding half a mile away at Lisahully which was used by the young people of the area. Brendan and I joined The Campbell's and McCauley's for sessions on the brae outside Annie O'Connor's house at Lisahully railway crossing. There very little traffic in those days so we spent hours enjoying sliding and sleighing in the frost and snow while they lasted.

Ballyshannon Main Street was a terrific place for sleighing. Starting up at the junction of Bishop Street and Main Street there was a long steep descent down and over the bridge as far as Paddy Doherty's shop. Fortunately there was a dip in the road just before the bridge which slowed the sleigh down just in time before reaching the junction of East and West Ports. The Ballyshannon sleigh was a really big one which carried eight or ten boys. It had a small steering section at the front where a small boy could fit. A bigger boy at the back was able to steer the small sleigh at the front with long reins. I never got a spin on it but saw it in operation. It was quite a sight seeing and hearing it thundering down the street to the sound of shouting and cheering from all on board.

The first few months in Templenew were exciting as we explored the house, farm and surrounding area. However, by the following summer, with the turf shed empty and little hay left in the hay loft we had to make a start at replenishing them. Our first priority was to get turf from the bog. As was the custom, individual farmers had access to their own 'bank' of turf in a nearby bog. Our turf bank was about a mile and a half away. To get there we either cycled or walked. We exited the farm via the avenue and turned left on the Beleek road and travelled three hundred yards to McCormick's Bridge, a railway bridge over the Great Northern Line that ran from Belfast to Bundoran. From the bridge we travelled on a narrow road up towards Doherty's farm. At Doherty's we climbed a steep brae and from the top of the brae we could see the bog. Our turf bank was about half a mile from that vantage point.

Working in the bog was hard labour as far as my brothers and I were concerned but we had to do it. Our father accompanied us when he was not away at cattle markets but most of the time we were on our own. Peter, being the eldest did the cutting with the 'slan' or turf spade. Brendan caught individual turf as Peter sliced into the turf bank and slung each dark brown, soggy and slippery sod to him. Brendan placed these on a side-less barrow which he wheeled from the turf bank for me to spread his cargo out to dry. When a section of the turf bank was cut down to a depth of about eight feet a new portion of the turf bank had to be pared back to access more layers of peat below.

Cutting, catching and spreading turf were strenuous and back breaking activities and soon worked up an appetite. Sometimes we brought food with us for lunch but more often than not our mother accompanied by Angela and Monica would arrive with tea and sandwiches. For some reason they always seemed to be late. We would keep watching to see if there was any sign of them coming down Doherty's brae. Our mother, knowing that we were waiting patiently would give a 'co-ho' from the top of the hill and this was music to our ears.

Our 'picnics' in the bog were always enjoyable because we got a break from the hard work and sated our hunger. Our sandwiches, scones, hard boiled eggs and apple tart were eagerly eaten with tepid tea that our mother and sisters had filled into lemonade bottles sealed with paper corks. The food seemed to taste better in the open air. Reclining in the heather with the dragon flies skimming over the stagnant water of the dark brown bog holes and butterflies and bees flitting among the clumps of purple flowered heather and the larks singing in the high clear air our lunch break was a joy. The difficult part was getting back to work.

After the turf was spread out it took several days for the sods to dry, depending on the weather. When they were dry enough they were raised into footings, three leaning against each other in an upright position. This dried them right through and then they were put into clamps which were bigger arrangements which meant that even if there was rain the inside turf were protected by the outside ones and the outside ones, being dry already, didn't get soft again. All of this took time and effort and was not the most favourite form of work but it had to be done.

By August it was time to draw the turf home. When Finner was sold 'Snowball' the gelding was sold also. My father bought a pony, a black mare that we named Nellie. She had one 'star' of white hair in the middle of her forehead. She spent most of her time grazing in 'Nellie's Field', the one on the Ballyshannon side of the avenue but was hitched up to a cart when required.

Horses are gregarious and like company, so when any of us went out to the field to catch her she resisted at first because she knew that she was going to have to work but she liked our company, so with a bit of coaxing she allowed us to put a halter on her and bring her down to the shed that housed her harness and cart. Peter, Brendan and I quickly learned how to put on the harness and hitch Nellie to the cart. A bridle with a steel bit and blinkers went on first followed by the collar and hames which were secured around her shoulders. Next was the harness saddle which was held in place with a girth. Then came the breeching, which went over her hind quarters. Two chains or traces were attached at either side through the breeching and the shoulder collar and attached to the cart after Nellie was backed into position between the shafts. Finally a belly band was slung under her belly to stop the shafts rising up.

When we got to the bog we filled the cart with turf and hauled the load home. Because Doherty's brae was very steep we had to stop half way up to allow Nellie to get her breath before continuing the climb. On one occasion, when I was about fourteen, Peter, Brendan and I ran into a serious problem when, having strayed off the hard path that led to the turf bank we travelled over a soft part of the bog and suddenly both Nellie and the cart began to sink. Nellie started to panic and Peter and Brendan jumped out and tried to push and pull the cart out of the hole we were in. Sizing up the situation I immediately unhitched Nellie and freed her from the sinking cart. Once we got her out of danger she settled down and we were then able to manoeuvre the cart out of the soft ground on to the hard path and re-hitch Nellie again.

Now that we were living on the Beleek side of Ballyshannon our weekly cinema visits to the Sunday matinee were to the Erne Cinema. The most popular films for me at that time were the Westerns. I got to see Roy Rogers, 'Hopalong' Cassidy, The Lone Ranger, The Cisco Kid, Gene Autry with his horse 'Trigger', Wyatt Earp, Buffalo Bill and of course Indian and Apache tribes such as the Cherokee, Blackfoot, Cheyenne, Cree and Mohawk. What I admired about the Indians was that they rode their horses bareback. I too had a horse without a saddle so I used to go out and put the bridle on Nellie and gallop her through the fields imagining I was in a Western movie. I even tried to get her to jump over the little burn that fed the stream in the big field that led to Ednagor. Nellie decided that she was not a jumper so I sailed over her head and that put the idea of jumping out of me.

Over the years we spent at Templenew Nellie was used for drawing home the turf and for helping to bring in the hay or haul logs from felled trees from far parts of the farm but apart from that she spent her time grazing. Eventually she got fat from lack of activity and developed some disease. The vet was called and he recommended draining off some of her blood. This was a temporary solution and eventually she had to be sold for slaughter.

Saving the hay in the fifties was a laborious and tedious business. We had to get a local man called John Gault who had a small Massey-Ferguson tractor to come and cut the hay for us. John was very fussy about going into strange fields and always asked us to make sure that there were no stones lying about because hitting them with the cutting bar would damage it and halt operations. If the weather was dry we went out three or four days later with wooden rakes to turn over each sward of cut hay. A couple of days later we had to shake out the hay to make sure it was thoroughly dry before moving on to the next stage of raking it into large heaps for building haycocks. This was the critical stage because if the haycock was built with hay that was not thoroughly dry it began to heat. We wound strands of hay together to make hay ropes which we then used to tie down each haycock anchoring it with wooden pegs. If the haycock started to heat it had to be dismantled and the damp hay spread out again to dry. We used to test each haycock a few days after it was built by putting a hand right into the middle of it. We knew right away if the hay was okay just by the temperature.

With our father away at cattle markets Peter, Brendan and I and sometimes Angela and Monica had to get the hay saved. We were not always as thorough as we should have been and sometimes rushed the operation, especially if the weather was unsettled, with the result that haycocks overheated to the point where steam could be seen rising from them. Our mother kept an eye on our efforts and sometimes had to intervene with, "Wait till your father gets home and I tell him about the way you boys let the hay lie in that field until the rain came on". If we were a bit slow in taking remedial action she used to go out and start demolishing the haycocks that were heating and this shamed us into activity.

In the autumn John Gault returned for carting in the hay to the hayloft. He had a low loader attached to the tractor. He backed up to each haycock and dropped the tail of the loader. Next a chain was slung round the base of the haycock and it was winched on to the sloping low loader. When the haycock reached a certain point on the loader its weight tipped the front of the loader down to the horizontal and the tractor brought it in for forking up into the hayloft. This was a dusty business especially if you were in the hayloft where there was little ventilation. My brothers and I were glad to see the end of another hay-saving season.

As the eldest, Peter was in charge of the farm in our father's absence. In late spring/early summer when the potatoes were dug he was the main help to our father in putting them into pits. The potato of choice was Kerr's Pinks. When they were dug they were heaped up into long piles, covered with rushes to protect them from the frost and then provided with a layer of soil over the top of the rushes. This kept them in good condition through the autumn and winter. When the pits were opened in the spring the potatoes were still hard and fresh.

Not having electricity in Templenew in the first years we were there my brothers and sisters and I had to take turns at filling several oil lamps with paraffin. Our father bought a large 40 gallon oil drum which was mounted on a stand in the basement just inside the back door from which we drew supplies to fill the lamps. We trimmed the wicks and filled the lamps with paraffin making sure to be especially careful with the Aladdin lamp which had a gauze-type assembly over the wick that glowed very brightly when it warmed up. This produced a very bright light which was needed for the large dining room where we sat around the big table at night and did our homework. Sometimes a black scar appeared on the side of the glowing gauze diminishing the glow but by sprinkling some salt down the globe the black scar burned off. Our mother bought a paraffin heater which also had to be filled every day and in addition to the range in the kitchen she had a paraffin cooker which also had to be replenished.

Other chores that we had to carry out routinely were to stock the turf box in the dining room with turf and blocks of wood and of course milk the cow and clean out the byre every day. The bullocks and heifers that made up the animal stock had to be given fodder throughout the winter. Fresh water had to be pumped up from the well into buckets and brought into the house for drinking and cooking. We didn't mind going to the well but we all detested having to pump the fresh water from the rainwater tank up to the storage tanks high up in the attic.

It took about two hours to fill the storage tanks. We knew when they were full because at that point the overflow pipe started to spout. We were usually assigned fifteen minute slots. Peter and Brendan, being the older and stronger children did the lion's share but gradually Angela, Monica and I had to do our bit. Our parents also did their share. If we were a bit slack at the pumping our mother would take off her apron and go down and start pumping herself. Even though she was fit and healthy she had suffered from asthma since her childhood and had to use a spray from time to time to alleviate the symptoms. Seeing her engaged in the strenuous activity of pumping water was enough to shame us into activity. Some years later her asthma suddenly disappeared never to return. To her it was a miracle.

Having saved the turf and the hay and thinned the carrots and turnips and got into the habit of doing the chores that summer of '54, it was time to start secondary school. When we came to live in Templenew we brought one gent's bicycle with us from Finner. In the basement of our new home were two bicycles that our father had bought in the auction. One of them was a small lady's bike and the other was also a lady's bike but was larger and much older. It had blue grips on the handlebars and so was called 'The Blue Swallow'. Peter was still at school in Limerick so Brendan used the gent's bike to cycle to the vocational school in Ballyshannon. Angela had changed school from the St.Louis Convent in Bundoran to the Mercy Convent in Ballyshannon so she used the small lady's bike. Brendan acted as her minder going to and from school because the convent school and the vocational school were on the same street. I had the use of The Blue Swallow to take me to the De La Salle Secondary School which was in the same building in St. Joseph's on The Rock. Monica transferred from the convent in Ballyshannon and was able to walk to the primary school called Rockfield which was just a quarter of mile down the Beleek road. She used to take the shortcut up through the front hayfield, cross the wall at McCormick's bridge and continue on down the road to the school. She was always the first home from school. Our mother would sometimes greet her as she arrived home with "You are my sunshine, my only

110

sunshine, you make me happy when skies are grey. You do not know dear how much I love you; oh please don't take my sunshine away!'

Moving from the primary school to the secondary in September '54 proved difficult for me right from the start. Having skipped a class in Primary school I was up to a year younger than my classmates in the secondary wing of the school. Classes were bigger and there were pupils who had transferred from Bundoran and Beleek and Ballintra. We also had different teachers for different subjects. Although it was a De La Salle Brothers' School there were some lay teachers, one of whom was Master Moran who used to give me and my brothers a lift to school from Finner on those occasions when we missed the bus. It turned out that the aforementioned Master Moran, originally from Kerry, controlled his classes mainly through fear. He was a strong advocate of corporal punishment and administered it liberally and at times mercilessly. He was an expert at wielding a bamboo cane which he could bring down accurately on the middle of an outstretched hand. At five foot eight he didn't overpower us with his physical appearance but he had an air of authority about him. He always dressed in a tweed suit with matching waistcoat, shirt and tie and leather shoes which made a distinctive noise as he approached down the wooden-floored hall from the small staffroom up the corridor. With a pale complexion and a bald head he had the professional appearance of a bank manager. He kept pieces of chalk in one of his waistcoat pockets and from time to time he lit up a cigarette or a butt of one as he walked around the classroom. Sometimes he arrived in the classroom with the bamboo cane crooked over an arm. At other times he would send someone to the staffroom to fetch it. Sometimes I was sent for it, not to punish me but to inflict punishment on someone else.

The combination of new classes and strict teachers unsettled me and I began to miss school. In the mornings I would get physically sick at the thought of facing into what for me was a hostile environment. My mother became concerned and got Dr. Kelly to examine me. He suspected appendicitis and recommended surgery. Neither he nor my mother knew that my appendix was probably fine, that at the root of my problem was anxiety.

The thought of going into the Shiel Hospital in Ballyshannon did not bother me because it meant that I did not have to go to a school that I hated. I was put into a male ward with several adults who didn't seem to be too ill because they talked and laughed a great deal among themselves and with the nurses. I remember Nurse Mc Dermott preparing me for the operation by painting my stomach with some sort of coloured disinfectant. On the morning of the operation she gave me an injection and I was ready for theatre. Going down to theatre didn't bother me so I presume the injection was some sort of sedative. Unlike my experience of having my tonsils out in Strabane hospital at the age of five when I had experienced a sense of suffocation when the anaesthetic was administered, this time I became unconscious immediately following an injection.

Back in the ward I was soon on the way to recovery. The biggest problem was trying to avoid laughing at the comments of my adult companions because every time I laughed my stitches hurt. During my week of convalescence in the hospital I had the usual visits from family members. An unexpected visitor was Brother Daniel. He was concerned at the amount of time I was missing from school. He brought out a copy of the Latin Grammar that we were using in school and told me to study it on my own so that I would keep up with my classmates. I agreed but in fact learning Latin verbs and constructions was the last thing on my mind.

Back in Templenew I relished my time at home and did not look forward to returning to school. I missed about six weeks of the first term and struggled to make up that lost time right up to the Leaving Certificate. Brother Daniel was right. The first couple of months learning new subjects are crucial for understanding the basics especially in subjects were progression is incremental such as language or mathematics. Not surprisingly I did poorly in the first Christmas Test coming near the end of the class. By the time of the Summer Test I had recovered some ground and managed to climb to the top end of the class but I always knew there was a gap in overall understanding. Repeating that first year would have been better for me but that was never suggested.

Brother Daniel was the head brother who hailed from Waterford. He was a tall man with thick black hair swept back without a parting. He applied liberal amounts of byrlcream, so a hair was never out of place. His soutanne was always clean and the double white teaching tabs of his collar were always starched and without creases. He used a cane from time to time but also induced pain by raising pupils up by grabbing them by the hair at the side of the head. Brother Luke was a highly organised teacher and used a cane sparingly. He liked promoting sport and went to great lengths to improve our meagre facilities. He marked out a tennis court at the side of the school by turning over the turf and set up a basketball court next to it. Occasionally he led groups on treks up Ben Bulben. Such outings suited the town boys better so I never took part in them. These initiatives encouraged us to participate in sport at lunchtime and after school. He was replaced by Brother Columba who came from Kilkenny. Not unsurprisingly his sporting passion was hurling and he quickly got us interested in playing it.

For some reason I was picked by Brother Daniel to deliver messages for him. On one occasion he sent me up the road from the school to the parochial house to deliver a message to the curate Fr. O'Neill. When I got to the house the door was answered by the housekeeper who told me that the priest was down the town but was expected back soon. I delivered the message to her and set off down the road back to school which was a distance of about a quarter of a mile. On my way I met Fr. O'Neill and told him that Brother Daniel had sent me to the parochial house with a message for him but not finding him there I had given the message to the maid. Fr. O'Neill thanked me but informed me that the person to whom I had given the message was his housekeeper and not the maid!

At other times Brother Daniel would come into the classroom and ask me if I had the bicycle with me. This seemed an unnecessary question because if I was at school then I had cycled there. On being told that I had the bicycle he would give me a written message which I was to deliver to the housekeeper in the Brothers' residence which was across the town in College Street. I used to love getting out for the ten or fifteen minutes that I took to cross the town and deliver the message. I felt liberated and important to be out of school and mingling with the townspeople who were going about their commercial business. Crossing the bridge over the Erne as a messenger of the school and climbing Castle Street up past the town clock made me feel a part of the Ballyshannon scene. Like footballers of a winning team I ran down the clock at my leisure and took my time getting back to the confines of the classroom.

The other times when I liked being over the town were when there was a circus and at the harvest fair. Duffy's Circus arrived each year and set up its big tent on the fair-green opposite the Abbey Ballroom. Posters were in every shop advertising the various acts of daring, exotic dancers, rare monkeys and performing elephants. Most people in the town and surrounding district attended during the circus week. When I had been at primary school I went up after school one day to get a look at the elephants, lions and monkeys. I got too close to the monkey cage and one of them caught me by the hair, much to the amusement of my schoolmates.

The Harvest Fair, in addition to being a normal cattle fair attracted a variety of street traders, hucksters, three-card trick merchants and charlatans of different kinds. One charlatan that I remember well was a black man who had his stall in the Diamond and was selling crocodile oil as a cure for all sorts of arthritis. He was the first black man that I had ever seen. What struck me about him was that although he was black the insides of his hands were pink.

Brother Daniel liked swimming and boasted to us about his daily dips in the sea at Creevy pier. "Nine degrees centigrade yesterday at Creevy," he would inform us, as he walked around opening windows to let fresh air in. We thought he was bonkers but admired his asceticism. He was always opening windows, either to let the stale air out or to dispel the lingering smell of cigarette smoke left by Master Moran. However he had to balance the freshness of the air with room temperature, so from time to time he would dispatch Liam (Busty) Higgins to put more turf into the furnace that heated the school.

As head brother he was in charge of finances. All through the first term we got a constant refrain from him, "Fees, boys, fees. I need you to get the fees paid as soon as possible". Another function of his as principal was to start the day with assembly in which he would lead the senior classes in reciting some decades of the rosary. I was usually rushing in late for school most mornings and often had to make my entrance in the middle of a decade. Through the winter months it was difficult to cycle the three miles from Templenew without getting the odd soaking. Brother Daniel would ensure that on such occasions I sat near a radiator to dry. I didn't think there was any need for making such a fuss. Ironically I used to present him with a sick note from my mother telling him that I had been kept off school on account of a cold or stomach upset. On reading such notes, which were frequent, he used to look at me quizzically as much as to say, "Do you really expect me to believe this?"

Master Frank Daly, another Kerry man was less severe. He lived in Cliffoney and in his first years of teaching he travelled with the pupils on the bus from Bundoran. Then one day as we were walking up the Rock from the bus stop he passed us in a brand new Volkswagen Beetle. Just as he turned left to go through the main gate the car lurched forward and he smashed into the pillar at the right side of the gate. This was a humiliating event to happen to a teacher in front of the pupils. For weeks afterwards he parked outside the grounds until he felt ready to drive through the gates.

He used a flat broad strap which was not nearly as painful as the cane. The strap was more of a deterrent while Moran's cane was meant to punish and humiliate. Daly had a dry sense of humour. He would remind us that he was an expert in religious education. He told us the evidence for this claim was in the gospel account where it said that Jesus 'taught daily in the Temple'. We thought that was a poor enough joke. He was always impeccably dressed and set a good example in good manners and decorum. He would say things like, "Don't slouch when you walk young man. Hold your head up and pull your shoulders back when you walk." He smoked a pipe at lunchtime and if we had him for an afternoon class there was a fragrance of tobacco smoke off his clothes. The one thing I didn't like about him was his cynicism. He would criticise the government and tell us that most of us would end up on the emigrant ship.

Although I had to go back to school and put up with the harsh regime I exploited every opportunity to avoid it by going to local fairs with my father, or persuading my mother that I had a cold coming on or helping my father with moving cattle or some other farm activity. As I moved up the school I changed my attitude from one of fear to one of defiance. I knew that Moran would beat me, not for misbehaviour but for falling short of the standards he expected but it was the same for us all. If we were doing geometry and I missed a day I was behind in proving the current theorem. Sure enough I would hear Moran say, "Eugene McElhinney, come out and prove theorem 26". I was good at geometry so I would proceed to prove the theorem but Moran would have the upper hand because he would say, "And how did you reach that conclusion?" I would say, "Because we proved that part in the previous theorem." That answer was not good enough for Moran so I would get three or four slaps across the fingers with his bamboo cane and told to go back to my seat. And if we did not learn our Latin vocabulary Brother Daniel caned us for each mistake. Despite the corporal punishment there were parts of school life that I enjoyed especially as I got to know my classmates better.

In our first winter in Templenew we got used to the routine of keeping the house heated with turf, wood and paraffin and looking after the many lamps needed for light. There was always a good fire in the dining room which doubled as a living room. The kitchen was okay for breakfast and light meals but the dining room had a large table and with the convenience of the hatch connecting the two we could sit as a family round the one table. The radio was also in the dining room and it became a focal point for popular programmes. Brendan who was learning about electrical circuits in the Technical School hooked up an extension speaker which he placed in the kitchen so we could listen to it in both rooms.

A radio in those days was known as a wireless. In the 1950's people without mains electricity had to buy battery operated sets. However, two types of battery were required to power different circuits. A wet battery, basically an acid filled jar that produced a low voltage powered the valves while a dry battery with a higher voltage powered the circuits. While it was easy to buy and connect the dry battery the wet battery required periodic recharging. This meant that a stand-by wet battery had to be used to take over from a spent one. Murphyy's electrical shop in the West Port, Ballyshannon charged these wet batteries for a small fee but the battery had to be left in the shop for at least forty-eight hours to charge it fully. Sometimes we didn't get the standby battery charged in time and had to wait for it to be recharged. We knew when the serving battery was getting low in power because the volume began to reduce. By switching off and resting it overnight we could extend its life a bit. Our father liked to hear the news so we had to ration our listening so as not to drain the battery.

We also needed to rest the battery if there was a particular sporting event being broadcast that we did not want to miss. One such event was the European featherweight title contest between Billy (Spider) Kelly from Derry against Ray Famechon, the reigning champion from France on May 27th 1955. We, but especially our father being from County Derry, were supporting Spider Kelly. The fight was very close but Famechon was given a narrow point's verdict. We could hear the reaction of the crowd and the commentator referred to scuffles breaking out in the crowd. Our father was very disappointed.

Popular programmes at that time were the rugby internationals, the All-Ireland GAA series, "Take the Floor" a mixture of Irish singing, céili dance music and comedy. The comedy was provided by the host of the programme called Din Joe. This was broadcast on a Sunday afternoon and was very popular. It was followed by a quiz programme called "Question Time" hosted by Joe Linane. Our mother and father and Aunt K liked this programme because it tested their general knowledge; similarly with 'Twenty Questions' which invited a panel to figure out some item which was animal, vegetable or mineral. Another popular programme was "Living with Lynch", a mixture of songs, sketches and jokes hosted by a Cork man, Joe Lynch.

One thing that I liked about the wireless was the access it gave to different countries and languages. On the dial were places like Hilversum, Madrid, Lisbon, Rome, Paris and Vienna. By moving the dial it was possible to hear all the languages of Europe. One programme that appealed to me was called "Journey into Space", a science fiction programme about space travel. It was broadcast by the BBC in the late evening. Unfortunately its transmission time clashed with the time which was set aside for the family rosary. If my mother was busy and delayed starting the rosary I could hear my programme but often she would intone the opening prayer and I had to turn off the wireless or if I was a bit tardy she would turn it off for me. When it came to saying the rosary everything else took second place.

During the cold months we said the rosary as a family gathered around the fire in the dining room. Our mother was in charge. She said the opening prayers and we took turns at reciting individual decades. When we got to the end our mother took over again with 'the trimmings', various prayers for different intentions, one being for the conversion of Russia. Also included in the trimmings was the litany of the Blessed Virgin which she knew by heart. I was intrigued by the closing section which included a multitude of titles attributed to Mary. They were,

Mirror of justice
Seat of Wisdom
Cause of our joy
Spiritual Vessel
Singular vessel of devotion
Mystical rose
Tower of David
Tower of ivory
House of gold
Ark of the Covenant
Gate of heaven

Morning Star
Health of the sick
Refuge of sinners
Comforter of the afflicted

I understood some of these titles but others escaped me, like Tower of David, Tower of Ivory, Mystical Rose, and Ark of the Covenant. Despite my weariness at having to kneel for twenty minutes answering the various parts of the rosary and trimmings I admired the lilting beauty of the litany and was struck by my mother's fervour throughout. This was particularly so when we recited the rosary during the warmer months before the statue of Our Lady which had a prominent place on the landing at the top of the first flight of stairs. My brothers and sisters and I knelt on the stairs. Sometimes we would jostle with each other and try to unbalance whoever was next to us on the step. A pause and knowing glance from our mother focused us back on our prayer.

Our mother had great devotion to Our Lady and during Lent she used to use the dolour beads instead of the rosary. This prayer recalled seven sorrowful events in the life of Mary. So, instead of having five decades of ten we had seven 'decades' of seven. Either way we ended up reciting 50 Hail Marys more or less. Before going to sleep each night our mother would visit each one of us, sprinkling the room with holy water and 'putting a prayer' on each forehead, "My Jesus of Nazareth, King of the Jews, preserve Eugene from a sudden or unprepared death this night Amen." She continued doing this until we left home. As I grew into my teens I began to feel that that this practice was a bit over zealous but looking back on it I now realise what a beautiful act of love and concern it was. I have never forgotten that prayer and to this day repeat it each night before sleep.

Going to Sunday Mass had its own ritual. We had to wear our 'Sunday best' and be ready in good time for the taxi which arrived to take us to St.Joseph's Church on the Rock. Willie O'Brien was out taxi man. He drove a red Ford Anglia which he kept in immaculate condition. He always had a cigarette in his mouth and before setting off he would say, "Right said she, and you never wrote."

As we sat in the car our mother had a good opportunity to check that we had washed our ears. Sometimes we did not pass her inspection so she would take a new handkerchief, moisten a corner of it with spittle and clean the unwashed ear. Sometimes Peter or Brendan would remind her to check my ears just to annoy me. On one occasion our taxi broke down and did not arrive. Even though missing Mass on that occasion was not our fault our mother promptly got us all to kneel down and say the rosary. At the end of it we all began to get up when she began the sorrowful mysteries followed by the glorious. It was the first and only time we recited all fifteen mysteries. Although we didn't say anything I think that all but our mother thought this was a bit over the top.

When we went to weekly Mass in St.Joseph's we sat as a family three quarters of the way up the church on the right. If we were a bit late seats would be scarce, so my mother and my sisters would go up the aisle as usual while my father and my brothers climbed the stairs into the gallery. In the centre of the gallery was an organ and an enclosed area for the choir. The near side of the gallery was usually full but by going round the back of the organ it was usually possible to get a seat on the other side. The problem was that the narrow passageway behind the organ had a bench on which sat men who liked to have a chat during Mass. They were big country farmers with rough looking hands that were heavily sunburned with working in the open air. I found them a bit intimidating the first time we looked for a seat in the gallery but discovered to my surprise how gentle they were, as they assisted me to get past them.

After Mass there was the obligatory stop at Paddy Doherty's to get the Sunday papers and an ice cream. A few doors down from Paddy's was Kelly's, bar which opened at twelve o'clock. Our parents often drew our attention to the dangers of alcohol, so Kelly's bar would have been perceived by us as a place to avoid.

I used to go into Paddy Doherty's shop often, to buy sweets, an ice cream or a comic. His was a general store with newspapers, magazines, confectionary, cigarettes, stationery and toys. Our mother used to buy a lot of Christmas fare from him. Paddy let out the room above the shop to Harry O'Brien the barber. Harry was from Bundoran and suffered from a bad ulcer which kept him off work from time to time. This barber's salon had a big window looking out directly at the bridge over the Erne. Through it there was a great view of the centre of the town dominated by the clock high up on the tower of the Bank Building. I liked Harry because he made a fuss over me when I arrived for a haircut. There were usually a couple of young men, members of the Aodh Ruadh Gaelic Club in the salon standing at the big window watching life on the street. Harry would cut some of my hair and then go over to these friends of his and I could hear snatches of conversations. Sometimes they discussed the latest performance of the Donegal Senior team, at other times they lowered their voices and I knew they were telling a joke that they considered me too young to hear. This double standard puzzled me. On the one hand Harry was polite and caring and then he seemed to be laughing at some smutty joke or other.

When we got home from Sunday Mass our father had the first read of the newspapers. I was interested in the sports pages and the comic strips such as The Lone Ranger, The Cisco Kid, Superman and The Phantom. Brendan was very good at drawing so he used to draw pictures of Superman and the Phantom. There was an American comic strip that appealed to Aunt K. It was called Blondie. It reflected American suburban life through the eyes of Blondie and her husband Dagwood. I didn't see much in it but one that did grab my attention was a science fiction story about the adventures of Buck Jones. It pitched my hero Buck against evil forces in outer space. Then one Sunday my admiration for Buck was cut short when the wicked queen from some strange planet managed to outwit Buck by luring him into a machine which gave her power over him. I was very disappointed at how Buck had allowed himself to be compromised in this way and so I didn't bother following the story any further. At least The Cisco Kid always managed to defeat the bandits. He had a horse called 'Diablo' and when he needed to chase the outlaws he would say to his horse "Dig dirt Diablo!" Superman and The Phantom always triumphed over evil so I preferred them to Buck Jones who allowed the power of evil to have the upper hand.

I was still reading The Beano and The Dandy at this time and swapped them with my school friends or borrowed their Christmas comic annuals. The Bash Street Kids, Desperate Dan and Dennis the Menace were popular items. My mother and Aunt K did not read comics as such but they knew about Desperate Dan and his liking for cow pies. At school we were encouraged to join the library which was situated down The Mall. I started reading the Biggles books as I moved on from comics. Biggles was a pilot in the Royal Air Force and the books told of his many adventures in different parts of the world. Unlike Buck Rogers or Superman, Biggles was a real person and it was easier to identify with him. He was a man of courage, integrity and had a sense of justice which led him to combat various forms of evil. Some of my schoolmates also read the Biggles books and so we used to discuss them.

When we moved to Templenew our father got a new dog to replace 'Doughery'. It was a white collie bitch which Angela and Monica named 'Guess'. They found it amusing when strangers asked about the name of the dog and started guessing when told her actual name. She was good at herding cattle and was a good guard dog and was protective of my sisters. One day

Angela and Monica and Guess were down near the wood when for some reason they strayed into an area that was littered with snails. Both girls started to panic and cry. Guess, sensing that help was needed ran back to the house and started tugging at the leg of our father's trousers. He realised that she was trying to tell him something. As she barked she moved back towards the field that led to the wood. My father followed her and rescued his frightened daughters stranded among the snails.

Guess slept under the stairs in the basement and Aunt K kept her out of the main house. Even though we would have liked to have had her staying with us upstairs we couldn't because of Aunt K's prohibition. If Guess perchance got into the main house and was spotted by K she was quickly banished to the basement. K would hunt her out of the sitting room with "Gad, who let that dog into the house". Sometimes Guess had to bolt as Aunt K's sweeping broom was hurled after her down the corridor that led to the basement stairs. My mother relied on her sister to help with running the house, part of which involved doing the cleaning and keeping the house tidy, so she sided with K. Like most children we were not as house-proud as our Aunt but we realised that she had authority in that department. She gave us pocket money from time to time which was another reason for keeping on the right side of her. She liked in particular to keep the sitting room neat and tidy. To make sure it stayed that way she locked it and kept the key. If we wanted to get in we had to get her permission. She also liked to control access to our telephone.

When it would ring she would pick it up and say "Ballyshannon 98." When the operator connected her she would enquire who was on the other end. If it was one of my schoolmates she would cover the mouthpiece of the phone and shout to our mother. "It's one of Eugene's school friends. Can he speak to him? My mother would usually reply, "Okay, but don't be on all night."

One area of the house that came under her jurisdiction was the front steps which she brushed regularly. If Guess was banned from the main house, mainly because she left hairs on the furniture, Goosie was banned from the front steps because of the mess she left. Both Aunt K and our mother became increasingly frustrated with having to use buckets of water to sluice the steps of goose droppings.

The problem was that Goosie was lonely and sought our company. Having been reprieved the previous Christmas at Finner she was now becoming a pet goose. The hens would have nothing to do with her and Guess ignored her. She formed a bond of sorts with Monica and followed her about, even going up through the front hay field after her as she walked to Rockfield School. During school time she would wander after our father as he did his farm chores. At night time she made her way to the byre but in the early morning out she came and settled herself on the front steps waiting for us to emerge. Hence the mess.

At one stage she didn't appear on the steps for a while. The reason was that she had started to brood. We knew about her nest in the stable and we gathered her eggs which were highly prized. They were large and quite strong so we shared them. Half of a goose egg was sufficient for us as children. When Goosie decided to brood she had no eggs to sit on but she solved this problem by scraping out one of the cobblestones in the byre which was about the same size as one of her eggs and proceeded to sit on it. This went on for a couple of weeks until the brooding notion went off her and back she came to fouling the steps. After that her days were numbered and that Christmas our pleas for another reprieve fell on deaf ears and our father wrung her neck. This was another painful lesson for us children.

In the following Summer Guess got ill with distemper and started wasting away. Our parents told us that she was dying and that it would be better to put her out of her misery than have her suffering. We accepted the sad news and waited for our father to shoot her. We heard the shot and when our father returned to the house I went out and found her lying on the grass between the back door and the orchard. Brendan and I dug a grave for her in a clearing in the orchard and laid her there. My heart was sore that day but I accepted that there was nothing else that could have been done for her. Within a short while our father got another collie which we called 'Raider'. He didn't last long.

He was a fair sized pup when he arrived, a collie like all the previous dogs but he had a rebellious streak. He began raiding the henhouse for eggs, hence the name 'Raider'. Our mother filled some egg shells with mustard to discourage him but this didn't work. He got away with this bad behaviour for several months but when it became obvious that he was not going to change his ways it was only a matter of time before our father became involved. Once our mother complained to him his fate was sealed. Out came the shotgun and Raider was shot out in the front field. He was replaced by another collie which we called 'Dusty'. He was better behaved than Raider until we moved into the town some years later.

In the springtime of 1954 the avenue lit up with the glow of a multitude of daffodils. It was the first time for us to see such a display at Templenew. In the field bordering Nellie's field there was a more stunning display. This field belonged to our neighbour Walter Semple. Apparently he had qualified as a chemist but had taken over his parents' farm after they died. He lived on his own and had peculiar habits. He dressed in breeches and leggings wore a khaki top and spoke with a cultivated accent. He seemed to have a liking for daffodils because the lawn in front of his two-storey house was full of them. One day that spring Angela and Monica were looking in through the tall gate at the entrance to his farm when Walter appeared. Monica piped up, "Semple", can we have some of your flowers!" He smiled, of course, and duly obliged.

I always admired Walter's field of daffodils next to us. The difference between his daffodils and ours was that his were singles. To me the singles were more beautiful and I wished that we could have had some. Our doubles did not have the delicate head and spacious centre that highlighted the pure yellow colour of the petals. Our mother had a big interest in flowers. Each year she planted sweet pea at the side of the house and in the plots at the sides of the front steps she grew hydrangeas and roses. She used some of these to adorn the statue of Our Lady on the landing and displayed others in vases throughout the house.

I got to know Walter Semple by having the odd conversation with him on my home from school. As I cycled up towards his front gate I dismounted to walk the last steep section of the hill just before turning in to Templenew and if he was at his gate he would quiz me about my progress at school. He had a particular interest in Latin due to his background in pharmacy. He visited my parents a few times and they were amused at the formal way in which he conversed. There was a large tree overhanging some of our outhouses and our father decided to have it removed. He got Dick Cleary from Ballyshannon, who bought trees, cut them up and sold as firewood to cut it down for him. Dick arrived and with his men he set about felling the large tree. He managed to bring it down but damaged the end of the roof of the hay loft in the process. When discussing this incident with our parents Victor opined that "I had the operation under observation and deduced that what was being attempted was a physical impossibility". The same evening he played a tune on our mothers' violin.

When Peter was in his late teens he used to visit Walter occasionally. He told us that Walter had a rugby ball which he and Walter kicked around the field behind his house. The most bizarre account was about the fate of a mouse that appeared on a shelf of the dresser while Peter and Walter were having a cup of tea. Walter had an air pistol beside his armchair and at the sight of the mouse he took aim and duly killed the mouse with one shot.

In that spring of '54 our parents were asked if it would be possible to provide board and lodgings to a group of five ordnance survey men from Belfast who were doing survey work just over the border in Fermanagh, which was a mile and a half away. The survey men needed accommodation for a few months from Mondays to Fridays but couldn't find a large enough house to stay in as a group. Bed and breakfast accommodation was not available much in those days and Cleary's Hotel in Beleek was small. Our parents agreed, since Templenew House was large enough to accommodate them and the extra income was welcome. They were given one of our large bedrooms and the spare room off the pantry.

So, at the beginning of May 1954 two jeeps drew up outside our front door and out got the survey men. The man in charge of them was Mr. Tommy Larmour from Armagh House, Ormeau Avenue, Belfast. We knew his colleagues as Mr. Smith, Mr. Ferguson, Mr. Jones and Mr. McGuinness. They were out all day doing their survey work and returned in the evenings. Our mother and Aunt K cooked and served them their meals. The big dining room proved its worth as they all could sit around the big table while Aunt K served their meals which our mother passed in through the serving hatch. After their evening meal they had access to the large sitting room. They were up early in the mornings and after breakfast they went off to work over the border.

We did not have much to do with the survey men. They kept pretty much to themselves but occasionally one or other of them would talk to us about our school work. Because they were there all through the summer they used to come out in the long evenings to stroll about or watch us playing Rounders. I remember one of them in particular, probably the youngest, who used to walk around reading his bible. Another one of them used to go out shooting rabbits with our shotgun accompanied by Peter. I got involved with them when a bat flew into their bedroom. With all the trees around Templenew it was common in the long summer evenings to see and hear bats on the wing, Occasionally one of them strayed in through an open upstairs window. Getting them out was not easy but I volunteered to become a bat catcher. Going into their room I followed the bat as it flew into curtains and on to the top of wardrobes. I used a chair to get access to it on top of a wardrobe. Now bats are not the most attractive looking creatures. They look like a black mouse with bony wings and have the most exquisite little ears and claws. I grabbed it and almost let it go again when it opened its little pink mouth and tried to bite me. Jumping down from the chair I ran to the window and threw it out. From then on I became the official bat catcher.

The survey men got on really well with our parents and Aunt K, that is, until one night in late August, when after a night out in Bundoran an incident occurred that upset our mother. One of the survey men was drunk and mistaking Peter and Brendan's bedroom for the bathroom he defecated in the corner. Our mother told Mr. Larmour that this behaviour was unacceptable and that she could no longer have such men in her house. And so the survey men left, but before they did Mr. Larmour wrote a fulsome note of thanks in the guest book.

A month later our parents got another request to provide accommodation for two English men from Stoke-on-Trent who had come over to install a new kiln in Beleek Pottery. First to arrive was Mr. Thomas Winterton. He was the man in charge of the project. He was accompanied by Mr. John Franklin. After a week or so Mr. Winterton went back to England and Mr. George Benn took his place. They stayed with us for a couple of months while they installed the new kiln. They made themselves at home and had lots of conversations with our father about his travels to markets in the north of England. John Franklin even helped to pump the water from the storage tank at the back of the house and joined us in the odd game of Rounders. He also taught us how to play cricket.

The example of Brother Luke marking out a tennis court by turning over the sod encouraged me to do the same on the lawn at the front of Templenew House. In the early summer of '55 I began this project. Our mother had a thesaurus which I looked up and found the dimensions for a tennis court. With Brendan's help we marked out a doubles court, hammered in two stakes at either side and strung the old tennis net that was in the basement kitchen between them. We had two old wooden racquets and so we had our first game on the new court. The summer of '55 was a very good one so we got to play on our grass court quite a bit.

That same summer a Dublin family called Connolly came for their holidays to Doherty's Farm nearby. The children were Paul, who was eleven, his sister Mary who was thirteen and another sister who was eight or nine. Whether they saw my brothers and sisters out playing on the lawn or were invited by my sister Angela I do not know but they arrived and joined in our games. Paul and I played lots of tennis and had many keenly contested sets. Although we did not have television in those days we followed the Wimbledon Championship through the newspapers and knew the names of the main players. We had our own 'world championship' which I tended to win more often than Paul. In between games of tennis Paul showed me how to play a Dublin street game called 'Jackstones'. It involved picking up small stones tossing them in the air and catching them on the back of the hand. The aim was to see how many stones could be tossed and caught like this. Paul was better at this than me at the start but gradually I began to compete and win the odd session. We played this game on the front steps of the house.

In the long summer evenings we also played Rounders as this involved the girls more. There were other games that we played involving running, catching, 'imprisoning and releasing'. At the end of the summer the Connollys went back to Dublin and I concentrated on football and hurling. With the encouragement of Brother Columba, who provided those interested with hurleys I began to practice my hurling skills at home. On arriving home from school I would go down to the 'ballroom' in the basement and spend half an hour hitting a sponge ball against one wall and try to keep striking it from every direction like in the game of squash. Sometimes I would go outside and practice taking frees or solo running with the ball on the hurley. I had an old football also and this allowed me to combine basic football and hurling drills. As I dodged around the trees on the front lawn with my hurley and ball or with my football I imagined myself as the great Cork hurler Christy Ring or the great Galway footballer Sean Purcell.

The De La Salle brothers encouraged us to play both games and Brother Thomas took charge of a juvenile team for the local GAA club, Aodh Ruadh. Football practice was held in the Fr. Tierney Park next to the school so this meant that I had to cycle into Ballyshannon in the evening for practice. We also had a school league which was played on a Wednesday afternoon, initially in the school pitch but later in Fr. Tierney Park. Peter had moved from college in Limerick to De La Salle and he was captain of one of the senior teams. As a result of playing in these competitions I got on the Ballyshannon juvenile team.

Being part of the Aodh Ruadh club was a big honour for me. Our first game was against Bundoran at home. We beat them and in that game I had the best performance ever. The return game was in Bundoran. They were too good for us on that occasion mainly because the game was played later in the year when all their boarding school players were home.

What I really liked about playing for the Aodh Ruadh club was the camaraderie between the players. We used to meet outside Paddy

Doherty's shop where Brother Thomas would announce the team. For an away game the club laid on a couple of taxis driven by John 'The Bishop' O'Brien and his brother Seamus. Later when I started playing minor football we travelled further afield for away games, to Donegal town and Ballybofey. We had a very good minor team and eventually went on to win the county championship in 1958.

Like most of my schoolmates I liked joining in at lunchtime in 'kick abouts'. Some boys played in around the goalposts while others played outfield. There was no organised game just kicking in and out with boys competing for possession. We did this even on wet days when the football, which in those days was made of pigskin, got wet, heavy and slippery. I reached up for a ball that had been kicked out but instead of a making a clean catch I made a clumsy one and dislocated my right thumb. This was ugly looking and very painful. One of my classmates brought me in to the school and knocked on the staffroom door. Out came Brother Daniel and when he saw the condition of my thumb he dispatched me immediately to the Rock Hospital across the road.

The Rock Hospital was basically a maternity facility but a nurse phoned a local GP, Dr. Kelly who arrived in and examined my dislocated thumb. He put me up on the operating table in the theatre and asked the nurse to hold me still. He then poured some of the contents of a bottle on to a piece of cotton wool and placed this over my mouth. I didn't know at the time that this was chloroform that he was using to knock me unconscious. I just remember that the nurse had to physically restrain me as I struggled to avoid what seemed like suffocation. Suddenly all went black and just as suddenly it seemed I woke up to find half my hand in plaster of Paris with my thumb and fingers protruding. With that Dr. Kelly sent me back to school and told me to come back in three weeks to have the plaster removed. Back in school I was the centre of attraction for a while. With my right hand in plaster I got off doing written homework.

My interest in football and hurling extended to other sporting activities as a result of competing in the school sports. Like most of the other boys I ran in races and attempted the high and long jumps. Although I was fast on my feet I couldn't compete with the taller boys and I was definitely too small for competing in the high jump. The long jump was different, where speed combined with the right technique made up for small stature. Although I did not win anything at the sports I came fourth in the long jump. This encouraged specialising in it so I made my own long jump pit with a jumping board under the beech tree in the field in front of Templenew house. In the good weather I used to practise jumping and measuring my progress. Even though this extra practice did not win me any prizes at school it taught me to persevere at projects that challenged me and like my football and hurling practices I got used to amusing myself.

That hot summer of '55 Brendan decided that it would be a good idea to dam a part of the burn and make a little swimming pool that we could bathe in. The burn ran through the big field between our lawn field and Ednagor. It then entered a wooded area before tumbling down towards the ESB reservoir. It was in this wooded area that Brendan set about making his swimming pool. He blocked the burn sufficiently to cause it to back up and by widening the area before the blockage he was able to create a pool which was about twelve feet by six. This was big enough and deep enough for a shallow dive and two or three breast strokes. It was here that I began learning to dive and to swim.

Angela and Monica didn't use our home made swimming pool preferring to bathe in the sea in Bundoran. There was a bus that travelled from Enniskillen to Bundoran on Sundays which was convenient for going to the seaside. Even though we had moved from Finner to the other side of Ballyshannon we still had access to Bundoran via that Erne Bus Company. Our father could swim and liked going for a dip in the outdoor pool that had been made in a little cove well sheltered from the large Atlantic breakers that pounded Bundoran strand. He taught Angela to swim there but Monica was too young to master swimming at that time. Peter, Brendan and I bathed there too. On one occasion after getting some help to learn the front crawl from a friend of his who was an accomplished swimmer Peter and his friend, on walking round to Rougey came upon a
young woman who was in difficulties in the deep water. Peter raised the alarm with the local guards while his friend jumped in and kept the young woman afloat until help arrived. She was taken to the hospital in Ballyshannon suffering from shock. Later Peter and his friend visited her there. The incident was reported in the Donegal Democrat.

Due to the mini heat wave of '55 our well ran dry. There was an inspection cover under the snout of the pump and by lifting it the contents of the well became visible. Normally the water level was quite high but in early August it was possible to see the bottom of the well about fifteen feet down with just a trickle in it. Fortunately there was another well in Ednagor belonging to the Boyle family to which we had access. This well was a quarter of a mile away which made it a bit wearisome carrying buckets of water every few days for drinking and cooking. We had to use the rain water sparingly. The storage tank at the rear of the house had filled up to the top with the heavy rain that fell just before the drought so that got us through the dry spell. With our frequent trips over to Ednagor we got to know the three Boyle families who had houses close to each other.

The 'Four Lifer' was a Friesian cow that we brought with us from Finner. Having suckled four calves at the same time she proved her worth as regards her milk producing ability. She was an even tempered animal and easy to milk. However, from time to time she would graze on parts of the farm that had prickly bushes growing and arrive in for milking with scratches on her teats. This made milking her difficult because it was impossible to avoid hurting her. My brothers and I took turns at milking her and we all had to put up with her reactions to squeezing her scratched teats. If she wasn't too badly scratched she would give us a slap with her tail to let us know to go easy. Her tail was not always that clean so to get a swipe of it was not very pleasant. If there were deeper scratches on her teats she soon let us know by kicking the bucket and our stool from under us.

I had learnt in school that a cow was a ruminant animal with four stomachs which allowed her to regurgitate the grass she had eaten and chew it again. This made me curious so when it was my turn to milk her I would study her behaviour. Sure enough after a spell of chewing the cud there would be a pause and by placing my hand gently under her throat I could feel a wad of grass being regurgitated. In the winter months I had to bring a hurricane lamp with me and hope that my cow hadn't been grazing through the bushes. I formed a bond with the Four Lifer and used to sing to her as I milked. As my brothers got older the milking chore fell to me. The morning session was the most difficult because I was always running late and had to try to get to school in time. Fortunately my mother stood in for me if I was really late. If she herself was delayed in getting down to the byre the Four Lifer would moo to be milked.

My mother did most of her week's shopping in Frank Kennedy's grocery store on the East Port. Feeding a family required frequent visits to the town to replenish the larder. Even though our mother baked every couple of days making bread, apple tarts, lemon meringues, rhubarb tarts, and several varieties of jam she needed other provisions to supplement here home baking. She had to buy different meals for baking purposes and other meals for feeding the hens. Kennedy's had a van for delivering large orders. Smaller orders we could carry on the back of a bicycle.

Sometimes we ran short of essentials like tea or sugar or we needed an extra loaf of bread. Fortunately Maggie Dillon, who lived just between McCormick's Bridge and Rockfield School, had a little shop to the front of her cottage and she stocked such essentials. Maggie was a widow with two adopted or fostered girls. The girls kept their own names so they were probably fostered. The little shop had a bell which was activated by opening the door. After a short pause Maggie would appear. She was a woman of few words. The only times I saw her were on the odd visit to her shop. She had old newspapers on top of the counter which she used for wrapping purchases.

Our father had been lobbying local politicians to use their influence in getting electricity to Templenew House and a few other nearby residences. Finally we got the news that we were going to be connected. We watched with great interest as a crew of ESB workmen arrived to put in the poles and wires. Because the house was already wired up for a supply it didn't take long to get us connected once the poles were in place. At last, in the late spring of '55 we put away the paraffin lamps and had the luxury of a supply of mains electricity. Right from the start our father insisted that no bulb was left switched on once a room was vacated. We got plenty of reprimands for forgetting to do this. Another great advantage of having electricity was that no longer did we have to get wet batteries charged. Now we could listen to the wireless without restriction.

One of the programmes that we used to listen to was one sponsored by Walton's Music of

Dublin. It was broadcast on a Saturday. It began with the announcer saying, "Your weekly reminder of the grace and beauty that lie in our heritage of Irish Song, the songs that our fathers loved" and ended with "If you feel like singing, do sing an Irish song". Walton's played all kinds of Irish music from traditional jigs and reels to popular ballads. Some of their recording artists on their Glenside Label were Joe Lynch, Delia Murphy, Charlie McGee and Noel Purcell. One of Charlie McGee's most popular songs was The Homes of Donegal.

Music was always important in our house chiefly due to our mother's piano playing ability. She could sit down and play complex pieces she had learned as a music pupil in the convent in Strabane. She could also play the odd tune on the violin. We often gathered around the piano in the drawing room on Sunday evenings while our mother played songs from a song book. Occasionally she played and sang 'Jeannie with the light brown hair' which seemed to be directed at me. I wasn't impressed and wished that she would play something else.

I was intrigued with how a piano produced such beautiful sounds and often would lift the lid while our mother played to view the action of the hammers on the strings. Bothe Angela and Monica went for piano lessons in Ballyshannon like many other girls in those days. Boys did not get the same chance to learn piano but I tinkled the keys of our piano and could pick out a tune with my right hand but that was about the limit of my music practice. I even tried to scrape a tune on the violin but found it difficult to tune.

There was a music shop in East Port Ballyshannon called 'Quigley's' that stocked musical instruments and sheet music. Our mother used to buy the odd piece of sheet music there. My friends and I used to stop and window gaze at Quigley's on our way home from school. On display were accordions, mouth organs, fiddles, flutes and the like.

One evening after tea my brothers and sisters and I heard music coming from somewhere upstairs. We couldn't figure out how this was possible because the radio was in the dining room and was turned off. We went up the stairs and there on the landing was Aunt K standing beside a gramophone which was playing a record of traditional Irish music. Beside the gramophone was a selection of records. Aunt K could see the surprise in our eyes, which obviously gave her great satisfaction. Being a spinster she had no children of her own to share her life with so being able to connect with us as part of the household seemed to become more important to her as we grew and matured. Surprising us with this gift of music was an example of how she could relate to us as a benefactor. Even though I was only thirteen I could see the pleasure our response gave her. She had a child-like reaction to being appreciated which seemed odd to me at the time but which I understand now.

The gramophone had to be wound up to get the turntable spinning and the needle had to be manually set on the record. This required a certain amount of care, so Aunt K was very particular about who could operate it. Not only that, it was kept in the drawing room which of course was locked so getting use of it required getting permission from K to play it and getting admission to the drawing room. She seemed to think that I was careful enough to wind it up and drop the needle so I got to play it more than the others. I used to play records by Joe Lynch and Austin Gaffney. One of my favourites was, 'If we only had old Ireland over here'.

During the summer of '56 I played juvenile football and hurling for the Aodh Ruadh Club in Ballyshannon and continued playing tennis against Paul Connolly. Paul and his sisters and Angela and Monica and the youngest of Maggie Dillon's foster children still played chasing and catching games. Most of the time these games were played on the lawn in front of Templenew House but sometimes we went up to Doherty's, where the Connollys were staying, to play in their yard. In the chasing and catching game if you were caught you were put in 'prison' and someone from your team had to break through 'enemy lines' to set you free. One evening in the late summer Mary Connolly and I were both captured and put into prison – one of Paddy Doherty's outhouses. Where previously I would not have paid any special attention to Mary, on this occasion I wanted to stay in 'prison' with this dark haired lovely girl. I hadn't really noticed her much before but now I found her strangely attractive. Unfortunately I was rescued by one of my team-mates and I had to leave the company of my dark beauty.

As that summer turned into autumn I was taken unawares when I began to dream about some of the school girls that I knew. Without warning, as it were, I had reached another of Freud's stages of psychosexual development. Overnight my boyhood had slipped away with my comics, my fantasy life in the tree that touched the ground, my 'Biggles' books and playing 'jackstones' with Paul Connolly. Since arriving in Templenew House I had tried, while standing on the threshold of the dining room doorway to touch the lintel but to no avail. In that late summer it was no longer beyond my reach. My adolescence had begun.

There was little information or advice about how to deal with the physical, emotional, psychological and social aspects of adolescence in Ballyshannon of the 50's. My father didn't give any guidance but that would not have been unusual in those days. It was even less to be expected of him knowing about his own upbringing. He had lost his mother when he was six and had a father who was stern so he had not experienced tender loving care in his youth. My mother didn't provide any information directly but she did make oblique references to certain 'urges', especially in men but didn't explain what they were. She had been raised in a puritanical era which had left her personally damaged by scrupulosity. On the one hand she was devout in her religious practice but on the other she suffered from an exaggerated sense of guilt which required her to go to confession more than required. Her reminder to us to go to monthly confession was probably her way of ensuring that our adolescent 'urges' were dealt with. In fairness to her she did make an attempt to warn Angela and me about any attempt by strangers to befriend us. Angela brushed her advice aside saying that she knew all about that and quickly changed the subject. And so an embarrassing moment passed, much to my relief.

School did not provide any sex education. On one occasion Br. Daniel, while going through a passage in the gospels explained to us what a eunuch was. We wanted to hear more but he didn't go any further. Br. Francis exhorted us to be worthy of our faith and to keep ourselves pure but he never explained what he meant. As always the best, if not the most discreet source of information was older boys. In crude and explicit terms they expanded on the 'urges' and their consequences. Although I didn't like their crude language at least I got the facts.

Another source of information on sexual matters was the annual Mission. A group of priests from some religious order or other arrived to preach and rejuvenate the faith of the parishioners. Redemptorists, Passionists, or Dominicans would take over the parish for two weeks. Extra early morning Masses were celebrated and each evening there was an hour devoted to the rosary, preaching and benediction. Stalls overflowing with all manner of religious objects were located near the church and the parishioners attended in great numbers. The first week of the mission was for the women and the second for the men. The separation of the men and women made it easier for the missioners to speak directly about the sixth and the ninth commandments. Addressing such topics to a mixed congregation would have been difficult in that era.

In the early days of my adolescence the references to the sixth and the ninth did not give any great cause for concern but as I grew older what they had to say began to sound a bit like my mother's reference to 'urges'. That along with the input from my older schoolmates set my moral compass from then onwards. The missioners did not mince their words when castigating the male population for their transgressions of the sixth and ninth and thundered on about the perils of being seduced by the world, the flesh and the devil. There were sermons about the other commandments also and how breaking them offended God but the sins of the flesh seemed to be particularly abhorrent. They seemed to be directly linked to the suffering of the Saviour. Graphic depictions of the torments of Hell and the depravity of sinful men got us all examining our lives more closely. After the sermons confessions were heard. The seats opposite each confessional box were packed by the contrite.

There was a lot of discussion in families and among the parishioners generally about the missioners and their message and opinions, about who the best preacher was, or who told the best jokes, but there was no reference to the specific preaching directed at the women and the men. The mission fortnight seemed to energise the parish and was greatly appreciated by everyone. I was impressed by the witness of the missioners and was drawn to the vision of integrity they proposed and I wanted to model my life on the ideals they placed before me.

There was a Franciscan Friary at Rossnowlagh, a quiet seaside resort just five miles from Ballyshannon that attracted many parishioners from Ballyshannon and surrounding area to its liturgies. Our mother and Aunt K were members of the Third Order of St. Francis, a lay branch of the order which linked them to the spirituality of St. Francis. When we first arrived in the Ballyshannon area it was easy to get to the Friary because the Donegal Railway Company still ran a service from Ballyshannon to Lifford, stopping at Rossnowlagh halt on the way. In the summer time throngs of people availed of the opportunity of getting to the beach this way. The railway service however ended in the mid-fifties so people had to get to the resort by bicycle or car. Our mother used to go there often on her bicycle. One great advantage of the Friary was that there was always a Friar on duty for confession which suited her very well. She had her own 'special' confessor, Fr. Cyprian who seemed to understand her scrupulosity. I always liked going to the Friary because there were people there praying privately, going round the stations or lighting candles. Occasionally a friar dressed in his brown habit would appear and swish down a side aisle on his way to one of the confessional boxes.

Another aspect of parish spirituality was evident every year during the month of May. This month was dedicated to Mary and in the town households made an effort to make a May altar. They placed a statue of Mary behind a front window and surrounded it with flowers. Then on the Thursday following Trinity Sunday the Corpus Christi procession took place. The route of the procession was from St. Patrick's Church to the grounds of the Shiel Hospital via Market Street and College Street. The Blessed Sacrament was carried in a monstrance by the parish priest under a liturgical canopy held in place by four De La Salle Brothers. Some schoolchildren scattered petals at the head of the procession. Hymns were sung and prayers were said in the hospital grounds and then the procession made its way back to St. Patrick's for Benediction. A guard of honour was provided by the local unit of the FCA at the entrance of the Church. An army bugler played a musical salute as the congregation was blessed by the monstrance.

In the spring of '56 our mother became ill. This was unusual because apart from her bouts of asthma she was very healthy and full of energy. She took to her bed and after a day or so she decided to consult the local GP. She had already diagnosed her illness as jaundice because her eyes were yellow and she felt lethargic. She phoned Dr. Moran and told him that she suspected that she had jaundice. He called out and confirmed her diagnosis. He prescribed medication and told her she would soon be back on her feet. Word was sent to our cousin Peggy in the Craigs so she arrived to help Aunt K with running the home while our mother was ill. Even though our mother was on the mend I remember wondering and worrying what I would do if anything serious happened to her. She was such a vibrant presence and so more approachable than my father that I dreaded to think what my life would be like without her.

Peggy usually brought provisions with her such as a plucked chicken, scones of bread or a side of ham. Since she stayed for a few weeks, on that occasion she decided to cook one of our chickens for the following Sunday lunch. Our father was en route from England so, not being present to kill a chicken Peggy set about it herself. I accompanied her to grab a plumb hen. I had only ever seen our father killing chickens by stretching their necks so I did not know if Peggy would be able to do the same. Well, she didn't stretch the hen's neck. Instead she took out a sharp knife, bent the chicken's head over and made a quick slash on the back of her neck. Unlike the flapping and shuddering that accompanied our father's method Peggy's victim just went limp as copious amounts of blood spurted from an artery. I was surprised and a little shocked at the business-like manner in which Peggy killed the fat hen.

An aspect of parish life that was special in those days was Midnight Mass at Christmas in St. Patrick's. Unlike today midnight meant midnight. Willie O'Brien arrived in his taxi at 11:30 p.m. and brought us to the church which quickly filled to capacity. High up in the gallery one of the nuns played the organ and a mixed choir sang the usual Christmas Hymns. Brian Campbell was the main tenor so he sang Holy Night as a solo supported by the rest of the choir. On one occasion the choir sang a less well known Christmas hymn, Noel, Noel. On the way out from Mass my father asked my mother, "What kind of a hymn was that they were singing, No Hell, No Hell"! In those days we fasted for three hours before receiving Communion so by the time we got home in the early morning we were ready for a big breakfast in the dining room under the brightly coloured streamers that had been strung across the ceiling.

A holly bush festooned with ornaments served as a Christmas tree.

The Christmas period of '56 was a bit special because in early December Ireland's golden boy of athletics, Ronnie Delaney won the 1,500 metres race at the Olympics in Melbourne. The news came through on the radio just before I set out for school. As I cycled in that morning I was thrilled that an Irishman had beaten the world's top middle distance runners. The papers had been full of stories about Delaney's chances. Having taken up an athletic's scholarship in Villanova University in the United States he had proved his potential as a promising middle distance runner. He had done well in the Olympics' qualifying heats but the majority opinion was that the local Australian John Landy would likely win. Other notable runners in the race were Murray Halberg, Gunnar Nielsen, Brian Hewson, Ken Wood and Klaus Richtzenhain. The one thing that favoured our man was his ability to 'kick' down the straight. Sure enough, Delaney moved up from the back of the field and sprinted past the lead runners to breast the tape in a time of three minutes forty-one point two seconds. Everyone in school was talking about the great victory but we had to wait to read accounts in the papers to get a full account of the race. The picture on the front of the Irish Press was of Ronnie Delaney kneeling on the track blessing himself, having crossed the line in front of Klaus Richtzenhain and John Landy. Later the highlights were shown on Pathé News in the Erne Cinema much to the delight of the audience. I was so proud of Delaney's achievement that, fifty years later, while attending an international seminar in Villanova University, Philadelphia I got permission to walk on the athletics track that he had trained on during his university days.

By the beginning of 1957 I was well into my third year of secondary school. Brendan was doing well at the vocational school where he had a particular interest in all things electrical. He used to bring bits and pieces home and construct circuits and motors, much to our amazement. In the autumn he used to go down to the orchard for 'windfalls' to bring with him to school. He was also getting interested in body building. The principal of the vocational school ran a fitness programme for boys which Brendan attended. Part of this programme involved working with weights so the boys in the programme could build up their biceps and triceps. Brendan got weights of his own and used a room in the basement as his personal gym. The principal of the Vocational School was also the commanding officer of the local FCA. Peter and Brendan joined the local unit and later on I served in it.

When Peter returned from the Redemptorist College in Limerick he finished his secondary education in De La Salle. He had had enough of the confinement of boarding school and wanted to be back home. Having completed his Intermediate Certificate in Limerick he felt that this was a good time to move. Our parents acceded to his request. Moving from one school to another was not easy but Peter quickly adapted and soon was playing a full part in school life. When Master Moran organized a football league Peter became the captain of one of the teams and also played for the Aodh Ruadh Gaelic Club.

Living just a mile and a half from the border meant that we made frequent trips to Beleek where some goods were cheaper than in Ballyshannon or where they had treats like Mars bars that weren't available in the republic. It only took a few minutes to cycle down the road, past Clyhore and on into Beleek. There were two customs huts to pass on the way. By going in the side road we had to pass the southern one while by going in via the main road we had to pass the northern one. None of the locals went in by the main road so we had only one set of customs officials to worry about. The northern customs didn't mind goods moving from the north to the south because this was good export business but their southern counterparts viewed goods coming out of Beleek as imports. Most of the smuggling was of a minor nature – a loaf of bread, detergent, ham and the like and the customs officials generally turned a blind eye to it. Nevertheless they were entitled to stop and search if they chose so we were always a bit tense as we cycled up past the hut with a bag of groceries hanging from the handlebars.

On one occasion our father decided to sell the 'four lifer' at Beleek fair. He got me to herd her down a lane that skirted the border. Nobody at the fair wanted an ageing cow so I had to smuggle her back again. Taking her back over the border caused me some anxiety but we made it home undetected. I was glad in a way that we hadn't been able to sell her because I had become attached to her.

Borders attract opportunistic traders and the border at Beleek provided a good example of opportunism. According to building regulations planning permission is required before the erection of any building but if the building is complete and roofed it escapes the planning permission requirement. So, one morning in 1957 Beleek awoke to the sight of a grocery store that had not been there the day before. A local man had hired a squad of bricklayers and joiners to work through the night and build a shop with a flat roof. He had built in a strategic position and began to trade profitably right away. His ingenuity was the talk of Ballyshannon for days.

While the border divided two economies it was also a very real political division and in late 1956 a smouldering resentment to the division of the island turned into a series of attacks against police stations and customs huts along the border. The Border Campaign as it came to be called could have been influenced by events elsewhere. In October 1956 the Hungarian Revolution was world news. People in the West were appalled by the way the Soviets sent in their tanks to Budapest and crushed the rebellion with brute force. By Mid November the Soviets had regained control. Our parents had told us about the persecution of Hungarian Cardinal Mindszenty, his trial and imprisonment when he opposed the Communist regime so we were very sympathetic to the revolution. Also in October 1956 there was the Suez Crisis when Egypt was invaded by Israel, Britain and France. I listened to various news programmes about these conflicts with growing interest. At thirteen and a half I viewed war and aerial attacks as exciting. However, both campaigns were over in weeks and this disappointed me. I had sympathy for the Hungarians but I didn't know enough about the Suez Crisis to understand the issues involved. It just seemed to end too soon,

In the Border Campaign Fermanagh bore the brunt of the attacks. The R.U.C. barracks in Lisnaskea, Derrylin and Rosslea were attacked in December '56. An R.U.C. constable was killed in the Derrylin attack. He was the first casualty of the Border Campaign. On January 1St 1957 Brookeborough barracks was attacked and two IRA volunteers, Sean South and Fergal O'Hanlon were killed. Just over a mile from Templenew House there was an explosion at the customs hut on the southern side. No one was hurt. We heard the explosion during the night but did not know what it was. In an enquiry afterwards a local customs official was asked about the incident. He told the enquiry that a man had come into the customs post with a parcel. He said he was busy on the telephone and told the man to "Put it there". The man with the parcel placed it in a corner and left. That night the parcel exploded and wrecked the customs hut. For some time afterwards "Put it there" took on a new meaning with the locals.

Beleek was famous for its Pottery, the facade of which dominated the entrance to the village when viewed from the bridge over the Erne. The ornamental china created there was world famous and the Pottery provided work to skilled artisans from the locality. The village was small but it was reasonably prosperous due to the employment provided by the Pottery and a thriving farming community. It had a special fair day on St.Patrick's Day which attracted a variety of street traders. I used to cycle down to it and spend an afternoon mingling with the large crowd.

There was another occasion when Beleek was in the news. A young seminarian called Edward Daly who was studying for the priesthood in Rome was given permission to be ordained in his home village because his father was dying and couldn't travel to Rome. In the event his father died before the ordination but the ceremony went ahead and Edward Daly was ordained at home. I cycled down for the ceremony even though Beleek was not my parish. The local church was packed but I squeezed in at the back and witnessed the ceremony. Seventeen years later I was present in St. Eugene's Cathedral Derry for his ordination as bishop.

Our father had an interest in books but he did not have access to many. One evening he went to an auction in a house of a recently deceased Protestant neighbour and arrived home with a large box of assorted books which he arranged on the shelves of one of the alcoves in the sitting room. Browsing through them I found the biography of boxing promoter Jack Solomons, a memoir of an English emigrant to Canada called 'A Manitoba Chore Boy' and an account of the first non-stop transatlantic flight by two British airmen, Alcock and Brown. The airmen flew a modified First World War Vickers Vimy bomber from St. John's, Newfoundland, to Clifden, Connemara. The fact that they landed in the west of Ireland made the story all the more interesting. I don't remember any of the other titles but I read these and was fascinated by them. I read the Manitoba Chore Boy twice probably because it recounted the life of a boy of my age forging a new life on the Canadian prairie. The sheer scale of farming on such large tracts of land compared to our few fields of hay impressed me. Alcock and Brown's transatlantic adventure was thrilling to read about and contrasted with my Finner memories of a small hovering helicopter. Through reading my horizons were extending.

Our father also had an interest in playing cards and dominoes. I didn't care much for dominoes but I did like games of whist and solo. In the long winter evenings when our father was not travelling to markets in England we used to have long sessions of solo. He particularly liked to get the better of us with a spread miser. This involved him displaying his hand while we tried to get him to win a trick. Sometimes we did but more often than not he beat us. Aunt K and our mother took turns at the whist and solo.

Our father was a good story teller and after a session of cards we would sit around the fire in the dining room and he would light his pipe and tell us about some of his exploits in Northumberland. We soon got to know some of the characters among his cattle dealer friends and English farmers. We heard about his contacts in Newcastle-upon-Tyne, Morpeth, Alnwick, Hexham, Yarrow and Whitley Bay.

We listened attentively, and even though many of the place names and people mentioned were unknown to us we got a sense of what life was like at the markets or father attended.

He told us he had also composed a song called 'Jasmine Deane' which had been published and there was a copy of it in the house which our mother used to play on the piano. Over the years it got lost. On one of his journeys from England a fellow cattle dealer died suddenly on the boat from Stranraer to Larne. This had a big impact on him because he told us all about it in great detail and had obviously been shocked by the incident.

I got to see my father at work a few times when I accompanied him to fairs in Ballyshannon or Kinlough. Going to a fair meant missing school for a day which suited me fine. If we had half a dozen cattle to sell we had to walk them from Templenew to Ballyshannon. This was far from easy. I would have to go ahead and guard any side road, entrance or gap in a hedge to ensure that none of the cattle went astray. Not being used to a public road or traffic young bullocks would sometimes try to get back into a field along the way, and occasionally did which meant I had to follow the stray, round it up and get it back on the road. Then going through the East Port and round the bridge and up Market Street to the green area opposite the Abbey Ballroom was particularly difficult. Once in the fairground things settled down as our cattle felt more at ease with other animals.

Once the cattle were in place it was a matter of waiting for buyers to show an interest in them. The cattle dealers were easy to spot because of the way they dressed. Unlike the farmers who were in rough clothes and wellingtons or boots the cattle dealers wore suits with long overcoats and had smart shoes. Some of them had their trouser bottoms turned up an extra fold to keep them clean as they walked through cattle slurry. My father would stroll around and engage his fellow dealers in conversation. Sometimes when a deal was hanging in the balance one of the dealers would act as a go-between and get the two parties to split the difference between them. There were some dealers who were known as 'Tanglers' whose sole mission was to get the two parties to move closer together on price and eventually do a deal. The 'Tangler' would get an unofficial 'fee' from one of the party's if he was successful.

I was always hoping that our cattle would be sold because then I was free to wander around at my leisure but best of all my father and I went to Mrs. McKeown's house in Market Street for our dinner. Mrs. McKeown and other women made good money on fair days cooking and serving dinners to hungry farmers and dealers. They served up roast beef, potatoes and vegetables, usually cabbage, followed by a sweet of apple tart and custard, a trifle or rice pudding. Some of the men went to the local bars for a drink but my father who was a teetotaller didn't. Being at the fair in Ballyshannon added to my sense of being a Ballyshannon boy. I was mingling with the local farmers on the streets of their town against the backdrop of the town clock and the chiming of the church clock high up on the tower of St. Anne's Church of Ireland church just off Main Street a short distance away and I was dining in one of the local houses. I was spending the day on the streets and not in school and that street presence tied me to the commercial life of the town.

It was during 1956 that Aunt K moved for a time to Booterstown, near Dún Laoghaire. I do not know why she decided to leave Templenew, whether she had fallen out with my mother or father or what. It seemed like an odd move to make. What might have influenced her was that her niece, and our cousin Peggy, was working in Dún Laoghaire as housekeeper to a prominent politician. The woollen mill in Convoy closed in the early fifties so Peggy had to find work somewhere else. She had a friend who worked in Dún Laoghaire and through her she secured her employment. Our mother received letters every so often from Aunt K and the following summer Peter got a postcard from her congratulating him on his success in the Leaving Certificate. After about eighteen months Aunt K returned to Templenew. Shortly after she had returned to Ireland she had voted in a national election which, unknown to her, affected her status as an American citizen. Consequently her social security payments were threatened and she spent months worrying if she would lose them entirely. Our father spoke to the local TD who worked on her behalf to resolve the matter and to her great relief her social security payments were protected but she never voted after that. We never really got to know anything significant about her time in the USA. She probably told our mother all about it but, naturally enough we were never included in such exchanges.

Throughout the spring and early summer of '57 my interest in football and hurling grew. I used to cycle into Ballyshannon to the Fr. Tierney Park for practice and to play games. A schoolmate

161

of mine, Paddy Mahon used to cycle home with me from school. He lived in Corlea just outside Beleek. He was a year behind me in school but we shared an interest in Gaelic games. He was also musical and played a button key accordion. Through him I was introduced to céili music. He used to go to the '98 Hall in Ballyshannon to play for Irish dancers. A local man Tom Magill, who hailed from the west of Ireland, was a great Irish dancer. He promoted traditional dancing and put on céilis from time to time. Going into these gatherings in the '98 Hall introduced me to Ballyshannon girls that I would not have otherwise met. Sometimes the céilis were held in the Rock Hall. On one occasion I was spun around by one girl so much in the Haymaker's Jig that I lost my balance and couldn't stand up right away as my head was spinning. Angela had her first dance in the Rock Hall when she was taken there by our father as a teenager.

There were girls from Beleek who used to cycle all the way to Ballyshannon to attend either the Convent or the Vocational School. One of them in particular attracted my attention and sometimes we cycled home together. On one occasion we stopped at Camlin Castle and climbed the turret together. Looking back on it we were both trying to initiate some sort of contact. I was too shy, so we got back on our bikes and cycled on. During that summer I found other girls showing an interest in me. When playing football the boys would leave their shirts at the side of the pitch when given a team jersey. At the end of the match some girls would have our shirts and we had to ask them to return them. Again my shyness prevented me from following up on these female ploys.

During the mid-'50s I was tuning in more to the popular music that was being played on the wireless because I was now at an age when the themes of love and romance were starting to appeal to me. I had already become familiar with hits like 'Stranger in Paradise', 'Love is a Many Splendoured Thing' and 'Let Me Go Lover' by our own Ruby Murray. Even our mother bought some of the current hits in Quigley's music shop. She used to sing and play the Rosemary Clooney hit, 'Where will the dimple be' even though some of the clergy thought that the words of that song were inappropriate. Because the wireless was the only source of popular music we heard a lot on the sponsored programmes on Radio Éireann and on the BBC Light Programme. Apart from those traditional stations there then emerged a new station which broadcast in English from Luxembourg. This became very popular because it played more of the popular music of the day.

From America came Rock and Roll. Bill Haley and the Comets introduced the world to this loud upbeat rhythmic kind of music that got people dancing. 'Rock around the clock' became an overnight hit. Alongside this new music were the romantic ballads sung by singers like Doris Day ('Que Será, será'), Frank Sinatra ('Love and Marriage'), Malcolm Vaughan ('St. Therese of the Roses') Our father, who didn't show much interest in popular music started listening to Tennessee Ernie Ford ('The Ballad of Davy Crockett') ('Sixteen Tons') (Ghost Riders in the Sky). He also liked Mitch Miller's 'The Yellow Rose of

Texas'. Our mother, being a pianist loved the piano style of Winifred Atwell in 'The poor people of Paris'. Then along came Elvis Presley with his 'Blue Suede Shoes' and 'Jailhouse Rock'. His long hair and raunchy style of singing didn't go down well with the older generation especially when phrases like 'Elvis the pelvis' were used about him in the local press. Our mother and Aunt K were not impressed. But then he signed up for national service and was posted to Germany. As a G.I. he got a crew-cut and put on a uniform and this changed his image with the older generation. As a G.I. he recorded a quaint German folk song called 'Wooden Heart' which became a hit and suddenly our mother and Aunt K thought he was wonderful! Our mother even started playing Wooden Heart on the piano.

Elvis grew in popularity especially among the young people. His hair style was copied and he made a few movies. The first one was 'Jailhouse Rock' which was a big success. I remember going to see it in the Erne Cinema. His energetic style and rock and roll beat was such a contrast to the old traditional ballads that the young people just loved it. Then Elvis started recording some ballads like 'Love Me Tender', 'I can't help falling in love', 'And I love you so' which endeared him to the older generation. Brendan was a big fan. Not only that but with Elvis' hair style and similar good looks he resembled him. As a handsome young Elvis lookalike it is not surprising that some Ballyshannon girls called him Elvis.

An annual event in Ballyshannon was the Drama Festival. During the month of March drama groups from all over the northern part of the country would arrive to compete and hopefully qualify for the All Ireland Final which was held in Athlone every year. Our mother looked forward to the drama fortnight and when our father arrived home from England on a Thursday or Friday they decided on which play to view at the weekend. On arriving home they would tell us about 'The Righteous Are Bold', 'Twenty Years A-Growing' or 'All my Sons' and discuss the performances of various actors. Our father, who had written two short plays and had acted in one, was obviously interested in stage productions. Our mother, who had studied Shakespeare, and used to quote Portia's monologue from 'The Merchant of Venice' about the quality of mercy, enjoyed the craft of the playwright and the interpretation of the players. Our parents made a point of being present at the final night to hear the judgement of the adjudicator. Back home they would tell us about the winner and best actors, giving their own verdict. As we got older we got to see the odd play with them but at this stage of my life I was more interested in 'the movies'.

The Erne Cinema had upgraded its projector and could now show films in cinemascope. This improved the viewing of Westerns and big period pieces. 'Gone with the Wind' which had been released in the early 40's was re-released in the mid-fifties and news spread that it was going to be shown in Ballyshannon. This was problematic for some of the older generation because of the film's depiction of infidelity. Our mother was certainly not impressed with the content and so we were banned from going to see it. It may have been that Aunt K had seen the first version in the United States and had told our mother about it. The Irish Film Censor had banned it when it was first released so it was not surprising that even in the mid-fifties it had its critics. Brendan was friendly with the projectionist in the Erne Cinema and he used to view some of the films from the projectionists' room. He brought home odd scraps of film that had been damaged or removed and we tried to project them on to a wall with a flash-lamp.

In late summer of '57 I started going out to Creevy Pier to swim. It was a favourite bathing area for the boys and girls of Ballyshannon. There were separate changing rooms situated several yards apart built of concrete blocks with a flat roof and windows just under the roof. It was not beyond some boys to sneak on to the flat roof of the girls changing room to see if they could peep in the windows at the girl's undressing, unknown to the girls of course.

Creevy was an ideal place for bathing because the pier acted as a breaker against the big waves that broke against that piece of shoreline. There was also a gradual incline from the sheltered shore out towards the end of the pier. Experienced swimmers were able to dive off the end of the pier and swim in the open sea. I was not experienced enough for that so I stayed in the 'pool' created by the pier.

One August evening I had cycled out to Creevy with a group of boys from Ballyshannon for a swim. After our session of swimming John Moran produced a fishing rod and invited me to accompany him out on a rocky headland to fish for mackerel. The only experience I had of fishing was when another school friend, Michael Travers came out to Templenew to fish in the ESB reservoir for pike. He had used a frog as bait and landed a huge pike that weighed 20 pounds. Michael was an expert fisherman. He lived down the Mall and used to fish for trout and salmon alongside Br. Francis on the pier opposite Inis Saimer. John Moran also lived down the Mall and probably learned to fish for trout and salmon in the Erne also but on this occasion he was interested in mackerel because they came in close to the shore in large shoals and were easy to catch. So easy, in fact that he handed me the fishing rod and I managed to catch three or four.

Back in Templenew as night began to fall my mother was going frantic thinking that something bad had happened to me. John and I had become so wrapped up in successful fishing that we did not notice the time passing. Finally we left Creevy and cycled homewards. I left John in the Mall and set off for Templenew. By then I realised that it was getting dark and became concerned about being stopped by the Guards for not having a light on my bike. With the upsurge of IRA activity the previous year during the Border Campaign there was a big Garda presence in Ballyshannon. They had a patrol car which used to travel out as far as Beleek. I got off my bike at the bridge and walked it down the East Port because there was nearly always a Garda presence at the junction of East Port and West Port. Luckily there was no-one there so I hopped on to my bike and cycled on but as I passed the turn for Killeen I could see the Garda patrol car approaching. I just prayed that they would ignore me. Thankfully they did. I sped on homewards, climbing the hills in my haste and as I turned into our avenue my mother and Angela were pacing up and down. I could see the relief on my mother's face when she saw me. She then began to chastise me for putting her through such travail. I tried to counter by producing four mackerel but she was unimpressed. I had learnt my lesson.

In the early autumn of '57 there was a big storm which brought down several trees on the farm. The big beech tree in the front field was one of them. Our father took advantage of the situation by getting out the cross-cuts and other smaller saws from the basement to cut the fallen trees into manageable blocks. This was hard work but Peter and Brendan were strong enough to use the cross-cut on the trunks of the trees while I used smaller saws on branches. Nellie was hitched to the cart and we brought the blocks of wood back to the house where we took turns at splitting them into smaller blocks with a hatchet. We did this at the back door where we also had two other important tools, one a turnip 'snedder' and the other a clothes wringer. The 'snedder' was a contraption comprising a hinged blade on a wooden block. We used to 'sned' turnips for feeding to the cattle and our mother and Aunt K got us to put washed blankets and towels through the wringer- a steel frame with two wooden rollers that were turned by a large wheel at the side.

When I moved into fourth year at De La Salle in the autumn of '57 our programme of study included physics which was taught by a part-time science teacher from the Vocational School. We studied such things as the properties of light and how it is reflected and refracted. We also learned about barometric pressure and how to construct a home-made barometer. This new scientific knowledge interested me. Living out in the country away from street lighting the starry sky on clear nights was a wonder to behold. I began to pick out some of the well known constellations and knew from my science classes that the light from the stars had to travel unimaginable distances. Then on October 4th at 7.28 p.m. the world heard that the Soviet Union had launched an object into space called a 'Sputnik' which was circling the earth emitting a radio signal as it did so. This created a new interest in scientific progress.

The Sputnik was the first artificial Earth satellite. The Soviet Union had launched it into an elliptical low Earth orbit. It was a 58 cm diameter polished metal sphere, with four radio antennas to broadcast radio pulses. It could be seen all around the Earth under clear skies. The newspapers were full of stories about the satellite and the possible implications for western nations in the area of space surveillance and exploration. It marked a definite start to the space race between the Soviet Union and the United States of America.   On the radio we heard about the Sputnik's orbits and the Irish Press gave the times when it could be viewed. I checked out the times and set my alarm clock for 2:30 a.m. to see if I could spot it. Everyone in school was talking about it. In the event there was cloud cover that night so I did not see it. We did not know it at the time but the launch of this satellite marked a new era in technological, military, political and scientific developments. My own view is that it triggered a shift in human thinking that contributed to the emergence of post-modernity. As a sleepy-eyed teenager looking out of my bedroom in Templenew House on an October night in 1957 straining to see the Soviet satellite seemed surreal.

In late 1957/early 1958 I was in the first year of the two-year Leaving Certificate. At lunchtime a group of us used to go down the town. A couple of older boys would go into Mrs Curran's little confectionary shop in Market Street where they could buy single cigarettes. She would open a pack of ten and sell the contents in ones and twos for a few pence each. It wasn't long before I was influenced by my classmates. While over the town we would see some convent girls though we did not have any contact with them. However they must have noticed us because gradually notes began to be passed on to us from particular girls looking to meet us or 'to go with them' as it was known.

There was one girl who lived in Market street who was very attractive. Her name was Marie and she became a tease for the boys. She had the figure of a model and long curly hair and an outgoing personality. I remember one snowy night when I was in town, probably with my friend Paddy at the Irish dancing we came across Marie and her sisters out throwing snowballs at various boys. She was wearing one of those stand-out dresses of the late '50's that accentuated her figure. It was not suitable for snowballing but looked terrific. There was one boy in particular, a tall blond athletic type from Gweedore who was working in Ballyshannon who seemed to be receiving more direct hits from Marie than the rest of us. It was fairly obvious that he was the object of her affections. He was a bit older than us and this gave him another advantage. Marie only had eyes for the handsome stranger.

Marie had a cousin who was not as glamorous. Like her friends she was on the lookout for a boyfriend. She passed a note to one of the Ballyshannon boys to pass on to me expressing an interest in me. I was flattered by her interest but she did not appeal to me, so I ignored her advance. She was not put off by this lack of interest on my part and accosted me on the street outside Paddy Doherty's and pressed her case. I told her that I was thinking of becoming a priest so would not be going out with any girls. This reply did the trick and she backed off. I don't know what she thought some months later when she would have seen me with a girlfriend.

Peter and Brendan were the objects of some girls' attentions too but pretty much unknown to me. There was, however, a girl who lived in College Street who fancied Peter. I think she was Kelly the butcher's daughter, a sister of the boy who had been our minder when we first went to the Brothers' school back in 1950. All I know is that any time I met her on College Street she would do a pretend swoon and ask me about my older brother.

It was around this time that Peter and Brendan joined the local platoon of the FCA. Previously known as the LDF (Local Defence Force) its name changed to the Irish version Forsa Cosanta Aitiuil. The Commanding Officer was Michael Anderson, the headmaster of the

Vocational School. His second in command was Lieutenant John Travers who worked for the Donegal Democrat. When Peter joined he started off as a two-star private but quickly progressed to corporal. The CO wanted him to attend courses at the Curragh Military Camp to get a commission but before he could do that he became a cadet in the Irish Naval Service. Brendan started off as a two-star private and progressed to the rank of corporal before he left the force. Many of the Ballyshannon boys in the final year of the Leaving Certificate signed up including me. We were all supposed to be eighteen years of age to enlist but many of us were just seventeen or in my case just coming sixteen. Paddy Mahon and I joined up at the same time. We lied about our age and the officer in charge, who was related to Paddy, signed us up even though he must have known that many of us were under eighteen. Being a member of the platoon had many attractions for young men. We got a uniform and a rifle to take home (but no live ammunition), we attended drills in the '98 Hall, went on manoeuvres at night, had shooting practice with .22mm. and.303mm ammunition. A highlight was a two weeks residential training course in one of the Regular Army's Camps, for which we got paid. Finner Camp, which I knew so well, was the Camp that I attended. Peter and Brendan chose Athlone for some if not all their residential courses.

Brendan was very particular about how he presented himself in uniform. His boots had to be polished to perfection as had his brass buttons. He even made a gadget to help him to shine the buttons without getting brasso on the uniform. It

172

was a flat brass plate with a slit that allowed him to slide it under the button, thus isolating it from the cloth. He even engraved the insignia of the FCA on to the end of it. Sometimes he got Monica to help him to shine his buttons. Peter and I made use of his invention too. Soldiers with basic ranks wore berets. Brendan used to place a piece of stiff cardboard inside his beret to shape it so that it had an angle at one side. His other trick was to make a 'bracelet' of lead weights on a piece of string and fasten it loosely around his calf. Then when he put on the trousers of his uniform the 'bracelet' of weights could be placed in the fold made by the leggings and this created a well defined fold which looked very smart.

One night when everyone was asleep a car drove down the avenue and suddenly there was loud knocking on the front door. Our father was away at markets and Peter had gone to the Curragh so our mother was too scared to open the door. The recent upsurge in IRA activity along the border had left people worried about more of the same so opening a door in the middle of the night in those circumstances would have been unwise. Brendan and I peered out through the dining room windows but we could not see anything. I promptly got my FCA issued .303mm rifle ready to point it at any intruder. I didn't have any live ammunition but I was banking on an intruder not knowing that. As a sixteen-year-old raw recruit I don't know how things would have developed had someone broken into the house. After about five minutes or so we heard the footsteps of someone walking away from the house and up the avenue. With that we returned to bed. When our father returned some days later he told us that a cattle dealer-friend of his had got into financial difficulties and wanted to leave his car somewhere out of reach of creditors and had picked Templenew House as a safe hideaway. He thought our father was at home when he made his dramatic call in the middle of the night.

Throughout the summer of '58 I played football and hurling with the minor team. I used to join my Ballyshannon team mates in the Fr. Tierney Park on the Rock for practice and to watch the senior team practising. Two new senior players had joined our club. They were the Tierney brothers, John and Felix who were county players for Armagh. One was a solicitor and the other was a civil engineer. They had moved temporarily to Donegal to work. I think they must have been past their best by that time because they did not particularly impress me with their play. There were a number of Gardai from different parts of the country on the senior team. One of them was Jim Long who came from Cookstown. He left the Garda some years later and went as a mature student to St. Joseph's College of Education Belfast in 1963. I got to know him there and was his best man at his wedding in 1970.

The Erne Cinema was still very popular with all ages in Ballyshannon and I attended regularly. Not only was it popular with cinema goers but it also provided an opportunity for courting couples to meet. Boys and girls who wanted to meet knew that the back seats were the best places because they could not be observed by anyone behind them. So, like other boys of my age I found myself in the back row sitting next to Ann

Doherty. I don't know whether she sat beside me or I sat next to her but gradually boys would try their luck at kissing the girl next to them on the cheek. If this kiss was reciprocated you now had a girlfriend. And that's how Ann Doherty became my girlfriend. After that initiation it was taken for granted that you would start 'going out' together. That meant arranging to meet and then going somewhere to talk and exchange kisses.

Back in the '50s the Catholic Church had strict attitudes to sexual matters. It didn't approve of close dancing and frowned on rock and roll music. Pregnancy before marriage was considered a disgrace for any girl who found herself in that situation. At the Parish Missions the men and boys were warned during the 'men's week' of the dangers of what was referred to as 'company keeping'. Phrases such as 'intimate touching' and 'heavy petting' were mentioned in tones that reinforced the missioners warnings about such grave occasions of sin. We were warned to be respectful towards girls and not to let our passions get the upper hand. I knew this and so I observed the guidelines laid down. My girlfriend Ann also knew what was expected on a date and so our company keeping was safe and innocent by today's standards. I used to meet her outside Paddy Doherty's and go for a walk down the Mall or up round the Rock and down to the East Port. Just beyond Quigley's Music shop was Flood's Garage so we used to go in behind it for our romantic rendezvous. Across the river were the grounds of the Convent and the Shiel Hospital. We never saw anyone over there so our little love nest was safe.

My mother and father knew nothing about my dalliance with a Ballyshannon girl and I had to be careful to keep it a secret. On one occasion I had gone to play a football match with the minor team but stayed on afterwards to go to a céili. I made up some story to my mother about being delayed at the football. The next day she was in town and Mrs Frank O'Neill mentioned to her that she had seen me at the ceili so I had some explaining to do when my mother got home. It wasn't that my mother disapproved of me being at the ceili but she wanted to let me know that I had been caught out in my deception.

Ann decided that we should meet somewhere different in mid-week. This was a problem for me because there was no football practice on mid-week so I had to come up with a solution. I told her I would meet her half-way between Ballyshannon and Templenew. She was to cycle out and I was to cycle to meet her. However, I had to have a reason for being away from the house. My father used to get us to check the cattle from time to time in case one of them broke out and wandered off. He was away at markets at this time so I told my mother that I thought one of the cattle was missing and needed to go in search of it on my bicycle. That allowed me to cycle towards town and meet Ann. During this time she gave me her photograph which I showed to my classmates and this earned me romantic credibility in their eyes.

After a few months Ann told me that she had met another boy, a footballer from Donegal Town and had to decide between us. I met her on Main Street and she told me that the boy in whom she was interested was nearby and she now wanted to go with him. I got a look at him. He looked quite handsome and was probably a better footballer than me. I was a bit put out by this news but our little relationship had run its course so I wished her luck and left her to the new love in her life. I often wonder what happened to her and how long her new boyfriend stayed on the scene. Ann was a good girl and I shall always remember her as my first love. Our innocent dalliance helped me to become a responsible teenager.

Around this time the local principal of Rockfield School, Mr Frank O'Neill, known locally as Big Frank was leaving the school. Local parents wanted to have a dance and presentation to see him off. They approached our parents to see if Templenew House could be used for this purpose. They were aware that we had a suitable room in the basement which would have been safe for dancing. Previous to this my mother had noticed that part of the ceiling had cracked and looked a bit unsightly. I prodded the cracked part and a portion of if fell down. We could see that the ceiling had been well constructed with meshed lattice work holding the plaster. Now with a section of it missing my mother suggested that we should strip the entire ceiling and I got the job of doing it. This was a bigger operation than either of us had anticipated so it took me a long time to strip the ceiling and dump the plaster. Having done that the joists were revealed so the end result was not as attractive as the previous ceiling even with the large crack. My mother and I had taken this project on without consulting my father who was away at the time. When he came back and saw what we had done he was not impressed. Luckily for me my mother took the major share of the blame. We painted the walls and this improved the overall look of the 'ballroom'.

The night of the dance and presentation was a big success. The locals arrived with homemade sandwiches, cakes and buns and an accordion player supplied the music. The local Fianna Fáil T.D. and the Parish Priest were there and they were entertained upstairs. A young female teacher from Big Frank's school was there. She was called Bridget Burke and lived in Bishop's Street Ballyshannon. She was known to her family and friends as Birdie. She took a shine to Peter and reportedly danced with him. We heard that they were going out together but we did not have any proof. Our mother used to tease him if he was outside when she was feeding the hens. She would say, "Here birdie, birdie" as she threw scraps to the hens.

Peter had finished his Leaving Certificate in May 1957. He had hoped to join the Air Corps and applied for a cadetship. As there were many more applicants than vacancies he was unsuccessful, so Brother Daniel asked him to fill in for one of the Brothers in the Primary School while he waited for another opportunity to apply. The following year he applied for the Army but, as he had physics in his Leaving Certificate, and that was a requirement for a Naval Cadetship, he was offered a cadetship in the Naval Service. Although he did not get his first choice he was glad to accept the alternative. Our parents were pleased that a career had opened up for him and the rest of us were proud that he had been successful in his application. Despite the celebrations, our parents must have been aware that Peter's departure was just the beginning of the loosening of the bonds that bind family members to home and hearth. Our father in particular would have been aware that with the eldest going and none of his younger siblings showing any interest in farming the long term future of Templenew was in doubt. As events played out that is what happened.

In the autumn of 1958 I began my final year in De La Salle. I was just back at school about five weeks when on October 9th Pope Pius X11 died. I felt some connection with him given that we shared the name, Eugene. He was Eugenio Pacelli and my mother told me that she had named me after him. I followed the news about his death and funeral on the radio and in the newspapers. There was much speculation about who his successor might be. A few weeks later the elderly Cardinal Angelo Giuseppe Roncalli, Patriarch of Venice was elected as the new Pope and took the name John XX111. At seventy-six he was regarded by many as a caretaker Pope. Within a few months they were proved wrong when he called into session the Second Vatican Council.

Like most boys of my age I was more concerned about doing my Leaving Certificate and finishing secondary education. At the same time I was starting to enjoy aspects of school. Brother Francis had discovered that the instruments belonging to the defunct Ballyshannon Brass Band were in storage, so he got permission to borrow them. He asked older pupils who were interested to form a new Band. I was interested but couldn't attend the practices that Brother Francis had assured us were needed. It only suited the town boys who could easily attend on a regular basis.

Having a piano at home and a mother who was an accomplished pianist encouraged me to pick out tunes as best I could but without tuition I couldn't learn to read music or advance through the grades. There were plenty of tunes to try, thanks to the songs that were played by the sponsored and request programmes on Radio Éireann. Hits such as 'Volare', 'All I have to do is dream' by the Everly Brothers, 'Who's sorry now?' by Connie Francis were very popular. The following year 'Smoke gets in your eyes' was a huge hit by the Platters.

The sentiments of these songs appealed to my adolescent longings and 'The Four Lifer' had to put up with me singing them as I milked her. She still gave me the odd slap with her tail but I don't think it was a response to my rendition of 'All I have to do is dreams', more a reminder that she had a few scratches on her teats. I still remember one glorious late summer evening singing one of these hits as I milked and then looking out over the half door of the byre to see the most wonderful red sunset over the orchard wall. I stood and stared as the crimson sun slowly slipped below the horizon and its afterglow softened the margin between earth and sky. It was one of those still evenings without as much as a gentle breeze. I stood transfixed by such beauty. And yet I was also conscious of the transience of the event for within an hour darkness had descended. Such raw and elemental aspects of life touched me deeply at the age of fifteen and also explains why the heavily charged emotions of the popular songs of the day such as 'Smoke gets in your eyes' appealed so much to me. The lyrics of the song, the dramatic arrangement and the expressive singing of the lead singer all combined to stir my emotions. While I was drooling over such sentimental songs my father was tuned more to the messages and humour of such songs as Sixteen Tons, sung by Tennessee Ernie Ford. If this song came on the wireless my father would put down his newspaper and say, "Turn that up 'till I hear it" and out would come,

'Some people say a man is made outta mud
A poor man's made outta muscle and blood
Muscle and blood and skin and bones
A mind that's a-weak and a back that's strong.
You load sixteen tons, what you get
Another day older and deeper in debt
Saint Peter don't call me 'cause I can't go
I owe my soul to the company store'.

My father obviously was attracted to the words of this negro spiritual on account of their reflection of the grim reality of life in the southern states of America and he would have appreciated its sardonic humour. The drudgery of work and the struggle to make a living through farming and in the cattle markets of Ireland and England would have chimed with the sentiments of the song. Other songs appealed to him such as, 'Keep right on to the end of the road' by Harry Lauder. No doubt he had heard this song on his trips to Northumberland which bordered Lauder's Scotland. This lilting tune with lyrics that celebrated the stoicism that is needed in life would have related to his experience. Another song that he liked and even tried to sing, despite not being able to sing in tune, was 'Come back Paddy Reilly to Ballyjamesduff'. He used to sing this as a party piece. Both Angela and Monica learned it from it and sang it themselves.

My mother was drawn more to songs with a strong beat and light –hearted humour, songs like 'Where will the dimple be?', 'How much is the doggie in the window?' Moore's Melodies also appealed to her. She played these on the piano and sang them to us as she played. She even bought some of the sheet music of these in Quigley's Music Shop. It would be fair to say that Aunt K was not musical, yet she enjoyed Irish music, instrumental and solo. For someone who spent such a long time as an emigrant, these musical items must have kept alive her musical memories of life in Glencairn and Urney.

For me the popular music and the dance tunes of the day met some of the emotional needs of a fifteen-year-old boy. At that age my ear was not tuned to the wider, deeper and profoundly moving musical explorations of the human condition that I would later encounter. Unknown to me fragments of this grand musical narrative were being introduced to my musical subconscious through my mother's playing of extracts from Beethoven's Moonlight Sonata on the piano and Anton Dvorak's 'Humoresque' on the violin. Both of these composers would have a big impact on my musical education a few years later. In the meantime I sang soppy sentimental songs to the Four Lifer, went to the céili dances in the Rock Hall and a year later took to the floor in the Astoria Ballroom in Bundoran.

It may also have been part of my emotional development as a teenager that the ephemeral nature of life that I saw around me also made an abiding impression on me. It is probably why certain passages in English literature in school touched me in the same way. One of the poems we studied for the Leaving Certificate was 'Elegy Written in a Country Church Yard' by Thomas Gray, the opening lines of which introduce the sombre theme:

> The Curfeu tolls the knell of parting day,
> The lowing herd winds slowly o'er the lea'
> The plough man, homeward plods his
> weary way
> And leaves the world to darkness and to
> me.

And later on we get the oft-quoted line, 'The Paths of Glory lead but to the grave'.

Among the books our father had bought was one that had within it a poem by Francis Thompson called 'The Hound of Heaven'. It begins,

'I Fled Him, down the nights and down the days;
I fled Him, down the arches of the years;
I fled Him down the labyrinthine ways
Of my own mind; and in the mist of tears
I hid from Him, and under running laughter.
Up vistaed hopes I sped;
And shot, precipitated,
Adown Titanic glooms of chasméd fears,
From those strong Feet that followed, followed
After'.

These poems, with their mixture of melancholy, regret and transience seemed to chime with my adolescent stage of development. Even though the words of 'The Hound of Heaven' suggest the musings of a mature and reflective adult they still spoke to me about an awareness of God. Other poems of a quasi-religious nature such as 'I see his blood upon a rose' by Joseph Mary Plunkett also contributed to that growing religious sensibility, as did Paul Robeson's rendition of 'I think that I shall never see, a poem as lovely as a tree.'

As the spring of 1959 gave way to early summer a decisive moment of my life arrived. A missionary priest called Fr. Liam McCartney arrived in school promoting St. Kevin's Missionary Society, which was based in Rathdangan, Co. Wicklow. He was a big man with a strong Belfast accent who spoke plainly and passionately about the ideals and attractions of missionary priesthood. He told us about his experiences working on the mission fields of Africa and gave us leaflets with pictures of the seminary. The leaflet had pictures of young seminarians at study, at rest and at prayer. Fr. McCartney spoke about the plight of the young African boys and girls of my age who didn't have schools to attend and who needed the help of missionaries to educate them and convert them to the Christian faith. I was struck my Fr. McCartney's sincerity and obvious commitment to the missionary life. His call to us to consider becoming missionary priests had an immediate impact on me. I knew that this was a challenge that promised to fulfil one of my deepest teenage desires – to have a positive impact on the world. What better way than to give my life to a cause that helped the disadvantaged and introduced them to the Christian faith? To do so under a rule that required poverty chastity and obedience seemed like a noble response. I cycled home from school that afternoon with the missionary's leaflet in my schoolbag knowing that I would have to give this matter serious consideration.

In the meantime I had to pass the Leaving Certificate, get the usual farm work done, play my football matches and do my military service. That was a busy schedule. Military service sounds a bit grand but the two weeks training that we had to do as members of the FCA was just that. Members of our platoon had the option of signing up for a course in Athlone, Mullingar or Finner. The obvious choice for me was Finner. I knew it so well as a boy that I wanted to see what it was like from a 'soldier's' point of view, a part-time one admittedly. So there I was, a sixteen-year old part time soldier who had just recently started to shave, reporting for duty at Finner Army Camp in early July and being assigned to a billet with nineteen other raw recruits.

After getting our bedclothes and a briefing from a sergeant we had to have a medical inspection. True to army procedures this was a no-frills inspection. The army doctor and accompanying officer entered the billet at one end. We were told to stand at the end of our beds and disrobe. So there we were, twenty naked young men being scanned by the army doctor as he went by. I don't know if he was checking to see if any of us had venereal disease or just wanted to make sure we were all male but the inspection was business- like and brief. The doctor stopped at one recruit who had blotches on his chest and questioned him about the rash and then moved on and out the other side of the billet.

The soldiers in my billet were from different parts of Donegal with two or three from Ballyshannon. The beds were firm but comfortable enough and when we eventually settled down for our first night at training camp I quickly drifted off to sleep to the familiar sound of Atlantic waves rolling in on Tullan strand.

The sound of reveille that I could ignore when living across the road a few years earlier wakened us up at 6:30 a.m. and almost immediately the sergeant in charge entered our billet and in a loud voice told us to get up, get washed and dressed and report for breakfast. After a quick shave in tepid water we put on our uniforms and reported for breakfast where lines of soldiers were queuing with plates for a stout breakfast of bacon, sausage egg and black pudding and toast. Returning to our billets we had to make our beds in a uniform way dictated by the sergeant and then report for early morning inspection by the Commandant who did not think twice about singling out a sloppy soldier and giving him a dressing down for his poor turn-out. We knew from films we had seen in the Erne Cinema that an army's discipline was essential to its functioning so we complied.

A couple of hours of drills followed on the camp square where non-commissioned officers put us through our paces marching in formation and handling our .303 Lee Enfield rifles in ceremonial formats, all through commands in Irish. The synchronised movements and sounds generated created a bond within each platoon and demonstrated the value and satisfaction of coordinated teamwork. As we marched 'Go Mear Máirseáil' or 'Go Mall Máirseáil' I could see my former home through the gaps on the billets around the camp square and remembered watching such parades from that perspective. It seemed that I had suddenly grown up even though I was still only sixteen.

What I really enjoyed was going down to the range and firing off rounds at the moving targets that I knew so well from the other side of the range during my boyhood days. The 'kick' given by a .303 rifle to the shoulder was bigger than I expected so it took some time getting used to it. We were warned that a firm grip was essential if we didn't want to end up with a broken jaw. As we discharged live rounds at the targets and heard the wide ones whistling past into the sand dunes behind I realised just how dangerous it had been for my brothers and me in our carefree days of playing among the same dangerous terrain.

We did other training on how to strip, clean and assemble a gun on a tripod and watched more senior soldiers demonstrate how to launch bazookas. The training that we got at Finner was varied, interesting and enjoyable. In the evenings we could go down to the football pitch to kick about or play an informal match. I had played on that pitch so many times with the regular soldiers that returning to it as an FCA soldier revived those earlier memories.

Some of my colleagues opted to visit Bundoran in the evenings and I joined them there at the one weekend that we spent away from home. With money in my pocket from my first week's course I went to the Astoria Ballroom which was the popular place for dance goers. This was my first time to attend a regular commercial ballroom. It was at the beginning of the showband era so all the popular songs and tunes were featured in the band's programme. I was not confident enough to ask a girl out to dance but Patricia McElhinney, a Ballyshannon girl who was older than me came over and asked me out to dance. Her family lived on the West Port near the Bridge and I knew her brothers who were fellow pupils in De La Salle. She must have realised that I needed encouragement to venture out on the dance floor. And that is how I made my debut in ballroom dancing.

At the end of the two weeks we had our passing out parade and then headed for home. I returned to Templenew with something in the region of £12 for my fortnight's training and gave half of it to my mother.

A few weeks later my Leaving Certificate results arrived. Jim Gallagher, our elderly postman used to deliver the post on his bicycle. When he turned into the avenue at Templenew House he used to ring his bell to encourage us to meet him half way down the avenue. I was waiting anxiously to hear the jingle of Jim's bell and when I finally heard it my heart jumped. Racing up the avenue I collected our letters. Among them was one addressed to me. Written across one corner was the word 'Congrats'. Seeing that, my spirits soared. Tearing open the envelope I quickly scanned the contents and was delighted to discover that I had passed all my subjects. My parents were pleased for me but thankfully they did not start discussing my future.

That night, without informing my parents I wrote a letter to Fr. McCartney expressing an interest in becoming a seminarian and posted it the next day.

I waited anxiously for a few days, listening for Jim Gallagher's bell to ring. I needed to get Fr. McCartney's reply before my parents knew about my plans. His reply arrived quite quickly. He thanked me for my interest in his missionary society and noted that my approach was quite late but that if I had not changed my mind I should 'take the bull by the horns' and arrange for a visit to Rathdangan for a medical. With this information to hand I now had to break the news of my interest in studying for the priesthood to my parents. I knew that I would have to tell my mother first.

My mother was more approachable than my father and even though I had never confided in her about my hopes for my future I knew that she would be sympathetic to this particular piece of news. My father on the other hand was not affectionate by nature and never had individual conversations of a personal nature with his children. While he often recounted stories to us about his early life or about his dealings with the farmers of Northumberland he never asked us about our feelings, hopes or plans for the future. If

189

I had ever needed a few pence to buy things in school like a nib for my pen, a copybook or a pencil I used to ask my mother before going to school but she would always say, "Go up and ask your father". This would usually be in the early morning and I would have to go up to my parents' bedroom where my father was still asleep and ask him for a three pence piece or a sixpence. He never refused. He used to say, "Look in my coat pocket and take what you need". Although he never refused I was always reluctant to ask him.

We all knew from his stories about his childhood that his father had been a stern man. Peter McElhinney was born in Rathmullan in County Donegal in 1860 when Ireland was under British rule. He joined the police, The Royal Irish Constabulary, met and married Kate McElwaine from Ramelton, whose father was a staunch Republican. Peter was promoted to sergeant and was posted to Kilashee in County Derry. It was there that our father was born. Our grandfather had applied for further promotion but was overlooked in favour of a Protestant member of the force, unfairly so according to our grandfather. He resigned from the force in protest and moved to Ballydun and got involved in a number of business enterprises and became a Justice of the Peace. Kate died in 1911 following the death of her fourth daughter Susan. Our father was six years old at the time. Peter, left with five children married Martha O'Kane from Ballydun and had a further four children.

Losing his mother at six years of age and adjusting to a step-mother must have been difficult for our father and could partly explain his lack of outward affection towards my siblings and me. One incident in his young life that he had recounted to us was revealing about his relationship with his father. He told us that his father had forbidden his children having pets. Young Hugh, however, arrived home one day with a pup. His father refused to let him have the pup and was about to punish his young son for disobeying his instructions when Hugh's stepmother intervened, reminding her husband that it was the boy's birthday. Peter relented but punished his young son the following day.

Knowing this, and being aware of the emotional distance between my father and me it was obvious that I needed to confide in my mother first about my interest in the priesthood. The way I did this was by showing her the letter I had received from Fr. McCartney. As she read it I watched her face to gauge her reaction. Then she looked at me and I could tell that she was pleased and was very supportive but told me I would have to discuss such an important decision with my father.

My father was in Nellie's field inspecting swards of grass that had been cut for hay-making. I felt awkward and embarrassed explaining to him that I wanted to join a missionary seminary and study for the priesthood. Unlike my mother's reaction, his was very negative. He didn't think it was a good idea at all. He pointed out to me that I was too young to make such a decision. He told me that a priest's life was difficult and that I was not mature enough to realise that. My heart sank at his words. I turned and went back into the house. Going up the stairs I met my mother on the landing and she asked me how I had got on with my father. I blurted out "He doesn't want me to go" and went into the bathroom where I sobbed bitterly. My mother obviously knew I was distressed because she was waiting for me when I came out of the bathroom. "Leave it to me Eugene", she said "I'll talk to your father". Those remarks gave me some comfort but I was still apprehensive about my future.

The next day my mother took me aside and told me that she had spoken to my father and that he had relented in his opposition and that I could write back to Fr. McCartney and make arrangements for my medical. I was thrilled at the news. Aunt K was informed and she was pleased too. I quickly wrote my letter and waited for the reply. Within a week I got details of the arrangements for the medical. I was to travel to Dublin by train and get the Rosslare Bus at Store Street Station and buy a ticket for Rathdangan. At Rathdangan I would be met by one of the priests and brought to the seminary for my medical at the end of August. I was excited by the prospect of seeing Dublin for the first time and of visiting the seminary that I had read about in Fr. McCartney's brochure.

In retrospect the persuasive power of my mother was the decisive factor in enabling me to follow the course I had chosen and I am eternally grateful to her for championing my cause. My father of course was being led by his head rather than his heart and from that perspective he was right. At sixteen I was too young to commit to religious life but at that time hundreds of other young men the length and breadth of Ireland were doing the same so I was not unique in choosing to try out my vocation. My father was also probably realising that none of his sons was prepared to stay on the farm which didn't bode well for the long-term future of farming in Templenew. With Peter already established in the Curragh as a naval cadet and Brendan enrolled in the ESB apprenticeship scheme for electrical engineering and now me going off to a seminary, where I would have to be supported financially for several years, it is easy to see his point of view.

Going to Rathdangan for the medical was an adventure in itself. I had to get the bus to Sligo and the train to Dublin all on my own and make my way to Store Street for another bus connection. I still remember getting my first view of the capital city as the Sligo train made its way slowly through the suburbs into Connolly Street Station. What struck me most was the forest of television aerials, some of them very high, attached to most chimneys. Ireland did not have its own television station at that time so the aerials were picking up signals from the BBC and ITV transmitting from the west coast of Britain. I did not know it at the time but these antennas sprouting from the Dublin skyline would invite into Irish living rooms a more secular way of life than we had been used to. So even before I stepped onto the bus to Rathdangan for my medical, the seeds of a cultural change had already been sown, a change that would in a short few years contribute to a transformation of the seminary scene in Ireland.

When I got to Store Street I checked the timetables and went over to the bus that was going to Rosslare. To make sure I had the right one I asked the bus driver if it stopped at Rathdangan. He assured me it did, so after taking my seat I was joined by a young man who said he was going to Rathdangan also. He had heard me talking to the bus driver and knew we were on the same mission. He introduced himself as Sean Kelly from Lucan. He told me that he had already been through university but thought he had a vocation to the priesthood and had chosen St. Kevin's Missionary Society. Like me he was going for his medical.

Meeting another prospective seminarian was a boost to my confidence. Sean was in his early twenties so I knew I was in good company. He told me he had family ties in Monaghan and had gone to St. McCartan's College which made him a sort of a northerner. We talked about football and shared school stories as we travelled the winding road to Rathdangan. In between snatches of conversation I looked out the window of the bus to see what County Wicklow was like. As we left the city we skirted along the edge of the Dublin mountains and headed southwest on the most important journey of my young life. To my left was the distinctive cone shaped Sugar Loaf mountain which stayed on the horizon for a good part of our forty-five mile journey.

Arriving in the small village of Rathdangan we were met by Fr. McCartney who made us very welcome. Puffing on his pipe he drove us the four miles to our destination chatting about the weather and enquiring about our journey. At this point the roads had narrowed and had little traffic. As we turned a corner we came to the entrance to the Seminary and its grounds. At the entrance was an ornamental gate with a wrought iron arch with St. Kevin's Missionary Society written on it. We drove through the arch and along a tree lined avenue with a canopy of leaves created by overhanging branches. At the end of the avenue we came upon a lake and up behind it were the College buildings. My first impression was that this was a magnificent setting for a seminary. Sean and I were dropped off at the central building and taken in to meet another priest. We were given some tea and biscuits and told that the local GP would soon arrive to conduct the medical.

Dr. Maguire duly arrived and did a basic medical examination. He sounded my lungs, took my blood pressure, listened to my heart, put his hand on my lower stomach and asked me to cough. And that was it. He declared me fit and healthy and left. Sean had told me on the bus that he had had some health problems as a child so his medical took longer but both of us were passed as fit for seminary life. Following this we were taken on a walking tour of the grounds. I was excited to be there. The buildings that had featured on Fr. McCartney's brochure were right in front of me and the expansive grounds with a lake and Wicklow mountains in the background made a positive impression on me. My visit reassured me that this place of great beauty, peace and tranquillity would suit me very well and vindicated my decision to apply for admittance to the seminary. Sean and I were provided with a meal and then returned to Rathdangan village where we got the return bus to Dublin. I got the evening train and arrived back in Ballyshannon quite late but I was glad that I had crossed my first hurdle successfully.

A few days later I received a letter from the seminary giving details of what I would need, a black suit, several surplices, shirts, socks, underwear, handkerchiefs and the like. I was told to ensure that all articles of clothing had my name sewn on to them. My mother bought all the necessary items and she and aunt K set to writing my name with black ink on a long strip of white tape which they then cut into sections and sewed to the insides of my articles of clothing. The letter also provided details about when I was to start and what bus I was to get from Store Street at the beginning of the third week of September. I now had a few weeks to wait.

Meanwhile my sisters were continuing their education at the convent in Ballyshannon and Brendan was attending Bolton Street Technical College in Dublin on a part-time course in electrical engineering. This academic side of the course combined with hands-on experience in the ESB's generating stations at Kathleen's Falls in Ballyshannon and Cliff near Beleek. He was later posted for a time to the turf burning generating station in Gweedore. With a great interest in body building and fitness generally he bought a new bicycle, a racer, which he used to cycle to and from work. He even cycled to Gweedore on it.

As the date of my departure for Rathdangan approached my mother announced that she would travel as far as Dublin with me. She said that she could not bear seeing me getting on a bus in Ballyshannon on my own. I would have preferred travelling all the way on my own: I had already done that but I knew that my mother would not agree to that. My aunt K started getting weepy at the prospect of me leaving. I could have done without all the emotion but at sixteen and a half I did not appreciate the effect of me leaving was having on my mother and my aunt. At that stage of my adolescence I was feeling the need to be independent without realising how that affected members of my family.

The day of my departure arrived. Aunt K travelled with my mother and me by taxi to Ballyshannon. At the bus depot my mother took a photograph of Aunt K, and me, a photograph that I still have. In it aunt K is fighting back the tears which surprised me because I always thought of her as rather stern and a bit distant. Before getting on the bus I went over to Paddy Doherty's to get a newspaper. I had been friendly with Paddy's nephews who worked in the shop from time to time. They must have told him that I was going off to the seminary because as I bought the newspaper he gave me a box of fifty cigarettes. I didn't expect such generosity so I thanked him and returned to the bus depot.

My mother and I got on the Sligo bus and as we crossed the bridge over the Erne I could see the lonely figure of aunt K waving limply after it. Before turning the corner down West Port I got my last look at the big town clock that dominates the centre of Ballyshannon and settled into my seat next a window to see again the places that had been the landscape of my youth from Ballyshannon to Bundoran. My mother was talking to me but I wasn't paying much attention as I watched with renewed interest the landmarks of Inis Saimer, Corn Hill, the army camp and our old home at Finner looking much the same as we had left it. By the time we reached Bundoran I was ready to see less familiar landscapes as our bus headed for Sligo. The blue jutting out shape of Ben Bulben was the last familiar image as we approached Sligo town.

Our train from Sligo got into Connolly Station a few hours before my bus for Rathdangan was due to leave. I put my suitcase in the left luggage section of the railway station while my mother and I travelled into the city centre. We had lunch in the basement restaurant of Cleary's Department store and then made our way to Grafton Street and turned into Clarendon Street to the Carmelite Monastery where Fr. Joseph McElhinney, my father's cousin, was the monastery's Prior. My mother asked to see him and after waiting a few minutes we were ushered in to the monastery parlour where Fr. Joseph was waiting for us. My mother introduced me to him and told him where I was going. I think she wanted to get his opinion about my decision to enter the seminary. He asked me about the motives behind my decision and seemed satisfied with my answers. After giving me his blessing we left and made our way back to Connolly Station.

Having walked the short distance to Store Street my mother said goodbye to me there as she had to go back to Connolly to get her return train to Sligo. I was glad to say goodbye to her before my fellow students arrived for the bus. At that age I still felt awkward being in my mother's company in the presence of other boys of my age. And yet my heart ached as I saw her leave but I knew that such is the price of parting. It must have been difficult for her going back on the train on her own but deep down she was probably happy for me. She had championed my cause despite my father's opposition and must have taken some pride in my choice. Before I could dwell much more on her departure I heard my name being called and turning round I could see Sean Kelly approaching. Having travelled with Sean for our medical I felt relieved to have someone I knew to sit beside me on the journey to Rathdangan.

Gradually other young men in suits began to arrive and by five thirty we were all aboard the bus. As we drove out of the city I looked for the peak of Sugar Loaf mountain on our left, the landmark that had impressed me on my earlier journey and I felt a gentle thrill at being already part of a group of young men embarking on a phase of life that would test our ideals and change us all for life.

Chapter 3   Rathdangan

As our bus travelled south from Dublin on that beautiful late September evening in 1959 I was full of anticipation. Even though I had already been to the seminary for my medical a few weeks earlier with one companion, this time I was in the company of young men from all over Ireland. Having Sean Kelly beside me put me at my ease as I listened to the babble of voices with a variety of accents. I could hear a few northern ones and was relieved as I knew that I would have plenty in common with them. I already knew what the entrance to St. Kevin's was like and felt a little thrill as the bus entered under the ornamental arch and swept up past the lake to the main buildings of the college.

We were known as Probationers or 'Probos' for short, and had a section of the college all to ourselves. Our accommodation consisted of four Nissen huts. Each hut had room for up to twelve beds with a basic washroom/toilets facility at the far end. A pot bellied wood-burning stove provided heat. The curved corrugated tin shell had some insulation which kept the winter cold to a minimum. Two large Nissen huts arranged back to back served as an oratory, lecture/study hall and recreation hall. Further along was a basketball/tennis court enclosed by a high meshed wire surround. Our dining hall was part of the main college. Behind the main buildings a new

200

college for theology students was being built which was due to be opened two years later. The senior students who were studying Theology used the old main buildings.

The prospect of using Nissen huts did not bother me having experienced the billeting provided at Finner during my FCA training. There was also something Spartan about these arrangements which appealed to my sense of sacrifice implied in leaving home comforts for a life of study and prayer. The basic facilities seemed appropriate for a missionary society and also appealed to my spirit of solidarity with the poor and disadvantaged.

Having disembarked from our bus we were assigned alphabetically to our sleeping quarters so that we could open our luggage and settle in to our accommodation. Supper followed and then we had a meeting with the priests who were going to be in charge of us for the year. There were forty-four Probationers at that first getting-to-know you session. Fr.McDonagh introduced himself to us as our Dean. He welcomed us warmly and outlined what our programme would be for our first week. He was in his late twenties, just recently ordained and came from Clones. He had qualified in music at University College Cork and we later discovered that he was keen to interest us in it. The other priest was Fr. Dunne, a quiet withdrawn man who was to be our Spiritual director. He sat with his eyes cast down for most of the session.

Our first evening ended with night prayer and then we retired to our respective huts. Sleeping in a dormitory was new to me, apart from my two weeks at Finner Camp, but I was happy enough having ten other teenagers sharing my hut. In keeping with the basic nature of our surroundings we were informed that our lighting was supplied by a diesel generator which delivered a lower voltage than mains electricity which meant that the light produced was less bright than mains lighting. It also meant that we had only battery power through the night when the generator was not in use.

Settling down to sleep on that first night in my dormitory I felt relieved that so far the experience had been a good one. I was happy to be part of a group of young men with the same plans in mind of testing our vocations. Fr. McCartney had emphasised during his talk to us in Ballyshannon that going into the seminary was a leap of faith, that it was a time of discernment to see if our desire to become a priest was a genuine vocation. As darkness fell on that September night the faint sound of the diesel generator throbbed somewhere in the background. I prayed that I had made the right decision in leaving Templenew that I had grown to love. Odd little scenes of my time there unwittingly came to mind in the darkness of the dormitory – Aunt K working on a jigsaw puzzle in the living room and complaining about careless children who had lost a couple of important pieces, the fun and laughter at Halloween as we ducked for apples and searched for the shilling in our portions of apple tart, the musical evenings in the drawing room when our mother sang as she played the piano, the story-telling of my father as we sat around the blazing fire in the living room, listening to his rendition of 'The Shooting of Dan Magrew'. The diesel generator suddenly stopped, interrupting my reverie and silence descended. Before going to sleep I recited my mother's goodnight prayer and realised that from now on I would have to say that prayer myself.

The next morning we were awakened by the sound of a bell at 6:30. We had been told the night before that silence was to be observed until after breakfast and that we should shave and get dressed and attend the chapel at 7:00 a.m. for Morning Prayer and Mass. This was to be the pattern for the year, the only change being a later rising time of 7:00 a.m. on Sundays. In the oratory we were allocated our seats alphabetically. This meant that I was near the back. The little oratory had room for about fifty so it was pretty full with forty-four of us and Fr. Dunne. After Mass we walked in single file up the hill to the refectory still observing silence right through until after breakfast. This was our first experience of the Great Silence. Following breakfast our next task was to make our beds and tidy up our dormitory and report to the study hall.

In the study hall Fr.McDonagh outlined our programme for the rest of the month. Each was to be measured for a soutanne by a tailoring firm from Carlow. They would be made during the following month of October when we would be on a thirty-day retreat. This retreat would introduce us to the spiritual life and would be very demanding. Like an assault course for young army recruits it would test our spiritual stamina and raise the intensity of our prayer. At the end of the retreat we would put away our civilian clothes and don soutanne, stock and roman collar and thus conform to clerical dress for seminarians worldwide.

We still had a few days to go before the beginning of the thirty-day retreat so these were spent getting into the routine of seminary life. We spent time in the lecture hall being briefed on the history of the demesne and various aspects of the Society; we picked football teams for Gaelic and Soccer leagues; we were assigned to work parties for manual labour and we were allowed over to the senior side of the college to meet the theology students, some of whom were in their final year before ordination. We also did a hike across country and up to the top of Carrig Mountain on a Sunday afternoon. This was a good bonding activity and allowed us to meet and converse with most of our classmates. We were also encouraged to write home to let our families know that we had settled in to our new surroundings and that correspondence would be reduced to rest days during the long retreat.

October arrived and our thirty-day retreat started. It was to be broken up into four sections, the first of six days followed by a one day break, then seven days, a break, ten days and a break and the final five days. Strict silence was required during each long section. Fr. Dunne was our spiritual director so he introduced us to the spiritual exercises of St. Ignatius which was the programme we followed. The title of the Exercises revealed its intent-'Spiritual Exercises to conquer oneself and regulate one's life and to avoid coming to a determination through any inordinate affection.' The first week dealt with the theme of Purgation. Sub-themes dealt with the problem of evil, global and personal sin, conversion and discipleship. The second week dealt with Illumination which drew on the life of Jesus as our model and a call to follow him. The third and fourth weeks centred on Union with Christ drawing on the example of His Passion and reflections on the four last things, death, judgement, heaven and hell.

Fr. Dunne was a small thin man in his early sixties with a piercing gaze. He used to glide into the oratory and take his seat at a table at the front. Speaking in a low monotone voice he gave a talk on a specific theme and then asked us to reflect on the import of the message. We heard a lot about inordinate affections and were encouraged to exercise custody of the senses. Custody of the eyes was particularly important because it helped us to avoid distractions and temptations. We didn't quite know what to make of our spiritual director. By his demeanour he appeared to us as an ascetic. This was confirmed by watching him picking at his food in the refectory and walking around with his eyes down. We did not see him socialising much with other priests of the college.

When not delivering a talk Fr. Dunne knelt at the back near the wood-burning stove that heated the oratory. We had to take it in turn to light the fire in the early morning and keep it stoked throughout the day. Woe to anyone who failed in this important task. Failure to light the fire before Morning Prayer or failure to keep it burning steadily throughout the day meant that the incompetent student had to repeat his rota following a blunt accusation by Fr. Dunne, "You let the fire out," delivered with what sounded like derision. When my turn came I was quite confident that not only would I have no trouble lighting the fire but keep it well stoked throughout the day. Hadn't I mastered the art of fire lighting in Templenew when with a few rolls of newspaper, a few scraps of dry turf and some lengths of well seasoned beech blocks I could have a blazing fire in either the dining room or the sitting room in no time at all? However, lighting and keeping Fr. Dunne's fire was a whole different challenge that I had underestimated. Trying to coax the potbellied stove into life with green laurel sticks on cold damp mornings was more difficult that I had anticipated. We were quickly learning on our retreat that pride comes before a fall so I fell quite easily as it turned out. Although I managed to get the fire going initially, one morning the wood was so wet that the fire went out just before Morning Prayer. It wasn't long before I heard the dreaded words, "You let the fire out!" as Fr. Dunne reprimanded me and put me on a second rota.

We quickly learned that one of the tasks our spiritual director set himself was to take us down a peg at every opportunity. There was to be no place for puffed up egos or smugness. True to the military-style approach of the soldier Ignatius, discipline and self abasement were required of the troops. If we thought that we could keep our heads down and avoid Fr. Dunne's piercing gaze we were mistaken because we had to visit him for spiritual direction on a regular basis and answer his questions about our perceived progress and accept with due humility any correction he had for us. These interviews were scheduled for us alphabetically. We made our way to his quarters which was in a building a short distance away from our huts and waited in groups of three or four in strict silence for our turn to present ourselves for spiritual direction.

Fr. Dunne's usual opener was, "How are you getting on"? Sounded innocuous enough but to answer "Okay" or "Grand" was not good enough. Just what did one mean by "Okay" or "Grand?", so one had to mutter something like, "I find the long silence difficult" or "I find my mind wandering all the time during meditation." At least this gave him the chance to upbraid us on our lack of understanding of the need for solitude to promote our spiritual growth, of the need to get control of our undisciplined minds. All one could do was to thank him for this excellent spiritual guidance and promise to try harder in the future.

One of the difficulties I found about observing the silence in the refectory was if anything remotely amusing occurred, like someone knocking over a sugar bowl or spilling some milk I had to physically restrain myself from laughing out loud. It was probably the strain of having to cope with the sustained silence that triggered reactions like this, especially in giddy teenagers. Such behaviour did not escape the hawk-like eye of Fr. Dunne. During one of my visits to his quarters he chastised me with "You were laughing during the silence at supper." Put like that I could not really deny it. He went on to remind me that I needed to act more maturely if I wanted to advance in the spiritual life. Needless to say I agreed wholeheartedly.

After the first five days of silence we had our free day when we could talk to each other. Following breakfast the silence lifted and suddenly there was an outburst of animated conversation. We hadn't realised the effect prolonged silence would have on a group of teenagers and wanted to share our opinions on the retreat so far. We discussed the content of the talks, the embarrassment of a student who had let the fire out, the uncomfortable visits to Fr. Dunne's quarters and the strange content of some of the spiritual reading that was available to us. Most of the books that we read were hagiographies of saints, some of them belonging to the middle ages. They were filled with bizarre accounts of the lives of ascetics who battled with all manner of temptation and evil spirits. Gullible as we were spiritually we were not drawn to emulate the asceticism of these strange saints. Instead we traded accounts and had a good laugh at some of them. Battle hardened as we all were from a secondary education that involved corporal punishment and humiliation we quickly recognized that Fr. Dunne was the bad cop and Fr. McDonagh was the good one. The latter was outgoing, engaging in conversation and even joined us for games of table-tennis at recreation time. He fancied himself as a bit of an expert with sweeping forehands and deft little back spins dropping dead just over the net. I don't think any of us ever beat him.

Our free day was soon over and we were back on silence again. By the second week we had got into the rhythm of the retreat of prayer, talks, meditations, work. The work was mostly outdoor manual activities such as maintenance of the grounds, wood cutting or clearing of overgrown shrubs in a nearby grove of laurel and holly bushes. We had to cut back a certain amount of laurel and store and season lengths of thick branches for cutting into lengths that would fit into the stoves that heated our Nissen Huts. We also had free time in which we walked through the woods or on the quiet country roads outside the grounds.

In mid to late October the leaves of the large deciduous trees of the demesne began to darken into shades of rustic reds, yellows and browns and already some of them were falling. None of the trees 'touched the ground' enclosing a world of make-believe or fantasy. Here the mighty oak, beech and sycamore soared upwards towards the heavens. Access to their high branches demanded risk, daring and danger. In my long retreat there was no room for make-believe.

Walking in the grounds in silent reflection gave me time to notice the beauty of this secluded part of Wicklow. Beyond the big trees of Rathdangan were the magnificent Wicklow Mountains stretching southwest from Carrig to Lugnaquilla and beyond them the Glen of Imaal. The backdrop of such beauty reflected God's creation and helped me to see it in the context of retreat themes.

These solitary walks also forced us to dwell on other themes of our retreat and re-evaluate our lives. What we lacked in experience of the world we made up for in youthful idealism. We shared the desire to make the world a better place and believed that we could do just that. With the

Gospel accounts of the life, death and resurrection of Jesus as the centre piece of the retreat we knew that no greater model was available to us.

We learned that during the course of the retreat we would experience periods of consolation when our spirits would be lifted and periods of desolation when the going would be tough. And so it was. On days of consolation as I walked in pale October sunshine through the woods and laneways of the seminary demesne in quiet contemplation I felt blessed to be among a group of young men who shared my hopes and treated each other with charity and respect. The sense of being part of a group enterprise was very real. On days of desolation the long periods of silence, the multitude of distractions and thoughts of home made it difficult to concentrate on prayer. We soon learned that seminary life, like life in general, had its ups and downs. The difference was that we could see these experiences as part of the warp and weft of the spiritual life. During rest days we were able to read any letters that had arrived for us during the retreat days. This was our only contact with home during October. By mid-October I felt confident about surviving until the end of the month and looked forward to a less demanding routine.

And so we endured the thirty-day retreat. Endurance it was, because for young men having to observe silence, listen to challenging talks, to learn how to meditate and submit to the correction of a spiritual director was difficult. One student found it too much and decided to go home without telling anyone. He left early one morning and made his way to Rathdangan village where he got a bus to Baltinglass. His absence was noted and a priest drove to the bus stop and on to Baltinglass and intercepted him. He brought him back to the seminary. Following discussions the young seminarian was allowed to go home. Even though I, like the others, had found the retreat very challenging I did not consider it beyond me. My father's Stoic spirit of 'Keep right on to the end of the road' came to mind and helped me to finish the course.

We had a free day at the end of the retreat and were given our clerical garb of soutanne, stock, Roman collar and biretta. This was a proud moment for us because we were now dressed like the senior students that we saw daily in the distance as they processed to and from the refectory adjoining ours. Leaving aside our civilian clothes marked a rite of passage of sorts while the donning of clerical garb signified our tentative membership of the society. We were now real seminarians, albeit probationers.

Following our long retreat we were now in seminary mode proper and began to follow a course of study and prayer. The study programme was of a general nature. We learned all about the society, its constitution, rules and regulations. We had classes on liturgy and liturgical music, apologetics and canon law. One of the rules of the constitution stipulated that students were not to have particular friendships. This meant that unlike a civilian college we could not choose a set of friends with whom to associate. Having committed ourselves to following the Lord he was to be our spiritual model and friend. In practice we had to be a friend to everyone. For example we were assigned to manual labour with particular students but this changed every term. We were assigned particular seats in the lecture hall, the oratory and the refectory. When going on walks after meals we walked with the first students we met rather than forming cliques. This brought home to us one of the requirements of community life and reflected a theme of our long retreat of not harbouring inordinate   affections.

Wednesday afternoons were given over to sport. In our class we had exponents of Gaelic football, soccer and hurling, some who had represented their counties at minor county level. Being on the young side I struggled to match the prowess of some of the older players but I enjoyed playing my part on the football field. Competition was fierce and like any group of young men games were very physical. The only difference between seminary games and those in civilian life was the absence of bad language or abuse of the referee. Well mostly. Tempers flared on occasions but that just reminded us that we were flawed human beings.

We used to make our way to and from the football field down past the Oratory and alongside Jimmy the woodcutter's yard. Jimmy was employed as a handy man and woodcutter who brought in loads of wood and cut them up for burning in our various stoves. He had an open shed with his own big stove which seemed to be lit all the time while he went about his business. There was always a sweet smell of wood burning in the air especially on dull windless November days as the smoke from Jimmy's stove hung over his yard and our huts. We were not to converse with any of the people working on the seminary estate so I used to nod to him going past.

The refectory kitchen was staffed with local women and girls. At meal times we were put on a rota to serve food from a hatch between the refectory and the kitchen. There was no communication with kitchen staff. They placed the food before us at the hatch and we served the tables from there. The girls in the kitchen liked to listen to music on the radio while they worked and sometimes they had the volume turned up quite high. Fr. Dunne would tell us to ask the kitchen staff to turn down the music. The kitchen girls liked listening to the current popular music so even though we did not have access to the outside world via the radio or newspapers we couldn't avoid hearing the latest hits. The kitchen hatch marked the boundary between religious and civilian life. This leakage, though unintended, was appreciated by us, reminding us of the worldly life we had left at the seminary gates.

We had our own music making when we gathered on special occasions in the company of the senior students for an informal concert in an improvised 'concert hall'. It looked like a renovated barn so we called it 'Dolphins Barn'. It was a long stone-built building with rough plaster and rough wooden floor with a stage and a 'green room'. There was also a cubicle at the back for housing a film projector. Two or three times a year we had a concert or film show, at Halloween, Christmas and St. Patrick's Day.

Fr. McDonagh had a passion for music and conveyed some of his interest to us. He provided a number of classes on musical appreciation as part

213

of our religious formation and formed a choir from our number. I was in the bass section of the choir and enjoyed the practices. Our first harmonic piece was 'Panis Angelicus' by César Franck, a well known Eucharistic hymn.

In addition to teaching us to sing in harmony Fr. McDonagh introduced us to classical music. He outlined the form and structure of the piano sonata, the overture and the symphony drawing on the works of Beethoven. He brought a good quality record player into the lecture hall and played extracts from Beethoven's works to demonstrate various features of the great composer's compositions. Two works that I remember vividly were the Egmont Overture and the Fifth Symphony. The sheer power and expressive force of these masterpieces swept me away and introduced me to the world of classical music. Snatches of the 'Moonlight Sonata' played by my mother on the piano in Templenew was one thing, but hearing the opening movement of Beethoven's fifth symphony took music appreciation to a higher level. Even though I was still a teenager and liked the popular music of the day this introduction to the classics was a revelation.

By the end of October we were well settled into seminary life. We got used to a programme of prayer, meditation, study, manual labour and recreation and began to bind as a group as we got to know each other. There was a farm belonging to the Society within the extensive grounds and although we did not have anything to do with it we spent one day along with some senior students helping with the harvest. Those seminarians who came from a farming background knew all about driving tractors and using threshing machines so with a large workforce we soon got the barley and wheat cut, threshed and stored. We slept very soundly that night.

There was one seminarian, a 'late vocation' called John O'Sullivan who was a gifted pianist. He had played in a band before joining the seminary so Fr. McDonagh decided to stage a musical with John's help. His choice of musical was Schubert's 'Lilac Time'. Auditions were held for acting and singing parts and rehearsals began. It was not anticipated that the show would be ready before Christmas because of the limited rehearsal time so a date before Lent was seen as a realistic target. The cast duly got to work, meeting during manual labour time. As the rest of us walked to and from our work we could hear strains of music coming from our 'concert hall'.

In Rathdangan we were largely cut off from the outside world, not having access to newspapers or radio. There was still no national television station but even if there had been we would not have had access to the new medium. Fr. Dunne informed us of developments in the world at large by reading out the headlines of the papers and through our letters from home we got the local news. Our families knew that we would not get home for Christmas and we resigned ourselves to celebrating the feast on our own. We sent Christmas cards home and I imagined what Christmas was like in Templenew without me. It would be the first time not going to Midnight Mass with my family and the first time to miss Christmas dinner in my own home. In the event we had our Christmas dinner in the priests' dining room in the main building and we were served by Fr. Dunne and Fr. McDonagh. This gesture by the priests reminded us the duty of a priest is to serve his people.

Following Christmas we returned to our weekly routine and set our sights on Easter. This was a special time in the seminary because it was then when ordinations took place in a parish church a couple of miles away. Our choir was told that it would sing Panis Angelicus at the ordination ceremony so we were looking forward to that. Another highlight of Easter was the visitation of seminarians' parents. My mother had already written to me about this and said that she and Aunt K were going to make the journey to see me. I am sure my mother wanted to see me but also she probably wanted to ask Fr. Dunne how I was coping with seminary life. In the meantime we continued with our prayer, study, work and recreation.

'Lilac Time' was going well in rehearsal by the end of January. With a few weeks to go before the first performance I was asked to join the cast. This came as a surprise to me because I had no experience of acting and was shy by nature. It turned out that I was being cast as a waiter with dialogue of one sentence which was, "Mr Shubert's supper sir". Even though this was a very minor role it drew me into the cast and made me feel very much an integral part of the production. It also meant that I could feel the excitement of being backstage during a show which is usually a highly charged experience.

When we finally put on 'Lilac Time' just before Lent we were confident that it would go well. All the rehearsals with the principals and chorus had prepared us for the opening performance. We had a dress rehearsal with our own class first and then did a performance for the senior students and one for visitors. I was a bit apprehensive about my tongue-twister of a line but in the end it all worked out. The problem with such a production with an all male cast was picking credible actors to play the female roles. The suspension of belief for these parts all added to the fun of the production. And, of course, one of the effects of the collaboration between members of the cast was a strengthening of the bonds between us.

By this time I had got to know all my fellow seminarians, some better than others. There were seven of us from the northern part of the country representing Donegal, Fermanagh, Down, Armagh, Antrim, Monaghan and Cavan. This allowed us to show the northern sense of independence and directness that northerners were supposed to have. Six students were from Dublin and they seemed to be more accomplished and confident. They had their own sense of humour that featured in-jokes about parts of Dublin that largely escaped the country boys. The rest were from the midlands and the south. Their accents were difficult to follow at first, especially those from Cork and Kerry but gradually we tuned in to their way of speaking. Like any mixed group of young men we poked fun at each other about particular pronunciations or turns of phrase.

From time to time we gathered in Dolphins Barn for concerts or 'hooleys' as we called them. One of the senior students would act as MC and anyone with a particular talent at telling a joke, reciting a poem singing or, playing an instrument was asked to perform. One of our probationers had a novelty act which involved playing a saw with a fiddle bow. Proved very entertaining. These gatherings were great fun and helped the probationers to mix with the seniors, some of whom had been at the same schools as us.

As I made my way to Dolphins Barn with fellow probationers to these entertainments I used to have a mixture of emotions. Although we were about to have an entertaining couple of hours, I was conscious that it would be over too soon and we would have to return to solitude and silence. Of course I knew that being a seminarian meant a certain amount of self sacrifice and that we could not allow the frivolous side of life to encroach too much on our more serious life of prayer and recollection. Like the popular music that the kitchen girls seemed to be listening to all the times we were in the refectory these snatches of secular culture had to be abjured. And yet there were occasions as we sat outside the lecture hall on a Sunday afternoon with little to do that someone would break into the strains of 'Living Doll' a Cliff Richard hit of the day. Leaving the world behind completely was not as easy as we thought.

We did not know it then in the spring of 1960 that a cultural revolution was on the way that would transform life in the West and impact severely on seminary life before the end of the decade. Cocooned in our retreat deep in the

Wicklow hills we did not see the straws in the wind signalling the oncoming changes that were about to impact on the Western world. Within a couple of years Pope JohnXX111 would summon the Second Vatican Council that would set in train huge changes within the church that would ripple out and change my life and the lives of my fellow seminarians. In the meantime we followed an outdated model and adhered to its orthodoxy.

During that first year I corresponded with my mother on a regular basis. She was anxious to know how I was getting on and I was anxious to hear how things were going at home. She also sent me pocket money. Aunt K also supported me financially and I was always grateful to her for that. In early March I received a small package in the post. I opened it and found a small box. Inside the box, wrapped in cotton wool was a brand new shiny watch with a red second hand. This was Aunt K's present to me for my seventeenth birthday. I was thrilled because I did not have a watch. I immediately drafted a letter of thanks which I knew she would appreciate. She had always liked being appreciated and showed it by the childish reaction of a shy smile and gentle laugh.

At Easter time the families of the deacons who were to be ordained arrived for the big occasion. We were not involved much as all the celebrations took place on the senior side of the seminary. We did however get to sing our Panis Angelicus at the ordination ceremony. Being at the ordination strengthened us in our commitment to seminary life and we were very happy to receive the first blessings of the new priests.

Other visitors to the seminary that Easter were parents or other family members of probationers who wanted to see the seminary for themselves and check how their sons/relatives were getting on. My mother took the opportunity to visit, with Aunt K taking the place of my father who opted to stay at home minding the farm. They were met off the bus at the nearby town by one of the priests and brought to the parlour in the main house where I was summoned to meet them. They were delighted to see me in my clerical garb of soutane and Roman collar. Even though we had exchanged news through the post we now had an opportunity to discuss things in more detail. Seeing the seminary and its grounds for themselves my mother and Aunt K now had a better understanding of my new life.

My mother updated me on how my brothers and sisters were getting on. She told me that Peter, or Peadar as he was now called since joining the Naval Service, would be moving from the Curragh in Kildare to the Naval Base in Haulbowline to continue his training. Brendan, she said was getting on well with the ESB and Angela and Monica were doing fine at school. Aunt K did not say very much but I could see that she was pleased to see me and hear of my progress. Fr. Dunne came into the parlour to talk to my visitors and I was sent back to my quarters but I was told that I could return later in the day to spend more time with them as they were not leaving until early evening.

In mid-afternoon following recreation or manual work we made a visit to the Blessed Sacrament and said the rosary. Following that I returned to spend some time with them before their departure. On leaving my mother hugged me warmly and Aunt K got misty eyed and I held back a tear as they were driven down the avenue from the main building. Their visit had unsettled me a bit but I returned to my quarters glad in the knowledge that I would be home for the summer holidays in a matter of a couple of months.

The rest of the year followed the usual pattern of prayer, study, work and recreation. We used to get the odd free day when we could cycle from the seminary to some of the towns round about. The senior students had bicycles that they used to lend us, so groups of us used to cycle up to twenty miles out and twenty back. Two popular destinations were Tinahely and Woodenbridge. Getting to them took us along quiet scenic roads through the Wicklow hills and into the Vale of Avoca. At the destination of our choice we spent an hour having lunch in a hotel or guest house before cycling back to the college. These excursions took us from our secluded religious life back into the normality of secular life where people worked and socialised in an open friendly and unhurried way. As we sat at lunch we could hear sponsored programmes on Radio Éireann playing the latest popular music. Sitting in the comfort of a hotel among the locals and tuning in to a rhythm of life that we were denying ourselves in the seminary challenged our commitment to religious life but not enough to affect our resolve. We cycled back to the college in time for plain tea and evening prayer and retired to our Nissen Huts and the Great silence.

The final months of our probationary year flew in and we prepared for the summer break. Fr. Dunne seemed to be satisfied with my progress and I was happy that I had completed my first year with all its challenges. The life of prayer, study, periods of recollection and silence spent in the company of other high minded young men had set me on a course that seemed right for me. And yet I knew that I had many more years to test my vocation and I was aware that not all of us would be returning in September. One had already left after the long retreat and a few more were thinking of not continuing. We swapped our Roman Collars and soutannes for black tie, black suit and black hat and packed for our vacation.

Most of us got the bus to Dublin for our connections countrywide. I had a couple of hours to spend in Dublin before getting the Sligo train so I strolled down O'Connell Street. There was a queue outside the Savoy cinema where 'The Nun's Story' was showing. It seemed like an appropriate film to watch so I bought my ticket and went in. The theme of the story resonated with my own because it was about a Belgian girl who had entered religious life against her father's wishes. Her life as a postulant resembled my own probationary year but as her story unfolded she went on to full profession only to leave the convent when faced with a challenge to her commitment. In 1960 the theme of a nun leaving the convent or 'jumping over the wall', as popular expression had it, was somewhat daring. It was a harbinger of things to come. I left the cinema preoccupied with the ending of the film.

Arriving back in Ballyshannon my mother was waiting to greet me. She gave me a huge hug as always and together we drove to Templenew in the taxi she had ordered. I was delighted to travel down the avenue again and admire my old home. I did a tour of it to recover the ambience of each room. Looking out the landing window I could see how even in late June the apple trees still had their blossoms. They tended to be later in this part of the country anyway, a reminder that I was back in Donegal. Things had changed somewhat during my year away. The 'Four Lifer' had been sold, Nellie had been sent for slaughter following her chronic illness and farm activity had reduced.

With his sons no longer engaged in farming our father had run down his cattle herd. There was now no need to save hay and with a surplus of turf available from neighbours he was able to buy a supply instead of getting some cut from our section of bog. With no 'Four Lifer' my mother bought milk from our neighbours. I was saddened by this situation and felt a bit guilty that I had chosen a life that not only didn't help to support the family but actually drew on its generosity.

In the meantime I tried to follow the guidance given to us by Fr. Dunne regarding how we should continue our life of prayer during holiday time. We were to meditate for half an hour before Mass each day, visit the Blessed Sacrament, recite the rosary and engage in spiritual reading. It was difficult for me to fulfil this programme living in the country. The half hour meditation was okay but getting to daily Mass meant that I had to cycle to St. Joseph's or St. Patrick's in the early morning. On good days I used to go for a walk

223

through the farm meditating as I did so. Sometimes I went down through the wood to the waters' edge at the margin of the ESB reservoir renewing again my love for the place where I had spent some of my formative years.

During that summer my classmate Sean Kelly called and stayed a couple of days. He had been visiting some relatives in Monaghan and decided to visit me on his way back to Dublin. We went to Bundoran at the weekend and attended the cinema and strolled along the beach. Sean invited me to visit his home on my way back to the seminary at the end of the summer.

Being a clerical student in those days meant that I was given preferential treatment and accorded respect by friends and neighbours. Being naturally self conscious I did not relish such attention and yet I was aware that as a seminarian I had a duty to represent religious life in the best light and felt privileged to be able to do so.

My summer holiday passed quietly in Templenew. I followed my prayer routine of meditation, spiritual reading, and visits to the chapels. I used to cycle into Ballyshannon and visit Tom Leahy who had run the céili dancing in the '98 Hall. Mrs. Daly who lived on the Rock had a son studying for the priesthood in a seminary in England. He was older than me but I knew him at school so I used to call at his house for cups of tea.

By the end of the Summer I was looking forward to going back to the seminary. However, in our second year we transferred to the philosophy house in Cork so I had to get the train from Sligo to Dublin, transfer to the Cork train which left Heuston Station and travel to Glenmire

Station in Cork City. My mother ordered a taxi and travelled with me to get the Sligo bus. I hated these good-byes because I liked being at home but knew I had to go back to the seminary to continue my studies. On this occasion I travelled two days early as I was spending some time with Sean Kelly in Lucan before getting the Cork train. Following my visit to Sean's house his father drove us into Heuston station for the Cork train.

There were quite a few other students on the train so I quickly caught up with their summer stories. I looked forward with a little excitement at the prospect of embarking on a course in philosophy in a new college. Peadar was continuing his studies in the Naval College in Haulbowline which was only about twenty miles from the house of philosophy in Whiterock, a suburb of Cork, so I expected to have visits from him from time to time. As the Cork train sped southwards my growing anticipation at starting my second year was tempered by a lingering concern about the future of Templenew now that it was clear that none of my brothers or sisters had any interest in farming.

Chapter 4 Whiterock, Cork 1960-'62

My first arrival into Cork differed from my first arrival into Dublin, due largely to the absence of high television aerials on chimneys. Being so far from the British coastline left Cork without a signal from the BBC or ITV, the only stations broadcasting at that time. It would be another year before Ireland had its own television service. Emerging from the railway station I got my first view of Cork. It didn't have the high skyline of Dublin city centre or the same volume of heavy traffic but seemed very busy nonetheless. My fellow seminarians and I shared taxis to take us the five miles to the Philosophy House which was in its own grounds on the outskirts of Whiterock and on the way I got a good view of the main parts of the city as we crossed the river Lee and drove westwards.

Unlike our residence in Rathdangan, with its basic Nissen huts, we discovered an imposing three-storey country residence set behind a grove of trees about three hundred yards back from the main road. A modern connecting corridor with large windows linked the old 'stately' house to a modern extension of two floors raised on concrete pillars. This extension had a flat roof bounded by a low wall which could be accessed from the second floor. As we drove in towards the main house we passed a croquet court and a grass basketball court. The grounds which covered almost six acres had extensive lawns with lots of various flowering shrubs. A fourteen-acre farm completed the area of the demesne. A gate lodge housed a land steward and his family. To the side of the main ivy-covered building were a number of outhouses and behind the entire block was an orchard. My first impression was very positive. I just knew that I would like my new home.

Of the forty-four probationers who had joined the seminary the previous year we were now down to thirty-six. We were sorry to have lost eight of our original number but we knew that this was not unusual and that some more would leave before ordination. Having successfully completed our probationary year we were now ready to be officially admitted into St. Kevin's Missionary Society. We had to take a pledge of obedience to the superior of the Society and make a will. We were all amused at the idea of making a will at our age but were given a will form and completed it. On the Sunday after our initial retreat we were presented to the bishop at Mass, and took our pledge of obedience. We were now full members of the Society and this made us feel connected to all its members worldwide.

The Philosophy House had three sets of seminarians: first and second year philosophy students and a group on a three-year degree course studying philosophy and arts or science in University College Cork. Of the thirty-six in my year twenty-four of us were assigned to the two-year residential course in Whiterock while twelve were assigned to the degree course in UCC. The university students were given their own rooms while the rest of us used dormitories in the first year and then had our own rooms in our second year. In order to keep the polished floors in good condition we wore slippers indoors, storing our outdoor shoes in the basement.

Having already spent a year in Rathdangan we were familiar with seminary routine so it did not take us long to settle in to life in Whiterock. We had a three-day retreat to tune us back into the rhythm of community religious life. The grounds were much smaller than at Rathdangan but we had several walks for the seventy or so of us. The flat roof was popular especially when it got dark. From that vantage point we could see the long muddy estuary of the River Lee and beyond it the twinkling lights of dwellings stretching eastwards towards Cork City. The estuary was a bird sanctuary so it was common to hear lots of different bird calls during our late evening walks on the roof.

Our lecture theatre was a large room in the big house. Lectures were given by the rector Fr. O'Brien and the dean Fr. O'Sullivan. We followed text books written by an English Jesuit, Frederick Charles Copleston that covered Logic, Epistemology, Psychology, Ontology, and Ethics. We learned that Philosophy dealt with knowledge itself and how we know things, about being and non-being, about good and evil. We also had classes in English and Latin and had debates in front of all the students.

Philosophy really appealed to me and opened up a whole new world of ideas that engaged my curiosity about the world, seen and unseen. I was engaged by the ideas of Plato, Aristotle, Augustine, Descartes, and Thomas Aquinas. The university students were studying these philosophers also and I used to enjoy having discussions with them while out on walks or during recreation time. A few of my fellow students were struggling with some philosophical concepts so I would try to explain my understanding of them. Fr. O'Brien was a great reader and used to tell us about books that he was reading and recommend them to us. He gave us essays to write and encouraged us to think and write clearly.

As in Rathdangan we all had to play our part in the running of the college. I signed up as a barber and gradually learned how to cut my fellow students' hair. There were three of us and each day we had a few customers. Using hand held clippers and scissors we did our best to keep our fellow students looking neat and trim. The students with fine hair were the most difficult to trim because any slight mistake showed up. Crew-cuts were the easiest because it was just a matter of cropping the hair short and flat on top and trimming the back and sides.

For manual work I was assigned to lawn maintenance. This involved keeping the lawnmowers in good order and cutting large areas of grass. Fr. Brosnan was the bursar and general 'manager' of the estate so he supervised the lawn mowing. He seemed pleased with my performance and got me, along with Tony O'Carroll, another student to treat all the trees in the orchard with fungicide. It smelt like Jeyes Fluid and the strong smell lingered on our clothes for ages.

During morning break in good weather the croquet court was popular and even the grass basketball court was used for informal games. Just like Rathdangan we had our teams for Gaelic football, soccer, hurling and rugby. Part of the fourteen-acre farm was set aside for pitches so we spent our Saturday afternoons battling it out in our team sports.

Early in our first term we had a day off to harvest the potato crop in a large field the Society had taken about a mile from the College. Any of us with a farming background knew what to expect but some of the 'townies' found it back breaking and finger-numbing. Fortunately with a large workforce we got the job done in one day.

On free days we borrowed bicycles from the university students and travelled up to twenty miles out and back to such destinations as Crosshaven, Middleton and Cobh. When we cycled to Crosshaven we spent a couple of hours in a Guest House overlooking the sea. We had our dinner there and spent an hour in the lounge relaxing. There was a piano in the lounge that attracted my attention. I used to sit down and play the few tunes that I knew. A couple of other students could knock out a tune too. Then we would cycle all the way back to Whiterock, passing through Carrigaline on the way. My aunt Martha lived in Cobh. She was married to Commander Christy Byrne the C.O. of the Naval Base in Haulbowline. Since Cobh was on our list of cycle trips I made a point of visiting her and my cousins. One of my cousins, Christopher later joined St. Kevin's and has spent a lifetime serving on the missions in Africa.

One of the rules of the seminary that we all disliked was reporting to the Dean every week or two to admit any breaches of the rules. For, instance, we were obliged to observe silence, at meals, during study and throughout the night. We were not permitted to enter other students' rooms or talk to lay members of the college staff. I always found it a bit silly to tell the Dean that I had said hello to the occupant of the Gate Lodge or that I had spoken to a fellow seminarian during study. Such conversations were brief and didn't abuse the spirit of the rule of silence.

Despite our insulation from the outside world we were already tuning into the changes that were taking place beyond the gates of the seminary, one being the emergence of a generation with a new perspective on the world. Post-war American youth began to have plenty of disposable income and, influenced by the music and films of the day formed their own opinions that were largely at odds with that of their parents. The 'Generation Gap' was born. Conscription at age eighteen ended in Britain in 1960 so this added to a new freedom and a new perspective of the group that had become known as 'teenagers'. American films of the mid fifties such as 'The Wild One' and the very popular 'Rebel Without a Cause' starring the teenage idol James Dean all added to the sea change that was transforming the attitudes of the new teenage generation. The music of Rock and Roll combined with the 'Beatnik' scene signalled a change. As Bob Dylan put it in one of his songs, 'The times they are a-changin.'

John O'Sullivan who had played the piano for 'Lilac Time' was studying music at UCC. One day he arrived into our recreation room and put on a record on the record player. We normally listened to classical or light classical music but on this occasion we were treated to a piece of jazz called, 'Rhapsody in Blue' by George Gershwin. John enthused over the piece and as I listened to it, although strange to my ear, I liked what I heard and subsequently took more of an interest in jazz.

Fr. O'Brien was quite progressive. He brought speakers from the world of the Arts in to give us talks and he arranged for us to visit the university to hear visiting professors giving lectures on secular issues. We had our own film shows but the films chosen tended to be old classics or with religious themes. During meal times we read material chosen by the rector. In our probation year in Rathdangan this material had usually been about the lives of the saints. In Whiterock Fr. O'Brien introduced less overtly religious books. One that I still remember was 'The Last Hurrah' by the American writer Edwin O'Connor. This book was about the real world of American politics and charted the changes that were taking place. It also highlighted the growing power of television when used for political campaigning. This exposure to a changing world even from inside the seminary appealed to me. On November 9th there was a knock on the large door of the lecture room. I was sitting near the back so Fr. O'Brien signalled to me to find out who was at the door. I opened it and found Fr. O'Donovan, a missionary priest home from the missions who was staying in the seminary. "Tell Fr. O'Brien that Kennedy has just taken California" he whispered, and quickly departed.

While I still wanted to deepen my spiritual life I appreciated the broadening of my horizons whether through my studies in philosophy or through an engagement with the wider world. Encouraged by Fr. O'Brien to read beyond our philosophy books I stared reading novels from the College Library, 'Of Human Bondage' by Somerset Maugham and 'Crime and Punishment' by Fyodor Dostoevsky. These were long and difficult books but I persevered and grew in my appreciation of literature. There was a photography club in the college so I joined it and learned how to develop negatives in a dark room. By the time of the Christmas holidays I had covered a lot of ground in my religious and cultural developments.

Peadar was progressing well at his naval studies at Haulbowline at this time. His class had been sent on trip to America to the American Naval Academy and while he was there he made contact with some of our American cousins. One in particular was Mrs. Kathleen Enright, formerly McCrudden. Her mother Teresa McCrudden was a sister of my grandmother Rebecca O'Flaherty. Teresa, who was my mother's aunt used to correspond with her niece from time to time so it was important for Peadar to make contact while in the Philadelphia area. Now that he was based just twenty miles away from Whiterock he was able to visit me occasionally. He was always generous to me on his visits with gifts or money.

Whiterock was a busy place with three different year groups sharing the same house. Where the probationary year had been geared to test our spiritual endurance and commitment, Whiterock allowed us to develop a broader approach to our vocations. The proximity of the city of Cork and the influence of the university students put us more in touch with what was going on in the world outside and combined to provide a balanced seminary education. By the end of first term I was very much at home in the house of philosophy and was looking forward to getting home for Christmas.

I travelled home by train from Cork, via Dublin and Sligo and then by bus to Ballyshannon. I was met by Angela at the bus depot. She had a bicycle ready for me so the two of us cycled out to Templenew in the dull twilight of late December. She told me about her progress at school and asked me about my new home in Cork as we cycled up past Kathleen's Falls and all the old landmarks onward towards Templenew. I knew every bump in the road and having been away since September I found it slightly odd to be travelling back along such a familiar road as a clerical student. As we turned in the gate at the top of Semple's hill and cycled down the gravelly avenue I was delighted to see the welcoming glow of light that lit up the front steps. Parking our bikes Angela and I entered the front door to be met with tight hugs from our mother and Monica. Aunt K never displayed her affection like our mother but I knew by her broad smile that she was pleased to see me again. My father and Brendan shook my hand awkwardly and we all retired to the dining room where my mother and Aunt K had prepared tea for all of us. Everyone was interested to hear about my life in Cork so I gave them a brief summary of what it was like. The next day Peadar arrived.

Even though I was back in my old home there was something different about being there in December 1960. The continuity of my earlier years was now broken and I was slowly drifting away from the life that I had led there in the fifties. I was changing and I could see how the trajectory of my life was taking me away from the old securities and seemingly timeless quality of family life of the previous years. Even though I valued my new independence I sensed a distance opening up between all our personal worlds. On the one hand this was no more than the normal feelings of growing independence of late adolescence but on the other there was a sense that my clerical life was setting me apart.

Following our traditional attendance at Midnight Mass on Christmas Eve our mother made a wonderful Christmas dinner which was served up in the big dining room. Alcohol did not feature at meals in our house in those days and we did not miss it. Even coffee was rarely brewed. Aunt K of course, as a returned 'Yank,' liked the odd cup. She used to buy ground coffee beans and make her own coffee. Occasionally our mother would buy sweetened concentrated liquid coffee.

Retiring to the drawing room our mother played some Christmas songs on the piano and we listened to some of the Christmas programmes on the wireless. At least we did not need to worry about the wet battery failing now that we had mains electricity. I was asked about life in Cork and was able to explain in more detail than I had done in my letters home what the course in philosophy entailed. However, there wasn't much point in discussing Plato's Ideal Forms, Aristotle's concept of substance or other philosophers' theories about the nature of 'Being'. It was this area of intellectual knowledge that began to distance me from the homely topics of popular music, sport and current affairs that I used to share freely with my family. I hadn't yet come to realise that the history of ideas and the lofty intellectualising of the great philosophers, while proving exciting to curious minds did not assist much in the daily struggle that is part of the human condition. In the meantime I had to leave the philosophical ideas to one side and re-engage with more mundane issues of life in Templenew.

Even though there was no television service in the Republic in 1960 some people in Ballyshannon erected high aerials to try to capture transmissions from Northern Ireland. Depending on atmospheric conditions it was possible to get a signal of sorts. Tom McGovern who traded in electrical goods had a very high aerial above his shop in Tirconaill Street. He placed a television set in the window which he kept on after closing time. Even though there was only the faintest of faint pictures visible on a snowy screen, passers-by used to stand and stare at this new medium. Then towards the end of 1960 RTE began broadcasting on television for the first time. The signal was very weak in Ballyshannon because the booster transmitters had not yet been commissioned but there was just about enough of a signal to see the opening programmes. One family at the top of Main Street was getting a picture of sorts so the neighbours all gathered in on New Year's Eve 1961 to be present on the historic occasion. I managed to squeeze in near the back of the crowd but I was too far back to see the screen. Like the others at the back we had to do with the sound of the commentary as President De Valera officially opened the new service and Gay Byrne interviewed various celebrities outside the Greshem Hotel in O'Connell Street.

During those Christmas holidays our Uncle Peter arrived on a visit. He was driving a van that he and Uncle Joe used in the drapery business that they had in Ballydun. In the course of one afternoon I had my first driving lesson. Uncle Peter showed me the controls, how to use the clutch and change gears and allowed me to have a go up and down the avenue. I was thrilled to be able to steer and change gears at the same time even though I found it difficult getting used to accepting that the view of the left side of the van as protruding far beyond the width of the avenue was an optical illusion. Gradually I got used to the new perspective. The next day Uncle Peter and my father went for a walk down to the wood and the ESB reservoir. While they were away I told Peadar that I could drive. He had been in town the previous day and had missed the driving lessons. So, he wanted to try for himself. The keys were in the dashboard so I hopped in and demonstrated my driving skills. Peadar decided to have a go. After a few initial starts and stops he managed to drive up the avenue. But that was not enough for him. Out the gate he went, turned left and drove up and beyond McCormick's bridge. Looking back on it this was reckless and dangerous. I told Peadar to turn immediately and go back before Uncle Peter arrived back at the house. He drove on as far as Clyhore where he could turn and made it back to the house in one piece. I was mightily relieved. Uncle Peter never discovered the rather delinquent actions of his two nephew boy racers. Over the years he had sent us money at Christmas so we were very appreciative of his generosity. I didn't want to spoil that good relationship.

I returned to Cork in early January 1961. As the taxi drove up the avenue taking my mother and me to the bus depot in Ballyshannon we passed 'the tree that touched the ground' and I was reminded of the times I had 'lived' in it. In my growing maturity I began to appreciate Templenew more, the place that had enchanted me with its 'stately character', whose trees and fields, orchard, wood and waterways had nurtured my love of nature; where music and prayer, sport and the drudgery of farm work had fashioned my character in ways that I did not realise. With a hug from my mother I boarded the Sligo bus in the shadow of the big clock on Main Street and glimpsed her forlorn figure as my bus rounded the corner at the bridge en route to Cork.

On my return to Whiterock I quickly resumed the seminary routine. We began the new term with the usual retreat to tune us back into the spiritual life that informed our religious development. Classes resumed and Fr. O'Brien continued to develop our extra-curricular talents. He emphasised the need for priests to communicate clearly and logically. To help us in this he asked us to prepare a talk for the student body which we delivered and which he recorded. Following our talk he presented a critique and played back some of it to illustrate our weaknesses.

As was customary it was decided to stage a play in our recreation hall in the second term. An Irish play was chosen called 'Na Gadithi'. It had a mixed cast so three students had to play girls' parts. I was selected for one of these. I wasn't particularly happy with dressing up as a girl but the play was a farce anyway so I got on with it. My part didn't have many lines so that suited fine. We had great fun rehearsing and performing the play. It provided a bit of light relief in the dull and dark days before Lent. Emboldened by my acting 'success', I volunteered to sing a song at a subsequent concert. My choice of song was 'Kevin Barry' a good Republican anthem. I did not sing it out of Republican sympathies as such but because I liked the melody. In a later production I teamed up with a Fermanagh student, wrote a sketch and acted it out. For another concert I put together a medley of songs with humorous links and performed it with two other students. As I matured I was growing in confidence although still quite shy.

Seminary life with its prayer, study, recreation and days of reflection continued through January and February. When March arrived I was looking forward to Peadar's commissioning as a naval officer. My mother and father were invited to the ceremony which took place on March 27th at Haulbowline Naval Base across from Cobh. I was given permission to attend. My father had hired a car for the long journey. He and my mother called for me at Whiterock. After a brief tour of the college we set off for the commissioning.

In those days it was possible to buy a driving licence without having to pass a driving test. With an afternoon's tuition driving up and down the avenue at Templenew with my Uncle Peter I reckoned that I was a driver so I applied and received my first driving licence. So, once we got clear of the city my father allowed me to drive part of the way to Cobh. Fortunately the roads were quiet in those days so I managed to drive ten or so miles.

The Minister of Defence officiated at the commissioning along with the senior officers in the Irish Naval Service. Three other cadets were commissioned that day receiving the rank of Ensign. The families of the four cadets were there to share in the celebrations. While we were there we had the opportunity of meeting again my Aunt Martha who was married to the Commanding Officer of the Naval Base Christy Byrne. Peadar's commissioning turned out to be quite a family affair. My parents dropped me off at Whiterock on their long journey home to Ballyshannon. I was glad to see them again especially on a day of celebration.

Sport continued to play a big part in our recreation time. Gaelic football proved the most popular and I was happy to be part of it. As in Rathdangan we had our leagues with weekly games. The difference was that we had a pool of players drawn from three years instead of one. This meant that some of the players were four or five years older than me, seeing that I was the youngest seminarian in the college. As in Rathdangan student games were robust affairs. So, on one occasion when I had grabbed the ball in the 'square' I received a hefty shoulder from a bigger and stronger player which sent me sideways towards an upright. The result was that I banged my head against the post splitting my left eyebrow in the process. As with any head injury there was a profusion of bleeding. I was taken immediately back to the college where one of the priests drove me to the nearest doctor's surgery where I had the wound stitched up. When I was called into the doctor's surgery he said to me. "Come in, let you." This colloquial turn of phrase amused me as did other phrases used by the Cork students.

My first year in Whiterock was drawing to a close. It had been a very interesting year. I was enjoying my studies and liked the college, its grounds, the regime that existed there and the camaraderie of my fellow students. I took pride in maintaining the lawns and applied myself to the religious demands of the seminary. Although I had just turned eighteen in March 1961 I still felt committed to the religious life. My spiritual director emphasised the need to maintain the same commitment while on holidays. Unlike our probationary year in Rathdangan when we did not have access to newspapers we were able to read the main dailies and so keep up with world and national news. In early April the big story was about the Soviet Unions' successful launch of a rocket which put the first human into space. Yuri Gagarin spent 108 minutes orbiting the earth in his spacecraft Vostok 1before landing in a capsule near Saratov in Russia. It had been only four and a half years since I had got up in the middle of the night in Templenew to try to spot Sputnik 1. The world was changing fast. Towards the end of June we had our last retreat of the year and left for our homes.

The feast of Corpus Christie was late in 1961. I had just arrived home and I was asked by the De La Salle Brothers to help with carrying the canopy that covered the monstrance during the procession from St. Patrick's Church across College Street to the grounds of the Convent beside the Shiel Hospital and back. I was honoured to be asked. Where before, as a schoolboy, I had been an onlooker, I was now part of the clerical part of the procession.

A former classmate of mine in De La Salle lived in Chapel Street. He worked in his uncle's shop locally and from his earning he had bought a Vespa Scooter. A couple of times a week he and I would travel on his scooter out to Bundoran and spend time on the putting green or strolling among the holiday makers. If the weather was bad I would call at his house and play draughts. I used to beat him quite often which he did not like one little bit.

I had made friends with other people in the town in the course of that summer of '61. McGinley's Bar in East Port had put up a high aerial and were able to get a reasonably good television reception of the BBC and UTV stations broadcasting from Northern Ireland. I used to go in and have lemonade and chat to Tom who ran the bar. He was always doing the crossword puzzle in the Irish Times and used to run the clues past me. One day when I was in watching the television in the lounge he told me that there was an English doctor staying in the local hotel for a week who was looking for someone to give his son a grind in trigonometry. He asked me if he could recommend me. I agreed and earned £5 for a week's tuition. In those days £5 went a long way.

Angela had just finished secondary school and was waiting on her Leaving Certificate results. In the meantime she had got a summer job in a Jewellers/Fancy Goods shop in Bundoran. In mid-August she received her results. She had done extremely well and within a short time she was offered a position with the Civil Service in Dublin. She was glad to accept even though it meant leaving home. Our mother was pleased Angela had acquired a position so soon because in the 60's it was difficult to get a good job. Monica was the only one of us still in secondary school.

During that summer I began to attend the cinema more than previously. Sally McGinley, a middle-aged spinster who dispensed the tickets, would always send me to the balcony even though my cheaper ticket was for the stalls. She obviously considered the patrons of stalls too uncouth for a clerical student. Sally had just acquired a new car, a Mini. She and her sister Mary used to go for the odd run in it. The Mini had just recently been launched and quickly became one of the most popular cars of the decade. The two sisters used to take me with them for a run out the country and even let me drive when we cleared the town boundary.

By early September it was time to return to Cork. My mother accompanied me to the bus depot as usual, gave me her usual tight hug and stood waiting for the bus to turn the corner at the far end of the bridge.

Returning to Cork as a second year philosophy student I was able to resume my studies with a new confidence. Being in my second year entitled me to my own room, and this gave me more independence. I knew the routine and was making good progress academically. We also had a new Dean, Fr. Kelly who was a northerner and he brought new insights to our studies. Fr. O'Brien included another priest, Fr. Lennon on the teaching staff so that added more variety to our lectures. He continued bringing in outside lay speakers to address us on such topics as public speaking, presentation of ideas and so forth. He told us that the Halle Orchestra was coming to the Opera House in Cork City at the end of term to play Dvorak's Ninth Symphony – the New World Symphony- and that he had negotiated a special rate for us. So that we would get as much out of the performance he proposed devoting some lectures to exploring the score. I was delighted to hear this news and looked forward to learning as much as possible about the symphony. Fr. McCarthy had already laid the foundations of musical appreciation in Rathdangan so I was ready to learn more.

Sure enough, Fr. O'Brien brought a good quality gramophone into the Lecture Room and during second study, when the university students were in the college, he devoted several sessions to an exploration of Dvorak's work, illustrating the dynamics of the score by playing respective portions of it. He explained how the composer had combined folk tunes with melodies evocative of city life to weave a musical tapestry that illustrated themes of longing, homesickness and adaptation. By the time we set off for the Opera House we had a good grounding in the work. It was the first time

I had been to a symphony concert so I was looking forward to the experience. I was not disappointed. Now in my nineteenth year I was ready to follow the musical journey of the New World Symphony with its mixture of brash and raucous sounds of city life counterpoised with the haunting and plaintive folk tunes redolent of an exile's homeland. The second movement spoke deeply to me of the enduring attachments to one's home and hinted at the future sacrifice missionary exile would involve. I had not really thought much about what that would mean. Now it posed the question.

There were a few of the older students who had record collections of classical music which they used to play on the gramophone that was at our disposal in the recreation room. I asked one of them if he would let me borrow a record from his collection for the duration of the Christmas holidays, one that he thought would be a good introduction to classical music. He very kindly agreed and gave me a recording of La Boutique Fantasque, by the French composer Hector Berlioz.

Fr. Lennon used to give us the odd free class during which time he would read us a short story. One of his favourite selections was the Fr. Brown series. He also introduced us to the short stories of Frank O'Connor. This combination of musical appreciation and literature added to the drier topics we studied in philosophy and gave us a rounded education. Fr. O'Brien's approach was ahead of the times as we discovered in subsequent years.

That first term of my second philosophy year had proved very informative and interesting. I went home for the Christmas holidays with a new interest in classical music. During that Christmas of '61 there was plenty to talk as each related their respective experiences. Peadar had plenty to relate about his experiences in the Naval Service and Brendan explained what his work entailed. I outlined what life was like in my philosophy course. Peadar was interested in elements of my studies so we had several discussions about them. He had read the controversial Jesuit palaeontologist Pierre Teilhard de Cherdin's book 'The Phenomenon of Man' which explored the theory of evolution from a Christian perspective so we had long discussions about that.

On resuming my studies after the Christmas holidays I learned that one student had not returned. A few other students had not returned for second year philosophy so our class was gradually getting smaller. Such departures caused us to reflect on our own decisions to stay the course. I was still committed to testing my vocation but as I matured I reflected more on the implications. The celibate life, despite its sacrifices had appealed to me and I was still committed to it but from time to time the realisation that a lifetime of celibacy precluded the possibility of having a family registered with me. Even though I was still only nineteen the thought of having a son or daughter began to appeal to me. Yet I knew that this was incompatible with celibacy so I dismissed it, seeing it as an obstacle to my vocation.

Following a short retreat we continued with our studies and seminary life continued to offer us extra-curricular activities. We had debates, concerts, film shows and visiting speakers and a full programme of football. And then the 'flu struck in February. It spread quickly through the student body disrupting daily life quite a bit. We had some seminarians who acted as infirmarians. They kept a supply of basic medicines and brought meals to the sick students who were confined to their beds. That February the infirmarians themselves were struck down so another student and I were appointed on a temporary basis to take their places. Before long we too contracted the 'flu and had to take to bed. Gradually the epidemic passed and normal college routine returned.

Peadar called to see me a few times and always gave me some money for which I was very grateful. I kept in touch with home through fortnightly letters. By Easter we were all realising that our two year philosophy course was coming to an end. Overall it had been a positive experience and I felt that I had matured quite a bit in Whiterock. The prospect of going back to Rathdangan and commencing Theology was appealing because it would mean that I would now be a senior seminarian and studying among a larger student body comprising of first divinity through to fourth. On my way home from Cork I travelled to Ennis by train, stayed overnight with a fellow student and then got the connecting train to Sligo and the bus to Ballyshannon.

That summer of '62 followed the same pattern as the previous one. I had the usual routine of morning meditation, mass, visit to the Blessed Sacrament, rosary and night prayer. In between were visits to the townspeople that I had befriended and visits to the cinema. Brendan was combining his studies in Bolton Street Technology

College in Dublin with on-site work in Kathleen's Falls; Angela was working in Dublin, so Monica was the only one still at home. Aunt K had fallen on an icy patch and broken her wrist. Even though she had got a plaster cast on it to reset the bone it still bothered her.

In early July we had a visit from Uncle Peter and Uncle Joe. They liked getting out of the North around the Twelfth of July to escape from the tension created by Orange Marches through Nationalist areas. Following discussions with my parents they offered Monica a job in their Drapery business which she could take up at the end of her summer holidays. The opportunity of getting a job in our Uncles' business at sixteen years of age with the added advantage of being able to stay with Uncle Peter's family was attractive. Monica agreed to take up the offer. In the meantime I was invited to spend a portion of my holidays in Ballydun. Our Father had told us lots of stories about growing up there so I was happy to accept the offer of a short holiday in the village that had played such a part in his upbringing.

I set off with my uncles in their Ford Anglia that July for the eighty mile journey northwards. My father travelled with us to spend just a few days in his old village. We crossed the Border at Killeen. I was back in Northern Ireland for the first time in twelve years. The first thing that I noticed was the better quality of the roads than in the Republic. We swept into Derry from the Letterkenny road and I got a view of the city from this high vantage that was new to me. I had no childhood memories of Derry as we crossed the Foyle and drove up past Altnagelvin Hospital en route to Ballydun. As we drove through Kilashee my father pointed out the Old Police Barracks where he had been born in 1905 and where my grandfather Peter McElhinney had served as a police sergeant at the turn of the 20th Century. Five miles further on we crossed the River Dun and entered Ballydun. Uncle Peter turned right just past the first junction into the grounds of his home, 61 Main Street. Going into his three storey house I met Aunt Anna and their four children, Peter, Michael, Mary, and Áine, ranging in ages from eleven to five. Uncle Joe ran the drapery business while Uncle Peter was the village Turf Accountant.

I had a very enjoyable holiday in Ballydun that summer. Uncle Peter, Aunt Anna and Uncle Joe treated me very well. Uncle Joe used to take me to football matches on Sundays, as far away as Cavan, to the Ulster Final. He always treated me to high tea in some hotel or restaurant on our way home. Uncle Peter used to give me pocket money every week. He had a television set with very good reception of the BBC and UTV stations which was a novelty to me. My father stayed just a few days. After two weeks I was invited to stay for two more. This took me into the middle of August. Uncle Joe drove me back to Ballyshannon and Monica returned with him to start work in the drapery business.

September came around quickly and it was time for me to depart again. This time it was back to Rathdangan. My mother left me to the bus as usual and off I went to begin first divinity. From Store Street I got the bus as I had done three years earlier but now I was much more mature and experienced in travelling. Many of my classmates were on the bus and we talked enthusiastically about the new challenge awaiting us.

Chapter 5:Theological Studies, Rathdangan 1962-1964

Unlike the situation in 1959 when we used the old Nissen huts for accommodation we now had a brand new modern building. This new college had been under construction during our probationary year so it was with pride that we moved into a modern complex of student rooms, lecture halls, refectory, chapel, and bell tower. The refectory was still not fully fitted out so we used the old one that was adjacent to the one that we had used as probationers.

We learned that Fr. McDonagh who had been our Dean as Probationers was now the Dean of theology students so we were happy about that. The Rector was Fr. McCarthy, an academic who had studied in Rome for a doctorate in Canon Law. We had a number of other priests on the teaching staff and a spiritual director. With four cohorts of students all in the same college, three of them senior to us we had to accept our rather junior status but we were proud to be now among the seniors. We soon settled in to our new surroundings and started first term with the usual retreat. Now that I was in the senior section of the seminary it became obvious that I now needed to be sure that my vocation was genuine and that priesthood was the right choice for me. The previous three years had flown by and I knew that being a senior demanded careful reflection from now on. We had been told about how easy it was to be carried along with the crowd and how we could move through the year from one highlight to the next without discerning the right choices. I prayed that I was doing the right thing and threw myself into my first term of senior house with enthusiasm. The Second Vatican Council was due to open in Rome on October 11th so there was great curiosity and speculation about what the results of this world-wide gathering of bishops would be. Broadly speaking it was going to address the position of the Church in the modern world. We all sensed that change was in the air.

In terms of teaching and learning, the big change for us as first divines was that we shared lectures with all the other students. We were at the back of the lecture hall with the fourth divines at the front. We also had to take turns at serving at liturgical services, reading in the refectory and ringing the bell that controlled the events of the day. All of this made us feel part of the senior house and reinforced the feeling of being at an advanced stage in our preparation for priesthood.

Now that we were part of the seniors we gathered as a body for the celebration of the liturgy. Every Sunday we had high Mass so we dressed in our surplices and soutannes and sang the parts of the liturgy in Gregorian chant. There was always something uplifting about being part of a male choir of over a hundred voices intoning the Credo or singing out the Gloria. In addition we had our cantors and our select choir who sang arrangements in harmony all of which added to the sense of solemnity.

The first and second divines had to take turns at ringing the big bell, reading in the refectory and serving at liturgical services. These responsibilities made me aware of my growing seniority on my journey through the seminary and I was happy to participate in them. Being on the bell for half a week demanded focus and discipline. I had to make sure that I was up before everyone else and get to the bell tower in time to ring for Morning Prayer. We had to ring for meal times, classes and liturgical services. The bell was rung by pulling down on a thick rope but this required pulling the rope enough to tilt the bell for a single peal. Pulling too hard or too fast gave a double peal which was not correct as it gave a muffled double sound. Like most first divines I didn't always get it right on the first ring.

As in the previous years we had silence at meals while some portion of a religious book was read. I had always been a good reader so I was quite comfortable fulfilling this role. In fact the rector, at one of his lectures, had emphasised the need for us to use good diction in public speaking. He asked me to read for all present to illustrate good diction and clear delivery. Generally speaking the students from the north spoke with accents that were easier to follow than their southern counterparts. Towards the end of the meal the priest in charge would ring a bell and the reader finished by reading a daily extract from the Martyologium Romanum, a record of illustrious deceased saints and martyrs from the early days of the Church. The last line of this was always 'Et alibi aliorum plurimorum sanctorum Martyrm et Confessorum, atque sanctarum Virginum', to which all answered "Deo Gratias", and departed in silence. The silence continued until we reached the main building so as we processed in twos, the more senior student began reciting Psalm 50 in Latin while the junior student responded. We had read daily extracts of the Martyrology during my two years in Cork so I was familiar with it. I always liked the poetic rhythm of these Latin cadences in this concluding line and relished delivering it. We did not know it then but not only was the use of Latin to fade away in priestly formation but also in the liturgy generally. By the time it came for me to recite the concluding line to the Martyrology towards the end of first divinity the bishops of the universal Church were already discussing the changes to priestly formation that would soon sweep away many aspects of our own formation in the early 60's. We were still being formed in an already outdated model without realising it.

The first indication we had that seminary life was changing was reports that Maynooth University College, the preeminent and largest Seminary in Ireland, was starting to admit not only lay students but female ones. In Rathdangan we noticed that the rector was giving the student body more free days than previously. He also set aside time for discussion groups to explore issues of theology and asked particular senior students to write papers on theological topics and present them to the student body. Looking back on it he must have had some information about the deliberations going on in the Council and was already preparing the ground for the changes that were to come.

Although as seminarians we were told to avoid particular friendships there were particular students with whom we had natural affinities as in any group of people. And so I made friends across all the years. I could talk quite easily to these students and share our thoughts about the challenges of seminary life. At the same time we did not abuse the rule and socialised with all the students as best we could. In Whiterock I had struck up a friendship with a student called John O'Boyle from Galway. He was in the year ahead of me. He became a sort of mentor to me and I valued his advice. At the end of my first year he moved back Rathdangan to study theology. When it came for me to move back to Rathdangan I was glad to meet him again and renew our friendship. Being three years older than me I valued his advice.

Following the Christmas break in Ballyshannon I returned for the second term and applied myself to my studies in theology. We had Old Testament Studies, New Testament Studies, Moral Theology, Dogmatic Theology, Canon Law and Sociology. All of these proved interesting and generated discussions between us during our free time and on our walks in the seminary grounds after supper. As in previous years we had football and hurling leagues. Now that we had four cohorts to draw from with the oldest seminarians in their mid twenties games were robust affairs. A few of the better players had played for their respective counties in football or hurling at senior level so the standard was quite high.

What was special about the senior house was that each Easter the fourth divines were ordained and at the end of the year the third divines became sub-deacons. The ordinations to the priesthood were great celebrations and they reinforced the reason why we were all there. They also made us reflect on our progress to that goal which we discussed with our spiritual director.

Ordination day itself was a highlight of the year. The deacons were on a final pre-ordination retreat as final preparations were made. If we knew the family of an ordinand we were assigned to look after them while they were with us. Members of the choir had rehearsed the music and third year students were chosen to assist the priests and Bishop at the ceremony which took place in a local church about two miles from the seminary. We all walked to the church and took our places. The choir intoned the magnificent Ecce Sacerdos Magnus as the bishop led the procession of assistant priests, and the deacons dressed in their white albs with stoles diagonally across their chests and their chasubles over their arms. As the Gregorian chant filled the old stone chapel the deacons prostrated themselves before the altar in an act of submission to the will of God. Following the incensing of the altar by the bishop and the Liturgy of the Word the deacons were asked by the bishop if they had come for ordination willingly. On answering "Yes" they were asked if they were ready to accept the responsibilities of priesthood with all that that entailed. Having been presented to the bishop by the Rector of the seminary each deacon received a silent imposition of hands from the bishop, a ritual that was repeated by all the priests in the sanctuary. There followed the prayer of consecration, the anointing of hands and presentation of chalice and paten, rearranging of the stole and clothing in the chasuble.

As I watched the beautiful liturgy of ordination and listened to the accompanying music echoing round the old church where countless ordinations had taken place I became aware of how significant this day was for the new priests. These were colleagues of mine, albeit several years my senior but I had sat with them in the refectory, sat behind them in the lecture theatre, walked in their company around the grounds, played alongside them on the football field. At the end of the year they would receive their inoculations against tropical diseases and depart for the mission fields of Africa. And when they departed I would move to the next stage of my vocation which was the reception of minor orders.

Progress through seminary life involves receiving various 'orders', minor and major. The minor orders are given after first divinity moving up to major orders in the two years before ordination. Minor orders involve exercising the roles of acolyte, lector; the sorts of roles that lay people carry out today. As the end of first divinity approached I had to think long and hard about minor orders. Throughout my time in the seminary I had consulted a spiritual director about my progress but I had shied away from discussing my doubts and fears. This was still the case in first divinity but I was drawn to approaching Fr. McCarthy, the Rector, for spiritual guidance. He had impressed me with his sanctity, his intellectual prowess which was evident in his lectures and by his approachability. Among his responsibilities was that of recommending first divines for the reception of minor orders. We were interviewed by a panel of priests who asked us questions about our studies and our progress in the spiritual life. Following a series of talks with Fr. McCarthy he said that I should defer going forward for minor orders for a year to allow me to work through the issues that concerned me.

I confided in John O'Boyle. He had already received minor orders the previous year so he advised me to wait. With the changes that were slowly happening in Maynooth and elsewhere there was more discussion about the current regime in seminaries. John and I talked at length about these things. He wasn't afraid to criticise the current arrangement and this encouraged me to reflect on my future.

During my time as a probationer a newly ordained priest had visited us. He had studied in Maynooth. I got to meet him and received his blessing. A couple of years later he and his housekeeper left the parish he had been assigned to and went to live together in England. This was a huge scandal in 1963 and was a big story in the local and national press. It threw into question the permanency of priestly vocation and sowed doubts in my mind about my own vocation.

Around the same time my mother wrote to tell me that Brendan had given up his job with the ESB and had gone to join the Shaw Savill Line as an electrical engineer on one of their ships called 'S.S. Gothic'. I didn't know what to make of this news. On the one hand I could see the attraction and sense of adventure of sailing round the world. Brendan had often displayed an interest in ships and the sea. He was an accomplished artist and often drew pictures of ships. Like a lot of young people he yearned to 'see the world'. Had he stayed with the ESB he would have had a job for life servicing the plant at the generation stations of Kathleen's Falls and Cliff. As already noted the '60's marked a cultural shift in our views as we learned more about the wider world. Travel abroad had a new appeal so travelling round the world and being paid for it had added appeal. In the event Brendan set off on his travels. The family unit was breaking up and at the time this did not affect me that much. We were all forging our way in the world which seemed to be the nature of things. My mother and father must have had mixed feelings, on the one hand realising that each member of the family had to find their own place in the world while on the other hand lamenting the end of a home-based family unit.

In early June we had a spell of really hot weather, hot enough for a swim in the lake. The Rector gave permission for us to take advantage of the scorching weather by taking a dip in its cool water. A large contingent duly donned swimming trunks on a Sunday afternoon and spent an hour or so diving and swimming in the lake that up until then we had simply considered as an attractive feature of the demesne. A few students from inland counties couldn't swim so we had to confine them to the shallows and keep an eye on them. My swimming exploits in Templenew and Bundoran stood me in good stead.

The youthful laughter of that afternoon that echoed around the college lake soon faded as we got dried, dressed in our clerical garb and retired up the hill to afternoon prayer in the chapel. With a short retreat a week later we packed our bags for the summer holidays and I headed back home once again

In the second week in July my Uncle Peter called. He invited me to spend part of my summer holidays in Ballydun as I had done the previous year. I accepted and spent a month there returning in mid-August. Monica had already spent almost a year there. She was staying in Uncle Peter's and combined her work in the drapery business with some housekeeping for Aunt Anna. After a month I returned to Ballyshannon and prepared for my return to Rathdangan. I hadn't told my mother that I had not taken minor orders because I did not want to have to explain to her that I was starting to question my vocation. If things worked out I would be able to take minor orders at the end of second divinity and I was hopeful that that would be the case.

I returned to Rathdangan to start second divinity that September just a month before the opening of the Second Vatican Council. Pope John XX111 had caused a stir when he said that he was going to open some windows in the church and let some fresh air in. Change was in the air and in the seminary we were looking forward to the Council's deliberations. We had seen changes in the wider world such as the Cuban missile crisis in the previous year, racist riots in the southern states of America and the beginning of the Civil Rights Movement in America. Dr. Martin Luther King's "I have a dream speech" was still echoing around the world as we began our studies that September.

We had a new lecturer in Moral Theology that year. Dr. Dominic Foley was a secular priest who had taught in Maynooth University College. I don't know why he came to Rathdangan, possibly because of the fall off of students to Maynooth, but he was different from the lecturers we had been used to. Not being a member of St. Kevin's Missionary Society he treated us simply as students of theology. He was good at Latin and occasionally would ask us questions in Latin and expect us to be able to reply. Thankfully he never asked me anything. He seemed to enjoy discommoding hapless students trying to argue theological points with him in Latin. Frank O'Sullivan, who was a fourth divine and a very able student seemed to be the only one who could take him on, much to our satisfaction.

Our studies continued through October and into November. At the end of supper on November 22nd the priest in charge informed us that President Kennedy had been assassinated. It was highly unusual for us to be given a news story in this way so we realised that this was an event of huge political importance. During the half-hour of free time before second study we tried to take in the implications of the news. For weeks after his death all sorts of theories were being discussed about the assassination. Later, I watched news reels of the events surrounding the killing in the Erne Cinema and like most Irish people felt that we had lost one of our own.

Peter, Angela and Monica were at home for that Christmas. We were living in the town at this time, Templenew House having been sold some time earlier. With none of the family committing to farming our parents decided to sell the property. My father had developed osteoarthritis in his hip following a minor accident at a fair in the west of Ireland when he was knocked down by a motorist. He was also approaching retirement age.

In the meantime he found a town house which they were able to rent. It was a three storey building, part of a larger ivy-clad dwelling adjacent to the Ballyshannon Players' Drama Theatre, a small rehearsal theatre used by the local drama group. An arch with a large wooden door underneath marked an entry at the side of the house to the backyard. There was a very small strip of garden bounded by a wall at the front with a few steps leading up to the front door. The area of the first floor was restricted by the presence of the entry to the rear. It consisted of a sitting room, with behind it a kitchen and pantry. On the second floor there were three bedrooms and a bathroom and on the third floor spare rooms. It was much smaller than Templenew House but it had a similar 'old style' quality about it. I was quite taken by it. That part of Ballyshannon had a number of old 'stately' residences, so the move from Templenew was not as big a wrench as I thought it would be. Every quarter of an hour the clock in the bell tower of St. Anne's Church of Ireland on Mullaghnashee Hill chimed, a reminder that we were definitely now living in a town.

Our mother had got a postcard from Brendan the previous August. His ship was passing through the Panama Canal at the time. He said in the card that he was New Zealand bound. He hoped to get there by August 12th. Following his return to London he planned to take a trip home. True to his word he arrived just after Christmas Day. We were all delighted to see him and hear of his exploits. He had a pair of cuff-links made of Páua shell that he had bought in New Zealand. When I admired them he gave them to me as a gift. After a brief stop and a visit to Kathleen's Falls Generating Station to meet his old colleagues he was off again on his travels. Aunt K had moved into a local hotel for the Christmas. She and my mother had started going to the whist drives in St. Anne's so that Christmas my father and I joined them. I had learned to play whist in Templenew so I partnered my mother and we did quite well.

I returned to Rathdangan and continued my studies. Under the direction of the Rector Fr. McDonagh we were having more free days than previously and more time out of the lecture hall to have discussions on selected topics. He brought in outside speakers and began to tell us about the deliberations of the Vatican Council. Things were changing in the Church and we were beginning to notice a loosening of the old rigid system.

I had continued my interest in classical music. We had a room in the recreation area with a modern record player in it and a selection of classical records among them Tchaikovsky's Violin Concerto in D Major. There was something about this concerto that engaged my attention. I could hear the soloist playing melodies that seemed to be challenged by the orchestra. Over the course of the concerto the solo violin struggles to escape from the clutches of the dominant instruments and finally breaks free in a soaring pure melody. It seemed as if the composer was trying to put us in touch with his struggle to break free from whatever burdens he was under. This musical struggle reflected my own state of mind in terms of my vocation. As we moved towards Easter and another ordination ceremony, discerning if I truly had a genuine vocation was my burden.

Following the usual celebrations that Easter, I had more discussions with my spiritual director. Having just turned twenty-one I felt it was time to make a decision about my future. As we moved into April I received news from home that Aunt K had been taken into hospital with a serious stomach condition. It appeared that she had been taking a lot of aspirin to ease various pains and these had caused some erosion of her stomach. The doctors had said that if she continued to haemorrhage her life would be in danger. As was customary in the seminary I posted a note at the entrance to the oratory requesting prayers for her recovery. A few days later the Dean informed me that my mother had phoned to say that Aunt K had died. I was shocked to hear this and felt helpless because we were not permitted to go home during term time. I felt for my mother and father who had to cope with the situation.

The question arose about where Aunt K would be buried. Although she had spent most of her life in America and the latter part in Ballyshannon her formative years had been spent between Glencairn, outside Convoy, and Clady in the parish of Urney. She had lived with her mother and sisters in Clady until she emigrated in her early twenties. The family grave in Doneyloop in the parish of Urney had interred in it her mother Rebecca, sister, Mary Boner, her half sister,

Helena O'Flaherty and stepfather Michael O'Flaherty. My parents decided that she should be laid to rest in the family grave. On April 26th 1964 her funeral Mass was celebrated in St. Patrick's Church Ballyshannon. From there her remains were brought to Doneyloop and interred beside family members.

All I could do that day was pray for the repose of Aunt K's soul. Looking back on it I think that she must have had a lonely life in America. She never talked about her social life there so we never found out if she had any or many close friends. The friendship that she had found in our family and the expressions of appreciation that she experienced from us from time to time seemed to mean a lot to her. She always appreciated getting letters of thanks from me for little gifts of money she sent me. It was almost as if such acknowledgements made up in some way for a lifetime of anonymity and social deprivation.

Following Aunt K's death my parents finalised their plans to move back to Northern Ireland. My mother wrote to me and told me that they were hoping to go there the following week.

In early May we had a day of recollection which gave me time to pray and reflect on my situation. There was a little wood of silver birch trees near the main building with a seldom used trail through it. It reminded me of the wood in Templenew with its mixture of hazel and birch and holly protecting the birds and giving shelter to the delicate crocuses and bluebells. I made my way into the little wood, sat on a clean rock in the middle of it and marvelled at the beauty all around me. Through the slight silver birch came streams of sunlight dancing round my feet. Rathdangan sits in the middle of an area of outstanding beauty. Even in this corner of the wood it was all around me.

I decided that I would have to come to a decision about my future that afternoon. Somewhere at the back of my mind a decision to leave was being formed. What was needed now was an examination of the reasons why I should not go. In those days there was still a stigma associated with clerical students who left the seminary. Terms such as 'spoiled priest' were used in a derogatory manner. I was conscious of this but knew that such perceptions were based on ignorance of seminary life and anyway such a rash judgement would not influence me.

The recent ordinations had made me realise the permanence of such a step, the news of the appointments of the newly ordained to the mission fields of Africa brought home to me the reality of 'going into exile', as it were. There was also the renunciation of the possibility of having children. I had to consider these issues singly and collectively. Now at twenty-one my boyhood dreams of priestly service were undergoing a reality check. A more serious consideration however was that of commitment. Having lived the seminary life for four and a half years I had plenty of time to discern my own level of commitment and that of my fellow seminarians. The litmus test was how I had maintained my spiritual engagement during holiday time. I knew in my heart that my personal relationship with Christ over and above the rituals of seminary life was not sufficient at this stage. Having admitted this to myself I knew that my decision had been made.

Fifty years later that lack of commitment was clarified for me in the words of an Abbot who said that what brings one into religious life may not be enough to keep one there. That neatly summed up what I had concluded in the little birch wood all those years ago. Later I also discovered some of the dynamics of faith development in the research of the American Psychologist, James Fowler, who held that teenagers cannot be expected to have reached a stage of faith as commitment since they are still involved in a search for identity and the quest for values by which to live. I know this now from experience. In terms of religious commitment I am now more in tune with the sentiments of Augustine when he wrote, 'Late have I loved thee, O beauty, so ancient, so new. For behold, thou were within me and I outside.'

Following the day of recollection I informed the Rector of my decision. He listened to my reasons and accepted that I had given it serious consideration. He accepted my decision and told me to write to my parents with the news. He added that he would have some paperwork to do in connection with my decision but that I could leave the following week.

Writing that letter was not easy but I knew that I had to tell my parents that in consultation with my spiritual director I had decided that I did not have a vocation to the priesthood. I had always told them that if at any point I realised that priesthood was not for me I would not hesitate to leave. My mother replied promptly telling me not to worry about my decision to leave, that I was doing the right thing if my superiors and I had so decided, and that she was looking forward to welcoming me home. This allayed some of my sense of disappointment that I had somehow let my parents down.

The following week a group of third divines was going to Dublin so I was able to get a lift with them. Before boarding the bus the Rector took me aside to wish me well. He pressed an envelope into my hand with some money to 'buy a suit' as he put it. His parting words to me were, "You're a good lad". He will never know how much at that particular moment I appreciated those words.

As our bus moved slowly down the hill from the main building we passed the Nissen huts which were still being used by the probationers. Only two of the four huts were now needed to accommodate a dwindling number of young men joining the seminary. I couldn't help remembering the chilling accusation from Fr. Dunne, "You let the fire out?" some four and a half years previously. Now in 1964 had I let out the fire of my vocation? I didn't think so, preferring to think that it had never been truly lit in the first place. That, after all was what discerning if one had a true vocation was all about.

Passing the lake my last striking memory of it was of the fun and laughter of our collective swim there the previous month, the last hurrah of my seminary days. Exiting the grounds under the ornamental gates marked crossing a border between the secular world and the religious one. The first time I had crossed that border I was going in the other direction and had felt a little thrill in the crossing. Now I had to accept that my ideals had been subjected to the rigours of reality and had been found wanting. Further up the road I scanned the horizon for the cone-like shape of Sugar Loaf Mountain, the striking landmark that had grabbed my attention back in 1959. There it was, as clear and permanent as the Northern Star guiding me back to my new northerly destination.

When we got to Dublin I said goodbye to my colleagues. As usual I had some time to spend before getting my connection northwards. The film, 'West Side Story' was showing in the Carlton cinema so I went in and found the sheer energy and lively music highly entertaining. I was still in my clerical black suit and black tie and even though I was technically no longer a clerical student I didn't feel any different. Leaving the cinema I decided to climb Nelson's Pillar, a central landmark in the centre of O'Connell Street. From the top of it the broad sweep of central Dublin lay before me with throngs of shoppers and tourists jostling against each other on each side of the street. Buses, taxis, lorries and private cars sped past in a continuous stream, halted briefly by traffic lights, reminding me that I was back in the hurley burley of the secular world. This was such a contrast to the environment I had left that morning. I knew that the transition to lay status would take some time. Even the spectacle of West Side Story had been a bit overpowering for me, with the impact of such a range of musical influences and syncopated rhythms that contrasted with the serene, detached and pure melodies of Gregorian chant that had been the background music to which I had become accustomed. I descended Nelson's Pillar not knowing that within two years it would be no more. Even though this potent symbol of the past would be swept away, the forces that put it there would still have some influence on the people who removed it.

Walking down Talbot Street towards Connolly Station I did not fully realise that my life as a seminarian would influence me for the rest of my life in ways of which I would not even be aware. From now on I knew that I would not be obliged to meditate, to pray regularly, to develop an interior life, to grow spiritually at the intensity and in the manner to which I had become accustomed. But, neither did I realise that I would never leave these aspects of my seminary life behind me completely. Fifty years on I realise that the religious sensibility that I first felt as a sleepy child in St. Columba's Church in Doneyloop in the midst of the monotonous prayers, discordant hymns and flickering candles of evening devotions never left me. Today it means the world to me.

With my parents now living in Ballydun I had to take the Belfast train for a bus connection to my new home. As I crossed the border, this time at Newry, I did not know what life had in store for me: that, as they say, is another story.

Lightning Source UK Ltd.
Milton Keynes UK
UKOW04f1523160316

270311UK00001B/4/P